MIKHAIL VOLOGSKY WAS THE MOST PROMISING CANDIDATE— FOR A TRAITOR

In terms of the job he had to do, Vologsky was a natural. He was a superb pilot, with a singular, agile mind. If any flier could steal a Foxbat and fly it to the West, Vologsky could.

But would he? That was the six-million-dollar question. And what would be necessary to persuade him? If every man had his price, what was Vologsky's?

Perhaps a combination of the carrot-and-the-stick. Either way, it was Kirov's problem. Manville had every faith in the Russian's ability to dig out the vital weakness in Vologsky's make-up which would turn him into a traitor. All he needed was the go-ahead...

A SKY-HIGH SUPERTHRILLER

FOXBAT

PETER CAVE

A JOVE/HBJ BOOK

Printed in the United States of America

Library of Congress Catalog Card Number: 78-70787

First Jove/HBJ edition published April 1979
Third Printing, April 1979

Jove/HBJ books are published by Jove Publications, Inc.
(Harcourt Brace Jovanovich), 757 Third Avenue, New York,
NY 10017

For Jack Kerouac, who lit the fire,
Mike Moorcock, who added the first fuel,
and Margaret, who blew the embers into flame again.

ACKNOWLEDGEMENTS

I would like to thank Linda Thorling, of Futura Publications, Ltd., and Peter Kellner of the *Sunday Times,* for furnishing research material.

Also the publishers of *Jane's All the World's Aircraft* and *Jane's Weapon Systems* for invaluable technical information.

Lastly, my thanks to the following authors and their books:
Hedrick Smith (THE RUSSIANS)
Joe Poyer (NORTH CAPE)
Charles Carpentier (FLIGHT ONE)

AUTHOR'S NOTE

On Monday, September 6th 1976, a lone Russian pilot stole a Mikoyan MiG 25 aircraft (NATO Codename: *Foxbat*) from his home Soviet base near Vladivostock, and flew it to the civilian airport of Hakodate, in Northern Japan, where he demanded political asylum.

This novel is based upon that known fact. The author wishes to make it quite clear that it is in no way intended to be a factual reconstruction of the events which led to the defection, and all characters portrayed in this novel are entirely fictional, but how far the chain of events described, and the suggested involvement of government agencies and organizations is possible, the reader alone can judge.

PART ONE: THE EGG

CHAPTER ONE

Paul Manville strolled unhurriedly through the VIP disembarkation area of Washington airport. He flashed his security pass under the eyes of the two armed guards posted beside the exit door. The nearest guard glanced at it, then ushered him through with a curt nod of his head.

Manville stopped dead in his tracks, whirling to confront the guard. He thrust the pass directly under the man's nose. "Read it, man, don't just glance at it. I could have just bought the goddamned thing out of a coin machine in the men's john."

The guard bristled momentarily, then took in Manville's security status. Cowed, he stiffened his stance, his eyes slightly downcast. "Sorry, sir." He studied the security card in greater detail, noting that Paul Henry James Manville was a member of that small elite within the CIA who enjoyed the privilege of a top-security 'Q' classification. That gave him priority access to The White House, the Pentagon, and all CIA personnel up to and including the top man himself. Manville was a very important cookie indeed. The guard scanned the color photograph on the pass more carefully, checking it against the listed physical description and the man himself. Age: 57. Height: 5′ 11″. Weight: 168 lbs. Hair: Fair and graying. Eyes: Blue.

It all checked, but the guard was taking no chances now, not in view of Manville's openly aggressive attitude. "May I see your left hand, please sir?"

"Certainly, soldier." With a thin smile crossing his lips, Manville extended his hand, palm downwards. The guard examined it in close detail, checking off the listed physical peculiarities. They were both there: the three-inch diagonal scar near the wrist and the permanent multiple fracture of the third finger, which gave it a twisted, arthritic appearance.

Hoping that Manville would be satisfied, the guard dropped his hand and executed a smart salute. "Thank you, sir. You are cleared to pass."

Manville returned the salute and pocketed his security card. He felt better now, reassured about his status. After all, he was a serving liaison officer between the CIA and the White House, even if he had been little more than a sleeper for several years.

Manville moved out through the exit, summoning a Yellow Cab from the nearby rank. One moved smoothly into position, its driver leaning back over his seat to unlock the rear door. "Where d'ya wanna go, bub?" he called through the open window.

Manville scowled at him. "Levitt Electrical Building," he snapped, climbing into the cab.

"Where?" The driver's face creased into a perplexed frown.

"Levitt Electrical Building," Manville repeated, settling back into his seat. "Corner of Seventh on Lincoln."

The driver's frown disappeared, to be replaced with a roguish, knowing grin. "Oh, you mean Spy House. Why the hell didn't you say so?" He slipped the cab into gear and eased away from the curb.

Manville nearly choked on the small cheroot he was in the process of lighting up. "Are you crazy or something? Don't you realize you could get 99 years in a Federal pen for shooting your mouth off like that?"

The driver shrugged carelessly, talking over his shoulder. "Listen, buddy . . . I got three kids, a 28 thousand buck mortgage and alimony payments to make to my ex-wife. So send me to Sing-Sing . . . I could do with 99 years of government-subsidized living."

It was not a line of conversation Manville wished to pursue. He lapsed into a sullen silence as the cab left the confines of the airport terminal and cruised up the turnpike onto the freeway.

The attitude of the airport guard, and the careless banter of the cab driver were both a sign of the times and the rot which seemed to have set in. It was symptomatic of a system going soft, falling apart at the seams. There was too much freedom, too much spare information and too many underground, potentially subversive media only too willing to spread it around. Watergate hadn't helped, of course. It had been like kicking the hell out of a two-hole outhouse; a lot of shit had gotten out and the stink rode free on the four winds. Security was shot to hell. Every mother's son personally knew his friendly local CIA agent who lived around the block. Kids bought short-wave radios at junk stores and then got their kicks bugging police patrol cars.

To a layman, it might all seem mildly amusing. To an operative of Manville's status, it was a tragedy. Levitt Electrical Corporation House had stood as a cover for over eight years. The fictitious company even got quoted on the Stock Exchange. Now every goddamned taxi-cab driver in town knew the building was a CIA administration center.

Manville brooded morosely on this topic as the driver manipulated his four-wheeled war chariot in between the busy traffic of the four-lane highway. He was taking his bloody life in his hands just taking a cab for six or seven city blocks. Sometimes, he longed for the good old days.

The cab pulled up alongside the destination. Manville glanced over the driver's shoulder, reading the meter. The fare was seven-fifty. Manville poked a ten-dollar bill through the driver's window as he alighted, keeping his palm extended for the full change. The cab-driver couldn't resist one last wisecrack. He held the note up to the light, pretending to scrutinize it carefully. "This ain't bugged, is it?"

Manville ignored the jibe. Snatching the change which was finally proffered, he pocketed it without a word and turned on his heel. Behind him, the driver muttered something predictable, then moved off. Turning again, Manville made a mental note of the cab's license number, more out of habit than anything else.

He moved across the pavement towards the building, glancing at his wrist as he did so. His meeting had been timed for three o'clock. It was just over one and a half minutes before that hour. Manville waited, finishing his cigar.

His digital watch and the clock on the wall of the administration building foyer tallied at three precisely when Manville finally strolled in through the glass swing doors and headed for the reception desk.

Inside the building, at least, security was still strictly observed, and the cover story maintained. The young receptionist gave no hint of recognition, even though she had seen him at least a dozen times before. She merely smiled sweetly. "Good afternoon, sir. Can I help you?"

Manville nodded. "I have an appointment with Mr. Abraham. My name is Elliot," he said quietly, using the agreed code names.

The receptionist smiled again. "Would that be Mr. D. Abraham, or Mr. J. Abraham?"

"Whichever is in the best position to help me," Manville responded. "It's in connection with overseas retail outlets."

The elaborate game continued. The receptionist gestured across the foyer towards the twin elevators. "Fourth floor," she murmured.

Manville chose the left-hand elevator. The one on the right went only to sealed-off sections of corridor on each floor, where any interlopers who had managed to get that far would be fobbed off with further charades designed to conceal the true function of the building. Inside, he stood stiffly under the ceiling light, aware that he was being fully scanned by concealed video cameras and metal detection equipment.

The elevator rose smoothly, then came to a stop. The twin doors sighed open, and Manville stepped slowly out into the corridor. Two guards, both armed with machine-pistols, stood stiffly to attention either side of him.

One of them moved slowly in, deftly reaching into Manville's jacket and removing the shoulder-holstered automatic that the detectors had pinpointed. "Security pass please, sir."

Manville nodded, producing his pass from his inside pocket. The guard scrutinized it carefully before handing it back. "Thank you, sir. Will you perform function S4 please?"

"Certainly." Manville turned back to the elevator, placing his right palm flat against the opaque plastic panel built into the wall beside the doors. In a matter of seconds, his fingerprints had been photographed and checked by computer against the central memory banks. A small green bulb concealed behind the panel flashed on momentarily.

14

"Thank you, sir." The guard returned Manville's gun and saluted briskly. "Go ahead, sir. You are expected."

Manville returned the salute. It was not obligatory, since he was, officially, a civilian. However, he regarded it as a mark of respect and discipline, and old habits died hard. He moved down the corridor and around the corner, where two more armed guards stood, alert, against either wall. Neither challenged him, and no salute was offered. Manville passed them, stopping outside a plain door. He rapped twice with the back of his knuckles.

"Come in." As the voice boomed out, the door open automatically, on an electronic security lock.

Manville paused to straighten his tie before stepping through. Inside, the office was spacious, but without any trace of ostentation. A plain, functional heavy-duty carpet led across to a large and uncluttered teak desk. Behind it sat a man whose physical appearance was out of all keeping with his professional stature.

Franklin Hayman's thin, wiry body was overshadowed by the large desk, even though he was seated on a swivel chair which had been adjusted to its maximum height. His narrow shoulders had a permanent forward-drooping hunch, with the result that clothes seemed to hang off him in shapeless folds. Even the most expensive and well-cut suit took on the appearance of a cheap off-the-peg item from a Hong Kong department store. To top this unprepossessing appearance was a thin, scrawny neck which seemed only just to support the weight of his head. His face, with its wrinkled, pallid complexion, looked for all the world like that of a nervous squirrel monkey.

But Franklin Hayman was small in size only. He was in fact one of the most important and influential men in Washington, feared and respected by Senators, Congressmen and the Military. His close-set eyes daily reviewed documents which would otherwise only be seen by perhaps half a dozen people—up to and including the President himself. As organizational head of all CIA operations on the North American continent, Hayman literally had greater power than heads of State or European monarchy. The lives of men could be snuffed out at one snap of his gnarled fingers—and frequently were.

Manville knew all this, and treated the man accordingly. Even in terms of his own quite awesome power he was noth-

15

ing but an underling in relation to his superior. When Hayman gave orders, Manville jumped. It was as simple as that.

But first, before the orders, true democracy had to be trotted out on the desk in front of the two men like a child's board game, the dice tossed and a couple of moves played. As ever when they met, they exchanged warm, friendly smiles, which supposed an equality both knew to be spurious, and intimated chumminess which belied the invariable gravity of their discussions and business together.

After the smiles, a brief exchange of harmless banter.

"Hope to hell this is important, Franklin . . . hauling me in off my vacation this way."

"Where were you?"

"Skiing in Aspen."

"Yeah? Snow good?"

"Fair. Too many ski bums about, though. Christ, there seem to be more of 'em every season."

"Well, sorry about that, Paul. Good to see you again, anyway."

"Yeah. You too." Manville extended his hand across the desk, making the penultimate move of the game. The two men shook hands perfunctorily, then Hayman settled back into his chair and his face became instantly serious.

"Want to get down to business?" Manville asked after a slight pause.

Hayman nodded. He reached across his desk to a small black metal box and triggered a switch. A red light flashed on, but there was no apparent sound. Both of them knew, however, that the scrambler equipment was now emitting a powerful high-frequency signal which would effectively blot out their subsequent conversation from any known form of electronic surveillance.

The meeting was for real now. Both men looked grim.

"Trouble?" Manville asked.

"Problems," Hayman conceded. "Our job is to prevent them escalating into trouble." He broke off to open his desk drawer and pull out a red card-file, sliding it across the surface of the desk towards Manville. The legend TOP SECRET. FOR YOUR EYES ONLY stood out prominently.

Manville brushed the folder with his fingertips, looking up questioningly.

Hayman nodded briefly. "Study it," he said.

Only with that official invitation did Manville open the file and pull out its contents. He took in the headlines.

INTELLIGENCE REPORT QUA/2779024/H9.

SOURCE: Herat, Afghanistan. (via Internal USSR unit K.165.)

SUBJECT: Combat aircraft Mikoyan MiG 25. (NATO Codename: FOXBAT)

Manville looked up, slightly puzzled. "This is old stuff, Hayman. I thought we wrote off the Foxbat some time ago. Our intelligence concluded that it was nowhere near comparison with our new Tomcat, didn't it?"

Hayman grunted. "Old stuff . . . but a new twist," he muttered. "We did originally conclude that the MiG 25 posed no real threat to our air defenses, but it would appear there have been some new developments. We know, for instance, that large-scale grounding of Foxbats has occurred on all major Red Air Force bases over the last few months. The question is, why? Logically, it would make sense to assume that the aircraft failed to come up to the standards of performance and aggressive capability which the Soviets expected of it. The trouble is, we now know that they are being re-issued . . . and we have cause to think that they might have undergone quite extensive modifications. Read on and you'll see what I mean."

Manville returned his eyes to the report, digesting it carefully. Finally he lowered the papers on to the desk and whistled through his teeth in astonishment, and more than a little dismay. "Do you accept such a vastly improved performance?" he asked Hayman.

Hayman shrugged. "I don't know," he answered frankly. "But the Soviets must have done something, that's for sure. We know that the projected new Ilyushin Y-type fighter aircraft isn't due to come into full-scale production much before the early 1980s . . . perhaps two more years before they are in full service with trained pilots and maintenance crews. That leaves the USSR with a pretty nasty gap to fill up, and the Foxbat was the best they had. It makes sense that they would really have gone to town on the modifications."

Manville laughed nervously. "Yes, sure . . . but a maximum speed in excess of Mach 4.5? That's incredible."

"Sure, by our current standards of technology," Hayman agreed "The original Foxbat had a maximum airspeed of fractionally over Mach 3, and a probable operational ceiling

17

of around 125,000 feet. That second fact, by the way, is based on an observed test which created a new world altitude record, 119,000 feet, some seven months ago. If, as this report suggests, they have replaced many of the main fuselage and wing members with titanium, rather than steel geometry, then we are dealing with a much lighter aircraft. It would only take a marginally improved thrust to give the aircraft a vastly improved ground-to-air time, a higher ceiling and a greatly boosted top airspeed."

"Jesus!" Manville was stunned. "But at that speed, and that height, the bloody thing could outrun a missle, for Christ's sake. We would have absolutely no defense against it."

"Exactly," Hayman said. "There is, however, another rather nasty conclusion to be drawn from those performance figures. If they are accurate, the new Foxbats can not only evade our missiles, they can attain the very top level of the stratosphere, and maintain a speed which is only marginally sub-orbital. That puts them within missile range of our satellites, threatening the entire SAMOS system. The Russians would have absolute superiority over not only the air, but space as well. Not a pleasant thought, you'll agree."

"Jesus," Manville said again, shuddering slightly. "So that's our problem."

"There's more, I'm afraid," Hayman said apologetically. He produced another file. "This is a quite separate intelligence report on a new, lightweight air-to-air missile the Russians are known to have developed recently. If they have been fitted to these new Foxbats, then the aircraft would have a potential complement of 6 to 8 AAMs in place of the current 4 . . . on top of its two wing-mounted 23mm electric cannon. That's a pretty formidable flying machine. Cutting back on missiles and fitting wing fuel reserve tanks instead would increase its range to well over 2000 miles. Finally, to make the position even worse, the Foxbat is probably also fitted out with a sophisticated anti-missile ejection pod and all conventional radar-blinding devices and tracking jammers. We wouldn't see it coming, we couldn't shoot it down when we did and we couldn't even chase the fucking thing home after it had hit us. Now read both these reports again, put them together, and tell me what you think."

Manville picked up the second folder, sighing heavily. There was a tight feeling in his gut.

Manville studied the material again for several minutes, saying nothing. Finally, he riffled the thin sheaf of papers together with his fingertips and slid them back inside the security folder, which he handed back to Hayman.

"Well? What's your opinion?" Hayman asked, as he carefully placed the folder back in his desk drawer and double-locked it.

Manville sniffed thoughtfully. "Impressive," he muttered. "Very impressive . . . if they're genuine, that is. What do the experts say?"

Hayman snorted in disgust. "So who has experts any more? Certainly not in the Aero-Space industry, that's for sure. In this age of specialization, what we got is a lot of brilliant mechanics working four to five years behind theoretic technology, and a few abstracted theorists working out in the unknown and each disagreeing with the other."

Manville shrugged. "No general consensus, then?"

"Totally inconclusive. Lockheed say no way, at least three years away from even the drawing board stage. NASA says yes, highly probable for a prototype to be flying tests, but doubtful to be operational for two years. British sources say they already have the potential power-unit and are half-convinced that the French may already be quite advanced in the aero-dynamics of the bodyshell. Sometime in the next two to five years they would expect to get together and do what they did with Concorde. Take your pick."

"Yeah." Manville laughed, without humor. "Point taken. As layman to layman . . . what's your gut reaction?"

"About the same as your instinctive reaction . . . guarded doubt. But there's that damned word *if* to content with. Small word . . . with massive implications."

"It could be a red herring," Manville pointed out. "Deliberately falsified information . . . to send us off on a wasteful course of negative research. How about the source? Reliable?"

Hayman nodded. "Usually highly so," he confirmed. "We received a three-year projection on the Soyuz program from the same cell . . . and that proved to be 100%. There's no real reason to assume anything has changed."

Manville shook his head dubiously. "I find that a shade inconclusive. Around that time, we were sharing a lot of material to work toward the Apollo link-up. I would have thought the Russians just about got ahead on a points average with that one."

Hayman waved the objection aside. "Nevertheless, I don't think we can afford to ignore it. A contingency plan, at very least, pending any further information."

"A spy plane?" Manville suggested. "We've come a long way since the U-2 fiasco."

Hayman shook his head. "If that report is anywhere near accurate, they could knock anything we have at present clear out of the sky. Anyway, the situation is delicate right now. We can't afford to be caught making what they would take as an act of aggression."

"I take it none of our satellites can gather any evidence?"

"The Russians are too clever for that. Any bases where these little babies are operating are going to be way off our orbital paths. They track every piece of hardware we got up there . . . just as we keep tabs on theirs."

Manville looked bewildered. "What, then? We have no agents who could get close to something this big?"

"Mohammed and the mountain," Hayman murmured, cryptically. "We can't get to it . . . so we bring it to us."

Manville took a deep breath, to let the implications of Hayman's words sink in. When they did, he whistled at the sheer audacity of the plan.

"It's the only chance we have," Hayman went on. "Somehow, we have to persuade one of their pilots to defect, bringing the plane with him. That way, we can strip the thing down to its last nut and bolt. We could jump our own technology ahead two to five years . . . at a conservative estimate."

"You'll never get official clearance," Manville said flatly.

Hayman's eyes bored into his, ice-cold. "I don't have to. You're the link-man. That's your job."

There was a long silence. Finally, Manville spoke. "Is that official?"

Hayman nodded. "It's official . . . as of now. You're on active assignment, Manville. I want full Pentagon and White House clearance in two months maximum. Meantime, we'll be getting down to the fine details." He broke off to unlock another drawer, pulling out a sealed buff envelope. "Here's your official brief. The operation will be code-named 'CUCKOO'. You appreciate the humor, I hope?"

Manville accepted the sealed orders, grinning wryly. "Very

apt," he agreed. "We get a foreign bird to fly into our nest and lay the biggest egg of all time. Let's just hope we don't get any of that egg on our faces."

"We do . . . and heads will roll," Hayman warned. He was deadly serious. "You know it, Paul . . . we can't afford to foul up on this one."

"It's not going to be easy getting clearance," Manville pointed out. "There will be a lot of nervous opposition, I can tell you now. Detente is a highly delicate subject right now . . . and we've been getting some bad press lately."

"Yeah." Hayman's monkey-like face twisted into a vicious scowl just thinking about it. "Those hallucinogenics experiments certainly stirred up a lot of shit."

"And the Cuban comedy show," Manville reminded him. "Exploding clam shells, for Chrissakes! The dumb bastard who dreamed that one up should have been strung up by his balls."

"He was," Hayman muttered.

"Is that it?" Manville asked, after a few moments of silence.

Hayman stood, extending his hand over the desk. "That's it," he confirmed. "The best of luck, Paul."

They shook hands. "I'm going to need it," Manville grunted.

CHAPTER TWO

LEVITT ELEC. CO PERSONAL ABRAHAM
  CUCKOO LP. 86003
  INTERIM REPORT 1. CODED TRANSMISSION. CHANNEL ONE.
  MESSAGE BEGINS STOP PRIMARY CONTACT ESTABLISHED
LEADING ORNITHOLOGIST STOP DOUBT EXPRESSED AS TO
MIGRATORY HABITS OF SPECIES STOP INITIAL REACTION
NEGATIVE STOP THUR 1630 EST STOP MANVILLE
APD/3700925/WP MESSAGE ENDS

Manville checked over his copy of the coded telex transmission before shredding it, unable to repress a bitter smile. He had never thought of himself as a master of the understatement, but his message to Hayman was something of a gem. "Initial reaction negative," indeed. It was true only if one accepted varying degrees of an absolute. What Ennis, the Presidential advisor, had *actually* said was: "Manville, have you got fuckin' rocks in your head or something?"

Belatedly, Manville realized that going in cold, straight to the top, had been a serious tactical error. Rejected at that level, he was back to square one, at a disadvantage. Now it would be a question of building up contacts again, putting up a case which would percolate up through the echelons of power, hopefully gathering momentum and authenticity as it

23

did so. If that happened, Ennis might conceivably be by-passed, or at least overruled.

Manville pored through his list of contacts, seeking the most likely allies. What he really needed on his side was some good old-fashioned redneck backing; a few influential voices bellowing the Battle Hymn of the Republic and waving the Star-Spangled Banner in tightly clenched fists. The old shock tactics didn't work so well anymore; the days of JFK and gunboats to Cuba were long gone. Detente, the cold peace, had started with the crack of a rifle in downtown Dallas, and the echoes could still be heard in the corridors of the White House. The Military were backed up against a wall and dis-orientated. Lacking the backing zeal of the last American hero, pulled out from Nam licking their wounds, they were like de-gutted bayonet dummies, crumpled paper tigers. There was a feeling of helpless impotence which permeated up through the ranks from GI to Supreme Command.

Then SALT. Another body-blow, another betrayal. Defense cuts, NATO falling apart at the seams as a near-bankrupt Great Britain trimmed her commitment back below the sur-vival level and the other European allies stopped considering the quality of their defensive and offensive hardware and be-gan worrying about sharing out the contracts amongst the EEC brotherhood instead. It had begun to look as though the Western powers had embraced the premise that no-one kicks a cringing dog.

Manville pulled himself together with a mental jolt. He was overreacting, for God's sake. One little rejection, the first suggestion of a problem, and he started to go to pieces, blame everyone except himself. It was getting to be more than just a bad habit; it was beginning to become an established part of his personality.

"On active assignment," Hayman had told him. Hell! What was so bloody active about being an overblown messenger boy? Being out in the field . . . that was active. Logically ex-tending a lifetime of military service in the defense of his country with a direct, positive approach. Not being afraid to do what needed to be done, without a moment's hesitation or doubt. Knowing the personal satisfaction of keeping body and mind wholly alert and fit, obeying no other master than his own conscience.

Body and mind . . . there was a bitter joke indeed. Some body, when it could no longer be persuaded to ski down a mountainside. A simple traverse . . . past the glacier then a quick christie round the moguls and a straight parallel run to the bottom Instead of which . . . what? Knees buckling, legs trembling like jelly, an undignified scramble down the ice on his ass and two days in a bar throwing down Bourbon.

All the time getting worse. The crack-up of personal confidence, the sheer bloody hell of facing every simple decision as a major crisis. Empty, impotent, gutless. Burying it all under a thick shell of bluster, bullying, slavish adherence to protocol and the discipline.

No way back now, of course. For Manville, there could never be another Dien-Bien-Phu, another Hill 24, another Czechoslovakia or Berlin Wall. Shit! They'd as good as killed him when they'd taken him out of the field. Co-ordinator, indeed. How the hell did a man stop being an agent and suddenly become a civil servant? How did a man stay a man when the one prop which supported him was knocked away?

Worse . . . who could he tell, what could he say? How does a man even try to explain that he is falling apart because he doesn't kill people any more?

Recognizing the all-too familiar symptoms, Manville fought against the gathering depression before it took too firm a hold on him. There was still a job to do, and although it might not seem much in comparison to the past, it was all he had left.

He returned to his contact lists, abandoning the military personnel and concentrating upon purely political figures. There were at least three Senators he could count on for verbal support, if nothing more. Willing support, that was. Marked off with a red asterisk were five more names . . . two other Senators and three Congressmen . . . whose apparent support for virtually anything was guaranteed by Manville's knowledge of their private indiscretions. That was all part of the job—dig the dirt and then turn it into pure gold. Manville's silence came dearly.

Eight voices then, and precious little else. It still wasn't enough to get past Dwight Ennis. What Manville needed was an argument with gut-weight, real pull. If only there was some backing evidence for the Foxbat report. With corroborating material, he could get people moving as though they had ramjets stuffed up their backsides.

It was a delicious, childish image. Manville toyed with it

25

for a few moments, imagining the corridors of the Pentagon and White House alive with zooming figures, gray-flannel covered asses farting tongues of flame. Chasing Foxbat, going into orbit.

Orbit. Faint bells rang, tumblers clicked. Again, Manville felt a slight sense of marvel at the processes of his own brain, his devious but quite unconscious way of running ahead of his own thoughts and frequently alighting on off-beat answers. It was a peculiar form of lateral thinking, inspired by instinct. In the past, the facility had rarely let him down. When it did, he covered up with bluff, and only rarely came unstuck.

The key to the whole business was not politics or national defense. It was more basic America than either of those two republican bastions. Money. That was the secret, the magic word which would open all the doors. The sacred, almighty dollar, the solid bedrock of American administration, ever since Manhattan island was bought for a handful of beads.

Manville concentrated, putting it all together in his head. If the reports on Foxbat were accurate, the aircraft represented the next five years of technology. Five years of research, countless billions of public dollars. From this solid standpoint, Manville looked back. Over the previous five years, where had the greatest money flowed freely? Not in urban development, not in city slum clearance, not in social welfare. Straight up, out of the atmosphere and into orbit—that was where the most staggering sums of money had gone. The space program; NASA. The small step for man had fired the American blood as no other single conquest had ever done. Belittle that, and you hit every patriotic American below the belt.

Manville grinned to himself. It was the only place to punch.

And punch he would. NASA was the immediate target. One known and accepted fact provided the argumentative weight he had needed, and could now build upon. The Mikoyan Mig-25 had established the all-time altitude record of just under 120,000 feet. Play on that, stress the suggestion in the new report that the improved craft was now on the verge of orbital flight, and it presented a real threat to the past achievements and the future development of all aero-space research. Foxbat could swipe satellites from the skies like irri-

26

tant flies; take the Russians leap-frogging ahead of the planned space shuttle program.

And wipe out the expenditure of thousands of billions of dollars. Money was the key, sure enough. Cape Canaveral was the lock in which to turn it.

CHAPTER THREE

Colonel Mark Woodrow Harris, USAF, eyed Manville across his desk, through black-framed, slightly tinted spectacles. He tapped one finger, reflectively, on the Foxbat report. When he eventually spoke, his voice was guarded, with a deliberate note of scepticism, despite the sporadic friendship the two men had shared over the years.

"Why have you come to me, Paul?"

Manville shrugged. There was no point in attempting to cover up. Harris was too shrewd. "I need some help . . . somebody with a bit of heavy armory to back me up."

"You've already been to the Pentagon and the White House." It was a statement rather than a question.

"Of course." Manville made no attempt at denial.

"And they weren't interested?"

"Interest isn't enough these days, Mark. You know how things are. Too many people sitting on the fence, exercising nothing but their asses. Dwight Ennis thinks this one is too hot to handle, under the present circumstances."

"Maybe he just doesn't believe this report," Harris murmured.

"No, perhaps he doesn't. I'm not sure I do myself. However, I don't think it's worth taking a chance . . . do you?"

Harris tapped the report once again. "For what it's worth,

I think this is wildly over-optimistic. I can't really go along with these performance figures—not given our last intelligence reports on the MiG projects into the 80's.

"An unexpected technological breakthrough? Something we haven't stumbled on yet? A damned sight more research money and facilities, perhaps?" Manville suggested.

Harris shook his head dubiously. "They'd need all three, and then some. I'll go along with some radical improvement to the turbo-ram-jet engine concept; perhaps a boost in top speed up to Mach 3.5, even 4 at a stretch of the imagination. But this sub-orbital capacity . . . no, I can't see it at all. Any winged craft has got to do better than Mach 5 to get into space. We know the MiG-25 already set a ceiling record of 120,000 feet. Even supposing they could have pushed that up to 150,000, 160 . . . we're still way off track."

"Some new form of rocket booster . . . detachable and expendable before re-entry?"

"Or have the Ruskies finally invented the sky hook?" Harris put in. It was a joke, not meant cruelly.

"You don't wear the rocket theory, then?"

Harris smiled gently, shaking his head. "I don't want to sound patronizing, Paul, but you're talking about a fuel-load/power ratio which is just not feasible. In strictly layman's terms, the amount of additional engine-weight and fuel that any supersonic aircraft could get off the ground would give a few minutes of sub-orbital time, if that. It just wouldn't be worth it."

"Wouldn't it?" Manville challenged. "Just think how much hardware we have up there, Mark." He jabbed his thumb at the ceiling to reinforce his point. "Supposing a couple of minutes is all these birds need? A small squadron could make a series of relay runs, each programmed for a few specific targets. In a matter of minutes, the Russians could completely destroy our entire SAMOS system of spy satellites. We'd be blind and virtually defenseless overnight."

Doubt flickered across Harris' face for the first time. He considered Manville's objection seriously for some moments.

Manville saw his temporary advantage, and seized it. "It wouldn't be just the SAMOS system, either," he added. "I don't know exactly what we have up there, or what stuff we are likely to be sending up in the next few years . . . but I'll take side bets on orbital weapons, either ready or in the pipeline."

Harris glared at him angrily. "You know orbital weapons are specifically banned under the SALT agreement," he snapped curtly.

Manville grinned, pleased to see that he had the man rattled. "Come on, Mark . . . don't try to bullshit me. I may be a layman in terms of aero-space, but I know my own country and I know military thinking. Just suppose such unspeakable treachery *had* been committed in Uncle Sam's fair name. It would be a trifle embarrassing, to say the least, if these airplanes gave the Russians the capacity to take a little look-see."

Harris continued to look both angry and worried. "You're treading on highly dangerous ground," he warned.

Manville took the hint. "All right, let's leave that. Take a few facts. Our major aero-space effort over the next decade is the space-shuttle system . . . right?"

"Right," Harris agreed, grudgingly.

"Then given the limited orbital performance of Foxbat, we face both observation and sabotage . . . still right?"

Harris was not quite ready to capitulate. He fought back bravely to regain the initiative of the argument. "But this 'orbital performance'. I don't think we can accept it."

Manville was not going to be put off now. He smelled victory. "You're going back on the defensive, Mark. We have already agreed that limited orbital time is feasible, and would have a purpose. That makes it a real, live possibility, and one which cannot be ignored, surely?"

Harris shook his head again, but now without real conviction. "No, there are other factors—other hangups besides the fuel and weight problem. Even if a human pilot could get those birds up there, he'd be flying on a kiss and a promise. A winged craft isn't like a rocket, or a satellite. It still depends on flow-patterns, even when the air is so thin as to be almost negligible. Variable wing geometry would cut the dangers down a little . . . but there are still CATs up there which could tear anything like a conventional aircraft apart."

"CAT?" Manville had not heard the term before.

"Clear Air Turbulence," Harris explained. "You cannot see it, you cannot measure it by instrumentation, but there are incredibly powerful air currents up in the stratosphere which can move at anything up to 300 mph. Imagine a craft slipping in to one of those in excess of Mach 5 and it would fold up like a paper dart in a wind tunnel. Add the dangers of

31

meteorite strike, burn-up on re-entry, compression blow-out, half a dozen other things . . . and each one of those planes and pilots might stand a one in ten chance of completing a three-minute mission and returning safely to base."

Manville dismissed the entire string of objections with a bitter laugh. "No contest, Mark. You're putting up candles in the wind now. Since when did men matter? If we're talking about World War III, even you and I won't get a look in. For the fifteen minutes it'll take, the computers will be completely in charge. A dozen flying machines and their pilots would be no more than a blip on a piece of magnetic tape. Infinitely expendable—and infinitely worth sacrifice, under the circumstances."

Harris sighed heavily. "My Christ, you're a cynical bastard, aren't you?"

Manville dismissed the words with an easy shrug. They weren't really meant as an insult. "I'm a realist," he said flatly. "In my job, it's a prerequisite." He lolled back in his chair to light a cigar, displaying the carefree indifference of a man who knows he had won the day. Eyeing Harris covertly above the flame of his lighter, he said: "Well? Do I get your backing or do I not?"

Harris evaded a direct answer. "I can't guarantee anything, of course. . . ."

"Understood. But you'll pressure the right people?"

Harris nodded.

"Then I should think we're in business," Manville said confidently. "I'll wire HQ to open up phase two."

"Is that wise, at this stage?" Harris queried. "I've told you . . . no guarantees."

"I have every confidence in you," Manville assured him. "Besides, it'll give Hayman something to get started on . . . find the right man."

"Will he, do you think?"

Manville laughed without humor. "That's his problem. The main thing as far as I'm concerned is getting official approval."

Harris was silent for a few moments, regarding Manville quizzically. "You're really pushing this one, aren't you, Paul. Why?"

With some surprise, Manville answered. "I always push, Mark. Whatever it takes to get the job done."

"No, not like this. This is something special. I can tell."

Still, Manville struggled to deny it. He didn't fully under-stand why he had personalized this particular project as much as he had. "Nothing special. I just don't like failure."

Suddenly, Mark Harris understood. "I didn't realize you'd ever faced it," he said, quietly.

CHAPTER FOUR

Lt. Mikhail Vologsky stared again at the buff-colored application form, so meticulously filled out, and so callously rejected. It had been returned to him almost exactly as he had sent it, with no covering letter or word of explanation. The powers-that-were did not believe in explanation. It presupposed question, active investigation into things which should not concern the individual.

The buff application form differed in only one important way from the half-dozen Vologsky had sent in the past. This time, there was an added touch of color upon it. Beneath the black-printed legend he had become accustomed to, there was a further, even curter message, in official red ink. In black— THIS APPLICATION HAS BEEN REFUSED. In red, the color of warning and danger—MATTER TERMINATED.

Vologsky seized the form, crumpling it into a ball in his palm. In a gesture of helpless fury, he hurled it across the room. Seeking solace, he stood and crossed the cramped living area of his two-roomed apartment and snatched up a bottle of Krepkaya, drawing the cork with his teeth. Spitting it on to the floor, he raised the half-empty bottle to his lips and drank down the fiery vodka in great gulps, as if to drown the useless curses which rose in his throat.

The burning spirit failed to cauterize the icy chill of rejection in his stomach, or disguise the bitter taste of ultimate failure in his mouth. Still, it helped a little, numbing his anger until it was no more than a controlled resentment.

Vologsky finished the bottle off and slammed it down upon the table. He walked to the small, single window and pushed it open, gazing up and outward into the night, at the friends he could never meet.

Pinholes in the sky, he had called them when he was a small child. Now, as a man, he knew every prick of light by name, could identify each constellation and its individual component stars. In his head, he could recall the exact distance, in light-years and kilometers, of at least half a dozen of them, and even work out the traveling time from Earth at the equivalent speeds of tram, train . . . or rocket.

The vodka completed its insidious work. The anger had turned to resentment, and now the resentment was replaced by maudlin self-pity. The bright images of individual stars elongated and blurred into melting crystalline shapes as bitter tears prickled in Vologsky's eyes.

He turned away from the window abruptly, pulling himself together. It was difficult to accept that a dream was finished forever. The past rejections he had been able to live with; there was always the hope that one day, sooner or later, there would be a vacancy for him within the Russian Space Program. Vologsky had constantly reassured himself that the repeated refusals were simply because his application happened to be made at an inopportune moment. By the law of averages, one such application must finally succeed. Now, he was denied even that slim hope. The curt red stamp on the returned application was a clear statement that any further correspondence would be regarded by the authorities with extreme displeasure.

Anger flared again to fill the void. Why had they rejected him? They had absolutely no right, no possible justification. From any rational viewpoint, he was supremely qualified to train as a cosmonaut.

At the age of 28, Mikhail Vologsky was at his peak, both physically and mentally. He was superbly fit, with the stamina of an athlete. His small but powerful 5' 8" frame was ideally suited to the cramped conditions of a space capsule, his body weight pared down to the absolute minimum for his build. He had repeatedly demonstrated that he had a greater tolerance of G-forces than most other men; Vologsky could take a full three minutes longer in the centrifuge chamber than any other member of his squadron. Under conditions where lesser men blacked out into unconsciousness, Vologsky could stay awake, alert, and able to manipulate delicate controls.

Mentally, he had a general IQ which was three points short of the genius level, and in the specialized field of mathematics, was far above it. From the age of six onward, Vologsky had been able to apply almost total recall to figures of any sort. He had a natural affinity with numbers, and could work out complicated equations in his head at four or five times the average human rate. On top of all these attributes, he was a superb pilot. Given his abilities and his natural desire to go into space, it should have been a logical extension of his career to graduate from the Air Force into the Space Program.

Yet he had been rejected. Not once, but six separate times . . . and now he had been warned off for good. There had to be some reason why, some factor strong enough to outweigh all his obvious qualifications.

It could not be political. Although he lacked any deep personal convictions, Vologsky had always trod the path of least resistance, done the right things at the right times. In his student days, he had been careful never to become involved in any radical movements, had joined the *Komosol* at the age of sixteen and become a card-carrying Party member before his 21st birthday. There was nothing in his past which could conceivably cast any doubts upon his convictions or patriotism. In his career, he had made satisfactory, if not spectacular, progress, was always suitably deferential to his superiors and fully conscious of the disciplines and limitations imposed by a military life.

Vologsky's sole transgression against the State and the system was his continued belief in the existence of God. He dared to be a Christian, in a country which had supplanted religion with a political ideal, discouraging worship without actually suppressing it forcibly. For an average man, a religious commitment would mean the faintest question mark against his character. In Vologsky's case, as an elitist member of the armed forces, it might well be considered a serious crime.

Yet he could not believe that the KGB could have discovered his one small secret. Vologsky was a Christian in his

37

mind, it was a deep, inner conviction which he guarded jealously. He had always been careful and discreet. He never attended any public ceremonies, where the ever-vigilant eyes of the KGB could pick him out and identify him. He kept no symbols of his religion to give him away to his comrades. He needed no Bible to remind him of the life of Christ, and if ever he felt the need for a symbol upon which to concentrate his devotions, he satisfied himself by making the sign of the cross with his fingers. When Vologsky prayed, he did it in silence and solitude.

Given that his secret was safe, what else could there be? What was it about him which prevented the realization of his ambition? As so many times before, Vologsky came to the end of the mental games he played with himself, dismissed the last hopeful excuse for his rejection and came face to face with the lonely bitterness of reality.

He knew, in his heart, the words which were doubtless stamped upon his private file. "Psychologically Undersirable". The very essence of his character was against him, creating doubts and rumors which would always stand in his way. Mikhail Vologsky was essentially a loner, in both the physical and spiritual sense. He had no family, no sweetheart, no real friends. Both his parents had died when he was only 15. The soulless, impersonal State had reared him since then, putting him through higher education and choosing his career for him. His adolescence and young manhood had occurred in a vacuum. As he grew to manhood, Vologsky had accepted that state of being as both normal and even desirable. Without relationships, a man could be a fortress within himself, dedicated to a career and a dream.

The dream was the stars. The need to go into space, an extension of the comforting vacuum. The military life had suited him perfectly, for within the confines of an Air Force Base, he could have companions without forming friendships. He was surrounded by other people yet able to detach himself. Taking orders without question removed the need to make decisions or involve himself with external matters. Vologsky's personal fortress had never come under attack. He was an island, self-contained and impregnable.

Such detachment could not, of course, go unnoticed. It inevitably gave rise to speculation amongst his companions. They could not understand a man who chose privacy rather than the comfort of comradeship and shared pleasures; who read books on mathematics and astronomy rather than drink in the mess with his fellow-officers. Nor could they understand a young, good-looking man who appeared to have no interest in girls. He kept no pin-up on his locker, he was never seen writing a letter of any sort, let alone a love-missive. Vologsky shunned the ribald laughter of his fellows as they boasted about their sexual conquests. He could not join in the telling of smutty jokes or the foraging expeditions for willing females.

Somewhere along the line, misunderstanding had bred resentment, and malice had crept in. Vologsky himself became the butt for smutty jokes and innuendoes. Rumors were born and spread. Mikhail Vologsky was a strange one, a homosexual.

Vologsky slammed his fist down upon the table as the injustice of it all descended upon him again. He felt the resentment building up in waves of pressure which threatened to burst his head open like an over-inflated balloon. Everything was so unfair, so bitterly frustrating. In the rigid and uncompromising structure of a society which constantly looked for negative, rather than positive factors, the faintest rumor was elevated to probable truth and doubt became a definite accusation. The whole system was tainted with a self-destructive weakness, for in striving for absolute standardization, it rejected the individual and automatically branded him a second-class citizen. In Vologsky's case, the very qualities which should have promoted him as a supremely efficient and dedicated cosmonaut turned and worked against him.

Somewhere, on a secret KGB file, a series of question marks stood against Vologsky's name and service record. Without the slightest shred of evidence, those nebulous question marks stood out like warning beacons. Mikhail Vologsky was not a typical young Russian. He did not get drunk with his colleagues, he did not share their dedication, even their ambitions. It seemed likely that his desire to get into space was a personal one, rather than a blind urge to serve his motherland. He might, conceivably, be indoctrinated with an obsolete religious belief, and he shunned company, including that of girls.

Resignedly, Vologsky faced the facts. The State had classified and rejected him. While the question marks remained, he would never be accepted as a cosmonaut. While he wished to become a cosmonaut, the question marks would never be investigated from a positive standpoint. He was boxed in by the final stupidity of total bureaucracy, reduced to a mere cypher in a computer which had been programmed to ignore him.

CHAPTER FIVE

LEVITT ELEC CO PERSONAL ABRAHAM
  CUCKOO LP. 86003
  INTERIM REPORT TWO CODED TRANSMISSION CHANNEL
one.
  MESSAGE BEGINS STOP EGG NOW LAID AND INCUBATING
NICELY STOP EXPECT HATCHING IN FEW WEEKS STOP
SUGGEST YOU CONTACT AVIARY AND BEGIN SELECTING
SPECIMEN STOP TUES 1100 EST STOP MANVILLE APD/
3700925/WP MESSAGE ENDS.

This time, Manville severely underestimated the speed of
the positive reaction which followed his approach to NASA.
Just three days after he returned to Washington, Hayman
sent for him again.

He was beaming with satisfaction as Manville was escorted
into his office. He leapt to his feet, extending a hand as Manville approached the desk.

"Congratulations, Paul. You've done a fine job. I received
official go-ahead this morning. You surely must have put the
fear of God into someone."

In contrast to his superior, Manville looked glum, morose.
He merely grunted, nodding his head.

41

"You'll want to get back to Aspen and your skiing now, I suppose?" Hayman said.

"Not really. I thought there might be more for me to do on this project."

Hayman's eyes narrowed, quizzically. "More Paul? You've completed an excellent assignment. You've cleared official sanction for Operation Cuckoo to go ahead. What more could you expect to do?"

Manville fidgeted nervously, chewing at his bottom lip. Suddenly, he made up his mind, and threw the nervousness aside. He stood, leaning forward to place his palms flat on Hayman's desk, staring down upon the still seated man. "Let me go live on this one, Franklin. Let me follow it through."

Hayman sat back in his chair, staring deep into Manville's eyes and noted the intensity of feeling flashing in them.

"Please," Manville pushed. "You know I can do it, Franklin. You know what a damned good agent I was—still am."

Hayman sighed uncertainly. "It's been six years, Paul. You've been out of the field for six years. Everything has changed . . . people, contacts, methods."

Manville refused to be put off by the objections. "Nothing changes that much in this business. I can soon pick up on the current contacts, get a good team together."

"No real need," Hayman muttered. Manville's obvious enthusiasm was getting through to him. "We have the ideal man right on the spot. Georgi Kirov . . . remember him?"

The name triggered off old memories. Manville let them flood back, smiling wistfully. "Sure, I remember him. The last time we worked together was in Prague, late Spring of '68 . . . just before the Czechoslovakian balloon went up. Christ! Is that old fox still alive?"

Hayman also smiled. "Alive and kicking. He's a good man."

"The best," Manville agreed. He couldn't resist putting in a plug for himself. "You see . . . you can't beat a veteran when it comes to the crunch."

"Maybe . . . but veterans deserve a bit of R and R. Why this sudden desire to get back into the action?"

Manville sat down again, taking time to relax and frame his words carefully. "It's not sudden," he said, finally. "And I don't really think you need to ask why. We went through the mill together, Franklin. We both know how it was. The only difference between us is that you have a wife and three kids. They are the only reasons you content yourself sitting behind that desk now. All I ever had was the job. It's all I've got now."

Hayman nodded thoughtfully. "Yeah, I guess I get a yen for the old days every now and again," he admitted. "A family helps quell it."

Manville played up the empathy he had established. "It probably sounds like a B-movie cliché, but I married my country . . . and I still want to serve her. Being a messenger boy just isn't where it's at. It's not enough."

"I can't send you over the wall, you realize that?"

Manville shrugged. He was willing to compromise. "OK. I accept that. Maybe I am a little bit past the fully active phase. But you could give me this project, put me in charge of the entire operation—and let me see it through. I can liaise with Kirov and any of his boys. He trusts me, we got on well in the old days. We're both pros."

Hayman thought deeply for a long while before making up his mind. "All right, Paul . . . you've got it. There's one thing, though. . . ."

"Give it to me straight," Manville insisted.

"There's no room for friendship or personal favors in this business, you know that," Hayman continued. "I'm turning this project over to you purely because it is my personal opinion that you can do it. Understand?"

"Of course," Manville nodded.

"If that opinion proves to be wrong, I don't carry any cans. The buck stops firmly with you. Do I make myself clear?"

Manville smiled wryly. "Very," he murmured. "But you don't have to play coy with me, Franklin. I remember the old rules, the important ones. I foul up, and I'm expendable—right?"

Hayman didn't bother to confirm the fact. It was enough that both men understood the facts of the situation, and each other. Opening his desk drawer, he drew out the current Operation Cuckoo folder, and in a calm, businesslike voice, got straight down to it. "I'd better appraise you of the situation to date. As of now, this operation is phase two status, active. Kirov has already supplied us with a list of the elite Soviet Squadrons equipped with the modified Foxbats. There aren't many, as you might expect. We are going to have to choose our bird from a very short list of names, none of whom are known to us, or have any political or idealogical weaknesses to play upon."

Manville shrugged. "We could hardly expect to find a crack Soviet pilot who is an open dissident. Politics probably won't be the right carrot, in this case. Knowing the way Kirov works, it might not even be a carrot. As a back-up system, the big stick always had a lot going for it. Kirov was always a master at inveigling innocents on to the wrong side of the system. If he can't lure our bird out with a promise, he'll drive him out with a threat."

"Push or pull—who cares so long as the job gets done," Hayman put in. "It should be a plus factor that you know Kirov's methods, though."

"Sounds like we'll need all the help we can get. I assume that you have already made some sort of shortlist from the names supplied? Mind if I take a look?"

Hayman pushed the folder across the desk. "Go ahead. It's your baby now." He paused while Manville opened the folder and drew out a typed list of names. When he had had time to scan it, Hayman spoke again. "You will notice that there are virtually no service records or personal details. I am making the assumption that Kirov will be able to fill in some of the blanks once we come up with a workable number . . . probably no more than three. From the very limited data we have there, you'll see I have marked off five possibles with an asterisk."

Manville checked the five marked names. "I'd cut that to three at once," he said confidently. He pushed the list over the desk, turning it so that Hayman could read it. He stabbed out two names with his forefinger. "We can cancel those two for a start."

Hayman stared at him in bewilderment. "Why? You don't know anything about either man."

Manville grinned. "I know enough," he murmured, secretively.

Hayman shook his head. He was lost.

"Both born in the Ukraine, you'll notice," Manville explained after a few seconds. "Intractable bastards, the Ukrainians. Bloody breeding ground for KGB men and members of the Politburo."

"A generalization?" Hayman queried, sceptically.

"An observation . . . from bitter experience." Manville

was adamant. "I wouldn't trust one of those bastards further than I could throw him. A Latvian, yet. They're solid, dependable people, with a sense of humor. The best bet of all would be a Georgian. Natural rebels, backed up with the guts it takes to buck the system. Kirov comes from Georgia, you'll notice. Completely different outlook from other Soviets. More Mediterranean than Russian in temperament. And the women—they're something else! Smouldering, dark-eyed beauties, wine in their bloodstreams."

"Personal experience?" Hayman asked, lightheartedly.

Manville's face clouded over as he remembered. "Yes, once," he murmured distantly. "East Berlin, '49."

Hayman leered suggestively. "One of the perks of the business? Seduction in the name of the flag?"

Manville smiled sadly, almost forgivingly. "No, it was more than that. I nearly defected for her, did you know that? God, I was a hopelessly romantic bastard in those days."

Hayman was intrigued. "What happened to her?"

Manville's brief memory exploded. "She was shot by the KGB," he said flatly.

It was obvious that the matter was closed, yet for some reason, Hayman felt compelled to say something, add some note of sympathy. "I never knew."

Manville shrugged. "There are some things that never do get written into reports." He broke off, picking up the list of pilots once again. "Can I study this in depth for a few hours?"

"Sure. You'll want an office. I'll have one placed at your disposal."

"Thanks," Manville said. "Who is the link-man to Kirov, by the way?"

"There's no direct link," Hayman told him. "Kirov is too important to us to take any chances. It's a three-man chain to make contact. You need only know the first, who is Alex Raneleigh, based in Brussels. It leaves a four to six day delay in communication, unfortunately, but it protects Kirov's cover. In the case of an extreme emergency, a red alert, there is a method of getting a brief coded message to him directly via Voice of America. At exactly 2100 hours their time on Tuesdays and Thursdays, the DJ will relay any short coded messages in the dedication for the first record he plays on the "Lovers Overseas" program. If you need to use that facility,

45

and I emphasize that it is for emergency use only, your contact at Voice of America is Felix Klamin."

Manville nodded approvingly. "Sounds like a nice tight little set-up."

"It is. And I want it to stay that way. Good people like Georgi Kirov are bloody hard to come by. He is not one of our 'expendables'."

Manville rose to his feet, nodding understandingly. "I won't forget it." He began to move towards the door. "Shall I see your secretary about that office?"

"Sure," Hayman answered. "Tell her to set up Room 403 for full scrambler equipment, and external telephone and telex communication connected into the central processor for monitoring. Any hassles, get her to buzz me back for clearance. Tell her you want that office fully operational by 0900 tomorrow morning."

"Right." Manville opened the door, pausing in the portal to look back. "And thanks, Franklin," he added.

Hayman snorted ironically. "For what? Posting you back to the Alamo?"

Manville smiled in return. With a faint shrug, he walked out, closing the door firmly behind him.

As the man's footsteps receded down the corridor, all traces of humor left Hayman's face. He snatched up the green telephone on his desk and punched out an internal number. The receiver gave out two faint clicks as the call was bypassed into the central monitoring system before being shunted through to the appropriate department.

"Internal security," a voice muttered finally. "John Collins speaking. Yes, sir?"

"Job for you," Hayman snapped. "Top priority, immediate action. Paul Manville is active again. I want a full counter-security surveillance mounted on him at once. I want his home and office bugged this afternoon. But do it discreetly. I've allocated him to Room 403, with instructions for all communications systems to be channeled through the central processor. However, I'd like an individual monitor plugged in as well. When you've done that, I want his file removed from the records department and brought fully up to date for the 'active' unit. Also please instruct records to make up a current personal dossier on Manville and all his known contacts. You got all that?"

"Yes sir. I'll get onto it right away."

"Good." Hayman slammed the receiver back into its cradle and relaxed, knowing that he had done all which needed to be done. He felt no sense of guilt in the betrayal of personal confidence. As he had made a special point of emphasizing; there was absolutely no room for friendship or personal favors in this business.

CHAPTER SIX

Manville did not regard his surveillance as a betrayal of trust, either. He both expected and accepted it as a matter of course. Forewarned by his intimate knowledge of Hayman's standard tactics, Manville identified his tail less than three minutes after leaving the Levitt Electrical Building. The knowledge that he was being followed sent a shiver of excitement through him, quickly followed by a flash of the old bravado, which had more than once, in the past, bordered on the foolhardy.

He changed taxis twice within three blocks, keeping a careful eye on the black Plymouth sedan which cruised sedately along behind both vehicles. At one point, when the cab driver crashed a late amber light, Manville thought he had shaken off his pursuer, only to identify the vehicle a few moments later as it re-emerged from another side-street.

Manville nodded to himself with satisfaction. The tail was good, but how good? It seemed like an excellent opportunity to put himself to the test, to see if his reflexes were as finely honed as they had been in the old days. He leaned forward in his seat, tapping the cab driver lightly on the shoulder. "An extra ten on the fare if you'll do me a favor."

The driver spoke over his shoulder. "Sure, buddy, what can I do for you?"

"Take the next turn right," Manville told him. "As soon as you get around the corner, put your foot down for a couple of blocks. When I yell, take the first available right again, drop me off quick and then keep right on going as fast as you like. Don't stop or pick up another fare for at least another five blocks after you drop me. Got that?"

The driver nodded. "I got it. You want to pay me now? The fare's six bucks dead." He reached back over his shoulder for the money.

Manville peeled off a twenty, tucking it into the man's palm. "Keep the change," he said generously. "Now, let's go."

Manville glanced back at the black sedan as the taxi surged forward. Caught off guard for a few moments, the gap between the two cars widened noticeably, before the cab screeched around a right-hand bend, losing it altogether.

The cab hit nearly sixty on the long stretch to the next set of lights. Luckily, they were green. The driver shot over the intersection and kept his speed.

"Now," Manville yelled, reaching for the door handle. The cab swerved in towards the curb with a squeal of brakes. Manville threw himself out, calling out as he did so. "Now get going." He dashed into the nearest shop doorway as the cab took off from the curb again and accelerated away down the street.

Seconds later, when the Plymouth came screaming around the bend, Manville was safely observing it from the inside of a record store window. He felt another little thrill as the car slowed and pulled in towards the curb. They were a good team, all right. The old gag hadn't fooled them for a minute. Manville saw the passenger jump out of the car and slam the door. Losing no more than five seconds, the sedan shot away again in pursuit of the cab.

From his safe view point, Manville observed the pursuing agent closely. He was young, maybe no more than 25. Manville didn't recognize him. It figured. Hayman would be unlikely to choose anyone known personally to his prey.

The young man looked carefully from side to side. Manville shrank back behind a display rack for a moment as his eyes moved towards the store window. Peering out a few seconds later, Manville saw him turn and begin to stroll down the street.

He crossed the sales floor quickly, snatching up a large paper sack displaying the emblem of the store, and flipping a quarter to the girl clerk. Hurrying to the door, Manville held the sack up so that it half obscured his face and walked briskly after the young agent.

Fifteen yards down the street, the man had come to an uncertain halt, his eyes searching both sides of the street for a glimpse of his prey. He never even saw Manville coming.

Manville jabbed his knuckles in the man's back as he stepped up behind him. "Freeze," he hissed. "This is a .44 Magnum."

The young man stiffened. Manville lowered the paper sack and placed one hand on the man's shoulder, spinning him around. "You just got terminated, son," he said.

The agent looked into Manville's eyes sheepishly, saying nothing.

"What's your name?" Manville asked him.

There was no answer. Manville shrugged carelessly. "OK, keep it to yourself. I can check with Hayman in the morning. You're for the high jump."

The young agent decided there was no further point in trying to bluff. "You gonna put me on the carpet?"

Manville nodded. "Yep. I'm going to recommend that you are taken off duty immediately and sent back for a three-month intensive retraining schedule."

"That's pretty rough."

Manville smiled indulgently. "Not half as rough as being dead, son." He turned away and walked across the street. There was a new spring in his step, a feeling of youthful zest stirring his muscles. Manville felt good all over, in total control of himself and any possible situation which could arise. It had been a long time since he had felt like that. Too damned long.

Manville had pruned Hayman's original shortlist of five to just two names, and added a third of his own choosing from the original dossier. The name meant virtually nothing to him, and a casual observer might easily have suspected that Manville had picked it out completely at random. Only two facts were known about the pilot at that stage; his age, 28, and his birthplace. Tbilisi. Manville was playing a wild hunch. He had picked out the only Georgian-born individual purely on the strength of his personal feelings.

He jotted the three names down on a slip of paper with a

51

gesture of finality and picked up the internal telephone, stabbing out the number for the code-room.

"Give me the chief cryptographer," he said softly, as a woman answered the call. There was a brief pause, before Emmet came on the line. "Yeah?"

"This is Paul Manville, in 403. I want to send a telex to Alex Raneleigh in Brussels. What's his current code, please?"

"Hold on," Emmet muttered. Over the receiver, Manville heard the faint rustling of paper. "Here you are . . . code 15. You want to draft out the message, or have me do it?"

"Thanks. I'll do it," Manville said firmly, hanging up. He reached into his desk and pulled out a current code manual. Laboriously, he began the complicated procedure of transcribing his intended message into apparently meaningless symbols.

Two hours later, when he had finished, Manville began to double-check it, by re-translating it all back into English. He was damned if he was going to code the easy way, using his computer. Manville only trusted himself, and to hell with the extra time manual effort consumed.

The message checked perfectly. He studied the English copy for a few more moments before dropping it into the shredder.

ORIGIN PAUL MANVILLE, LEVITT ELECTRICAL. DESTINATION BRUSSELS FOR EYES OF ALEX RANELEIGH ONLY. INSTRUCTIONS FORWARD REQUEST FOR FULL DETAILS OF FOLLOWING SOVIET AIR FORCE PILOTS TO GEORGI KIROV. ONE DMITRI PASSK, BORN KIEV 1943. TWO NICOLAS SOLVETIOV, BORN LENINGRAD 1946. THREE MIKHAIL VOLOGSKY, BORN TBILISI 1949. REQUEST URGENT REPLY IN CODE SIX

Satisfied, Manville picked up the coded copy and headed towards the dispatch room. Once the message was on the wire, he had little else to do except sit back and wait for a few days. Perhaps a quick trip back to Aspen was on the cards, after all. Feeling the way he did, there was no bloody mountain on God's Earth which could daunt him now.

CHAPTER SEVEN

LEVITT ELEC CO PERSONAL MANVILLE
   CUCKOO LP 86003
   ORIGIN BRUSSELS STOP RANELEIGH
   MESSAGE BEGINS STOP RE INSTRUCTIONS FROM AVIARY
REGARDING THREE SPECIMENS STOP FIRST CHOICE
UNSUITABLE AS HAS SECURE NEST AND TWO FLEDGELINGS
STOP CHOICE TWO POSSIBILITY BUT KNOWN TO FLY CLOSELY
WITH FLOCK STOP CHOICE THREE SEEMS HIGHLY PROMISING
AS LONE BIRD WITH POSSIBLE MIGRATORY TENDENCIES STOP
GROUND BAIT BEING LAID STOP WILL ADVISE LATER WITH
FULL OBSERVATION REPORT STOP MESSAGE ENDS STOP
MON 0800 GMT

Manville could not help himself gloating slightly as he digested the essence of the message. His hunch had been right after all. His own choice, Mikhail Vologsky, had proved to be the most promising candidate of the three. It seemed to be a good omen.

Manville thrust the telex aside and turned his full attention to the more detailed report which had followed the preparatory message just four days later. The speed and efficiency with which it had been delivered was impressive, and suggested strongly that Kirov had also worked largely upon intuition. He had provided merely skimpy further details of the first two pilots, dedicating his greatest effort to building up a detailed profile of Mikhail Vologsky. Dmitri Passk was a non-runner, with a wife and two children to hold him firmly to his homeland. To attempt defection would be to sign their death warrants, and no man could be expected to do that. Nicolas Solvetiov, the second choice, had no known family ties but was known to be a strong party man who toed the line. He did not appear to be the type which could be persuaded to turn traitor. Vologsky, however, was a very different bird indeed. Manville re-read his personal dossier with mounting enthusiasm.

Vologsky emerged from the mass of details as an almost archetypal defector. He was young, brilliant and alone. He had no parents, wife and children . . . not even a girl-friend who could be used as a weapon of enslavery against him. He did not even appear to get on well with his colleagues. He was a man who was isolated in his world, to such a degree that his immediate environment probably hardly mattered to him. A man such as Mikhail Vologsky would be equally relaxed in Moscow or New York, Leningrad or Los Angeles.

His record appeared flawless, yet there was an inconsistency which grated harshly, leaving room for a lot of speculation. Given his period of service, and his unblemished record, Vologsky should have risen well above his present rank of lieutenant, yet he had not. It suggested that there was something about the man, some unknown factor which made him slightly suspect in the eyes of the authorities. The powers-that-be were obviously a shade disenchanted with Lt. Vologsky. It followed, logically, that he might easily reciprocate those vague doubts. In terms of the job he had to do, Volgosky was a natural. He was a superb pilot, with a singular, agile mind. If any flier could steal a Foxbat and fly it to the West, Vologsky could. But would he? That, was the six-million-dollar question. And what would be necessary to "persuade" him? If every man had his price, what was Vologsky's?

Manville thought back to his earlier conversation with Hayman, the discussion of the relative merits of the carrot and the stick. Perhaps a combination of both? Either way, it was Kirov's problem. Manville had every faith in the Russian's ability to dig out the vital weakness in Vologsky's make-up which would turn him into a traitor. All he needed was the go-ahead.

Accordingly, Manville took out his code manual and began preparing an official sanction for dispatch to Brussels.

PART TWO: THE HATCHING

CHAPTER EIGHT

The elongated, slightly oval hummock could hardly be called
a grave, more a burial mound. What lay beneath it was totally unimportant, having lost all relevance to the world when
the worms, the termites and the bacteria had converted the
last shred of flesh into dust and let the dry bones to crumble.

Nevertheless, Alexai Ybreska gazed upon the weed-fes-
tooned mound with a beam of satisfaction. To him, it
represented life, not death. A good life, at that. Another successful task accomplished meant a further two thousand
American dollars deposited in his Tel Aviv bank account,
waiting for when he finally obtained his exit visa and could
flee to the new homeland.

Kneeling, Ybreska carefully rubbed the soil at either end
of the grave, making sure there was no buried stone or
marker which would identify it. There was nothing. The site
was perfect in every way. Ybreska glanced around at the
crumbling ruins of the old, derelict church. At night, perhaps,
a few peasants might find their way here, congregating for
worship like nocturnal pilgrims. By day, the area was completely deserted. The fields surrounding the churchyard had
long ago been relieved from private ownership and lumped
together into one huge collective farm. The few small cot-
tages which had once made up the village community had

59

been bulldozed into the ground and their occupants moved into the gray and faceless high-rise apartment blocks of the new urban development. Any farm workers who came near the site in the course of their daily work were too busy to lift their eyes from the soil to take in the surrounding landscape. or individual figures moving within it.

Yes, the grave would no nicely, Ybreska decided again. He need look no further. His Washington contacts would be pleased with him.

Find us a grave, they had instructed. Neglected, about ten to twelve years old and completely anonymous. In a quiet place, no more than ten miles from Tbilisi. Find that, and wait for further instructions.

Ybreska had never thought of himself as an agent, or a spy. Besides the fact that he was a Jew, he never even considered himself a dissident. He did not want to betray Russia, or even abandon her, for any ideological reasons. It was much simpler than that. At an early age, Ybreska had seen through the myth and realized that money was the sole power which kept the Earth turning. With it, life was good; without it, a struggle. There was no need to struggle.

He thought again of the bank account in Tel Aviv, manipulating figures in his head and converting them into possessions and acquisitions. It was a deliciously decadent daydream which stirred the blood, sending adrenalin pumping through his system. With one last glance around him, Ybreska confirmed the fact that he was alone and unobserved, and stood up, wiping the faint smears of dirt from his hands.

He began to walk away from the burial ground, his heart surging with excitement. It was all so easy, and so worthwhile. Ybreska laughed, suddenly, the words of a popular Western song breaking on his lips.

Ybreska vaulted over the low, crumbling wall surrounding the old churchyard on to the rough pitted track which led toward Tbilisi. A couple of hours leisurely stroll would get him to the Georgian capital shortly before dusk fell. He would meet Kirov and report his success. Well before the evening really got under way, he would have a couple of hundred roubles in his pocket, to be converted into a night of vodka-drinking and celebration.

Despite these optimistic thoughts, and his excitement, Ybreska stopped singing abruptly as he began to walk along the track. Such as it was, it constituted a public place, and he could no longer guarantee himself the seclusion and privacy of the deserted churchyard. One did not sing forbidden songs, in English, in a public place.

Silent now, Ybreska fell into a carefully measured pace, without even realizing the strange irony of his suddenly changed mood. It was not in his nature to reflect overmuch on things. He chose not to investigate the possibility that there might, after all, be other reasons why he wished to quit his homeland.

Georgi Kirov was waiting for him at the appointed place and time. He stepped out from the dimly-lit doorway of a sidewalk cafe to greet Ybreska with no more than a curt nod of his head. Falling into step together, the two men walked slowly and silently down Rustaveli Avenue, towards the open plaza where they could talk freely.

The plaza was a place for nocturnal meetings, although the majority were of a far simpler, far older kind than two men planning international espionage. Young lovers strolled quietly beneath the trees, or sat together on the few wooden benches, daring to snatch the odd, discreet kiss or embrace. Kirov and Ybreska walked among them, still saying nothing. They were just two friends, enjoying the cool evening air, perhaps walking up a thirst before repairing to a beer hall.

Finally, when Kirov was sure that there was no one within earshot, he stopped, producing a packet of cheap Polish cigarettes from his pocket and offering them to Ybreska. "Smoke?"

Ybreska accepted gratefully. "Thank you."

Kirov returned the packet to his pocket without extracting one for himself. He produced a box of matches, scraping one into flame and cupping his hand around it as he offered his companion a light. In the flickering illumination of the match, Kirov's lips moved. "You have had a successful day, Alexai Ybreska?"

He saw the excited, childish smile on the younger man's face and knew the answer. "The site you have found . . . it is perfectly suitable to our purpose?"

"Perfectly," Ybreska assured him. "It is exactly what you asked for."

"You are sure there is no marker . . . no signs that the grave has been tended in recent months?"

Ybreska shook his head. "No one has been there for years, I would swear it."

"Good," Kirov nodded with satisfaction. "Tell me the exact location, please." He continued nodding thoughtfully as Ybrska detailed the site. "Yes, it sounds ideal. You have done well, Alexai Ybreska."

"And the money?" Ybreska blurted out. "The two thousand American dollars? It will be paid immediately? Any day now, I shall obtain my visa."

"It will be paid at once. I shall authorize it myself tonight. You know that I always keep my word."

"Of course, Georgi Kirov," Ybreska whispered deferentially. He paused for a moment before speaking again, when his voice took on a slightly wheedling tone. "But a few roubles now, eh? On account?"

In the darkness, Ybreska could not see the sneer which curled his companion's lips as he answered. "Three hundred roubles, it is all that I can spare."

"That will be excellent," Ybreska murmured, hardly able to suppress his excitement. He had not expected that much for such a simple task. He heard the faint rustle of paper, then Kirov grasped his wrist and pressed a bundle of folded money into his palm.

"Go now, Alexai Ybreska. Do not attempt to contact me. If there is another errand you can run, I shall get in touch with you again."

"Of course." Ybreska pocketed the money and began to move away. He looked back, briefly, but Kirov had already melted away into the darkness.

Kirov gathered phlegm in his mouth as he strode away, spitting it onto the ground as a gesture of the disgust he felt. He despised the little Jew for his grasping, mercenary manner, despised himself for having to use such trash. In complete contrast to Ybreska, Kirov was a man of deep political and ideological convictions. He loathed the repressive State and the system which it supported. His heart cried out for his countrymen, forced to live gray, drab existences in a land where there was no freedom and little truth, but so much potential beauty. He was an activist by total commitment, and a professional. He was an agent, not of the capitalist West, but of the spirit of human freedom.

His brief anger passed, and a wistful smile crossed his

swarthy face. No, it was not really disgust he felt for people like Alexai Ybreska; it was pity. The system created them, forced their greed upon them. They were helpless little flies stuck fast to a sticky trap from which there was no escape. People like Ybreska were too afraid to have a commitment, even to openly express doubts. Ybreska would not ever think of his little errands as subversive acts. To him, they were something of an adventure, a small knock at the system which gave him the illusion of individual importance. The minor tasks which Ybreska performed were of no real significance to him, merely a means of making a little extra money *na levo*—on the side.

But there was one more, all-important reason to feel pity for Alexai Ybreska. Thus far, Kirov had received only a vague brief about his current project. His limited activities to date had been confined to an uncommitted setting-up operation. It was merely a process of putting out delicate feelers, testing the winds and establishing a rough but workable scenario to contain the plot. Everything he had done was just window-dressing, unimportant in itself. If and when the word came from Washington to advance Operation Cuckoo into the second, active stage however, things would be very different indeed. It would immediately become a project of prime importance, far too serious to leave any loose ends hanging free. Kirov knew only one way to work efficiently and safely—to always cover his tracks carefully behind him. It was a question of survival, both of himself and the operation. Once the project swung into motion, Alexai Ybreska became one of those loose ends, potentially dangerous, and therefore expendable. At that point, Kirov knew that he would be forced to eliminate the little man, without a moment's hesitation. Even if he did not do so by personal choice, the execution would doubtless be ordered from Washington as a matter of course.

But such thoughts were negative, non-productive. Kirov dismissed Ybreska from his mind as he strolled leisurely through the streets. In place of the pathetic, unimportant little Jew, Kirov focussed upon the main character of the plot, the pilot, Mikhail Vologsky. Now there was a man worthy of thought, deliberation. It was not only the pilot's importance. He was an enigma, a challenge, a man-shaped outline of a jigsaw puzzle, to be filled in piece by piece until a complete portrait could be seen. Without that, Kirov was fumbling in the dark, Operation Cuckoo was only an abstracted idea.

Kirov assessed the scant information he had managed to accumulate over the last few weeks. It was not much. He knew Vologsky's age, his birthplace and the fact that both his parents had died under vaguely mysterious circumstances in the mid-sixties. Hence the unmarked grave; still part of the window dressing. Vologsky himself had no knowledge of exactly how his parents had died, or where their bodies lay. The grave was Kirov's first contact point; a seed from which casual conversation and perhaps sympathy might be persuaded to grow. Show a man his lost mother's grave, and you invoked deep emotional forces which could be played upon, manipulated.

Kirov had already prepared that preliminary, and it remained alone, and somewhat nebulous. He needed more, several important pieces of the jigsaw puzzle before trying to establish direct contact. Vologsky's political affiliations were unknown; like many young men, he was a Party member, yet did he carry the card out of conviction or as a means to an untroubled life and career? That was of the utmost importance, and had to be answered quickly. Vologsky's career itself posed further questions. Had he chosen a military life through love of the Motherland, or had he been channelled into it by the State that had reared him? Was he committed to the role of protector, or did he just love flying? He was a Georgian by birth; did he, then, share the fierce nationalistic pride of his fellow-countrymen, or had his orphanage moulded him into one of the bland, rootless vegetables who regarded themselves as Soviet citizens?

So many questions. And no easy way to discover the answers. When it came to assembling facts and details, the system was a formidable obstacle. Russia was an information vacuum, in which questions were positively discouraged. To extract a telephone number, one had to furnish the full name, address, exact age and birthplace of the subscriber in question. To learn the departure time of a train, one had to pay 10 kopecks and consult a public information booth. Frequently, Kirov wondered if his Western contacts had the faintest conception of how difficult his work was, under the vastly different circumstances which prevailed in the two societies.

Immersed in his thoughts, Kirov reached his small tailor's shop without realizing it. Unlocking the door, he walked through the darkened workroom and slowly climbed the two flights of stairs which led to his cramped living area above. Pausing outside his living room door, he switched on the hall light and crouched down on his knees. He examined the bottom of the door carefully.

Three inches in from the portal, Kirov's keen eyes picked out the single human hair which he had fixed, with a smear of soapstone, between the door and the bare wooden floor. It was still in place, a sure sign that the door had not been opened while he was out. His home remained inviolate; his cover stood undetected.

He entered the room, crossing to the telephone. He picked up the receiver and carefully unscrewed the ear- and mouth-pieces, peering inside. Replacing them both, he upended the main body of the telephone cradle and took a small screwdriver from a nearby drawer. He removed the base plate of the telephone and examined the instrument's innards. The telephone was just as it should be, with no bugging device to turn his private conversations into public knowledge. It did not, of course, preclude a wire-tap upon the instrument, but then Kirov was too professional to use the telephone for anything but legitimate business or private conversation anyway.

These simple precautions observed, Kirov relaxed and sat down on the edge of his small cot, smiling with relief. Another day had passed in which he had remained safe and untroubled by the authorities. It was a milestone in his life. Every night was a milestone, and had been for the past fifteen years. Day to day. It was the only way a man in his lonely and dangerous profession could live. Sooner or later, he knew, would come the tramp of heavy feet up the bare wooden stairs, the harsh pounding on the door and the imperious, loathsome voice of the KGB. Then it would be over. Death or the camps. One and the same thing, really.

But not tonight. Maybe tomorrow, or the day after that. Maybe never, Kirov dared to reflect, in a rare moment of optimism. Perhaps this operation would be the last, perhaps his Western masters would finally decide that the old work-horse had given his best and deserved to be put out in rich pastures.

And then . . . who could tell? A comfortable little *dacha* in the peace of the countryside, perhaps, or a manipulated exit visa, a chance to get over the border and over the wall?

A dreamy smile crept over Kirov's face as he thought of

Vologsky again. How easy it could be for him—to simply sit in the cockpit of his Foxbat and fly to freedom. A man would have to be an idiot to turn down such a chance.

Feeling hopeful rather than confident, Kirov lay back on his cot and fell into a deep sleep.

CHAPTER NINE

The Foxbat was barely cruising at 700 knots, at an altitude of 50,000 feet. It was well over 2000 miles from home base, with no hope of returning there direct.

The aircraft was set on automatic pilot, leaving Vologsky little more than a passenger for the time being. With the relaxed detachment of a man who has an implicit trust in his technology, Vologsky cast his eyes over the bewildering array of instruments which made up the control panel, taking note of the few facts he actually needed to know.

The fuel gauge read a little over half full. Allowing for a 12% margin of error, that gave him something between eleven and thirteen hundred miles of flight at his present subsonic speed. If he needed to gain a lot of altitude, or make a run for it, that figure could be more than halved. The chronometer confirmed his flying time since the aerial refueling over Omsk, tallying with the covered distance on the on-board computer. It was also a reminder that it was nearly time to seek out his last visual co-ordinate and prepare to take over manual control of the aircraft once again.

Vologsky looked out of the cockpit at the sprawling terrain below. He had a clear picture, for there was virtually no cloud cover, with only a few wispy strips of cirrus streaked like vapor trails against the reddish-brown groundscape. It was an uninspiring view. The vast tracts of sterile desert land were broken only by irregular patches of short, dry grasses or rough scrubland. Vologsky was over some of the most useless and unwanted land in the world, where there was no rural life and many thousands of miles separated the few townships.

He smiled thinly, reflecting upon the scenery beneath. Useless and unwanted it might be, but that did not interfere with its importance. The majority of the vast Kazakhstan region was a no man's land, but it formed a deep buffer zone between the populated areas of the North-Western USSR and the Mongolian deserts which gave way to the Chinese border. It had to be constantly and carefully monitored, for if and when Chinese aggression ever came in earnest, that was where the tanks and the missile launchers would be concentrated.

Such was Vologsky's mission today; to overfly the very Sino-Soviet border at Alma-Ata then cruise along the Sinkiang border as far as the Turfan Depression taking photographic, radar and infra-red records.

The Foxbat's infra-red scanners, probing ahead, picked up Vologsky's visual co-ordinate first, identifying it as a large cold patch in the center of the surrounding wasteland. Vologsky adjusted himself in his flight couch, flexing his fingers before he gripped the control yoke again and prepared to switch the aircraft back to manual control. Reaching to the control panel, he flipped the auto-pilot to the off position. There was no sign, other than the winking of a small green light, that the aircraft had reverted to his control.

Easing forward on the yoke, Vologsky tested the change of control, putting the Foxbat into a gentle dive and taking it down to just over 45,000 feet. Ahead, and slightly to his left, he saw the patch of blue against the desert and knew that he was perfectly on course. Moments later, as Lake Balkhash slipped away below him, Vologsky made a minor adjustment and set the Foxbat on a course which would take it directly over the home missile bases at Alma-Ata. With that destination a good thirty minutes of flying time away, Vologsky climbed to 60,000 feet and snapped on the auto-pilot once again. He set about using the time to run a complete check on his detection and recording equipment.

A shrill bleep from the missile detection system gave him a brief forewarning that his aircraft was being scanned by radar tracking devices. The system, automatically self-arming, clicked into frenzied activity, locating and cross-checking the radar sources and seeking out the placement of active missiles within an area of several square miles. Fed through the onboard computer, the data was assembled and correlated in seconds. He was being scanned by his own people, and he had been identified. Accepting that the contact was friendly, the detection system shut itself down.

Vologsky took over control again, knowing that he must be within twenty miles of the outer warning ring around Alma-Ata. To be completely safe, he activated his automatic call-signal which would be picked up on the ground. It ensured that no trigger-happy missile controller would fail to observe the safety precautions and attempt a little target practice. Moments later, Vologsky received a two-tone pulse signal over his headphones, followed by a brief message.

"You are acknowledged, Timberwolf Seven. You are clear to fly over the inner ring defense system."

Vologsky punched out a sequence on the computer panel, which automatically locked him in to the local frequency. "Message received, Alma-Ata. Am now breaking contact." He flipped the two switches which plunged the aircraft into total radio silence. He was really on his own now, and in less than two minutes he would be flying over hostile territory.

As the last of the concrete missile silos of Alma-Ata slipped away beneath him, Vologsky made his final preparations for the mission proper. He activated the aircraft's radar scrambling unit, switched on the moving map display and set the detection and recording equipment for fully automatic sequence. The actual mechanics of the operation would take care of themselves. All Vologsky had to do now was to fly the Foxbat across the Chinese border and bring her out safely again. He smiled grimly at the thought. All! It was a small word, but one with a wealth of meaning. Thirteen per cent, the figure was. Every pilot in his squadron knew it by heart. The surveillance missions were frequent and regular. Out of every hundred aircraft which ventured over the border, eighty-seven returned safely. The rest were written off to the Chinese, who did not take kindly to violation of their airspace.

Vologsky squirmed in his flight couch, adjusting his position. He took several deep breaths, preparing his mind and body for the disorientating shocks of passing through the sound-gate and going supersonic. He fixed his eyes firmly on the Mach-counter as he began to throttle up.

The needle crept steadily up to Mach .99 and hung there for several seconds. Vologsky kept the power steady as he coped with the familiar, yet always unnerving, transition from sub- to supersonic flight. The vague red haze swam over his eyes for a moment, then cleared. The loose skin of Vologsky's cheeks and lower chin quivered under the increasing pull of the G-force and his entire body seemed to take on a couple of stone in extra weight. The numbing effect of complete spatial disorientation blurred his mind momentarily before it struggled to compensate.

He was ready. Vologsky throttled up gently, and the Foxbat shuddered through the sound-gate. There were two minor shock-waves from the nose of the craft, rippling through the cockpit before being shrugged off by the surging momentum of the sleek fuselage. Then, as the Mach-counter needle jumped over the center position, Vologsky felt the last of the physiological discomforts as his body seemed to become suddenly weightless, oddly detached from his brain and reality.

The brief, irrational mental jolts quickly followed. The plane was no longer controllable, flight was a scientific impossibility—it felt like a submarine ploughing through thick oil, rather than an aircraft knifing through rarified air.

At Mach 1.2, the Foxbat finally slouged off the world of sound with a dull, ominous rumble, and Vologsky surged with new enthusiasm and excitement, happy to be in perfect control of one of the fastest flying machines in the world. Acceleratng up to Mach 1.8, he took the Foxbat over the Mongolian border and began the first of his two runs down the Sinkiang-Uighur plateau.

So he was one of the eighty-seven! Vologsky congratulated himself as he streaked back across the border, his mission completed. He flipped the radio switches on again and transmitted his call signal to the base at Alma-Ata.

His headphones crackled into life. "Welcome home, Timberwolf Seven."

"Good to be back," Vologsky acknowledged. He was

jubilant, in an unusually chatty mood. "I'd still rather be up here than down there, though. You lads really are sitting in the middle of a hornet's nest."

The radio operator's voice came back, shaken and uncertain. "You are on open transmission, Timberwolf Seven."

The warning tone cut through Vologsky's ebullience. He had suddenly made a serious error. Any reference, however vague, to the Chinese arms build-up along the border was top secret, and highly delicate. The Alma-Ata operator was nervous and embarrassed merely overhearing Vologsky's verbal faux pas.

Vologsky snapped off transmission abruptly. With luck, the call might not have been monitored. If the radio operator kept his mouth shut, the transgression might not get to the ears of his superiors. He set a course for Omsk and cut in the automatic pilot, settling back to cope with the chain of niggling worries that his blunder had triggered off.

The arms build-up itself was very worrying indeed. Vologsky had not monitored all his automatic recording, but he had seen enough to know that things were really serious. The Chinese were massing huge displacements of heavy tanks and artillery all along the border. The regular border clashes were rapidly escalating towards a full-scale offensive. The missiles would come next; and from then on it would be a far lower percentage of survelliance aircraft which returned safely. It was not a happy thought. In Vologsky's squadron, each individual pilot fell due for such a flight every twelve days on the rota system.

But twelve days was a long time. Too long to brood and worry about vague possibilities. Vologsky forced himself to relax, shutting the matter from his mind. There were more optimistic things in the immediate future. After a ground refueling at Omsk, he would have a two-hour rest period before flying on to his home base at Kharkov. After debriefing, he was due for two full days of leave. That was something to look forward to.

CHAPTER TEN

Georgi Kirov packed the small Moskvich van carefully. Spreading a plastic dust-proof sheet on the floor of the vehicle, he lay two new rolls of fine Czechoslovakian serge cloth side by side, covering them with brown paper. On top, he placed two more rolls of cheaper, coarser home-produced material and an oilskin pouch containing the tools of his trade—finely-honed shears, measuring tapes and a selection of threads and stainless steel needles, carefully graded in size. A manual of current patterns and an album of stock materials completed the transportable tailoring business, and Kirov was ready to travel again.

Over the years, tailoring had proved a superb cover, and Kirov's specially cultivated clientele the source of much useful information. Carefully, painstakingly, he had built up the traveling side of his business, to cater for the elite in the hierarchy of State power. The small shop in Tbilisi was only a base, from which to order cloths and make tax returns. Kirov did little actual business there, for he had deliberately priced himself well outside the common market. Few ordinary citizens could afford to pay the 300 roubles which Kirov had set as a starting price for the most basic of suits. Instead, he had directed his talents to bolstering the vanity of the military and the higher-paid members of the Civil service. High-ranking officers were only too willing to pay vastly inflated prices for a little judicious alteration and improvement to their standard uniforms. They would happily pay out princely sums for completely new garments made from superior imported cloths. Important members of the KGB, the Politburo and the GRU walked about resplendant in clothes finely tailored by Georgi Kirov. Business was spread by word of mouth, a favor extended as bait for a favor to be returned. It worked out well. Kirov not only got to travel freely within military establishments and top security complexes, he was known and respected by important public figures. It offered a certain degree of protection.

Now, Kirov was putting all these advantages to work. Hopefully, they would provide him with the opportunity to make contact with the pilot Vologsky. He was on his way to the Red Air Force base at Kharkov, one of the main defenses of Moscow and its environs. That contact was now necessary and pressing, for Operation Cuckoo had advanced into its final stage.

Before preparing to drive off, Kirov returned to the shop and took one vital tool of his trade from its secret hiding place. Shielding the small .32 revolver beneath his armpit, he ducked behind cover of the van's open rear doors and secreted the gun in a small concealed trap cut into the vehicle's floor. Now he was fully prepared for both aspects of his profession. Before leaving for Kharkov, there was the matter of Alexai Ybreska to conclude.

Ybreska waited impatiently near the abandoned churchyard for Kirov to arrive. He paced the dusty road somewhat nervously, yet hardly able to contain the soaring enthusiasm in his heart. He had news . . . news which would doubtless upset Georgi Kirov, and he feared the man's negative reaction. Still, the aspect of that news which affected himself was uppermost in his mind, threatening to swamp such minor worries.

In the distance, Ybreska saw a vehicle approaching, throwing up huge dust-clouds as it bumped along the rutted track. He glanced at his watch. It could only be Kirov. The man was always exactly on time. Taking a few deep breaths to prepare himself for the encounter, Ybreska stepped into the middle of the road to meet his contact.

Kirov brought the Moskvich to a halt, recognizing Ybreska from a distance. He peered out through the windscreen and side-windows, scouring the surrounding countryside. It seemed to be completely deserted. Calmly and methodically, Kirov climbed from the driving seat and skirted round to the back of the van, opening the rear door. He took the revolver from its hiding place, quickly checking that all the chambers were full, and slipping off the safety catch. Satisfied that the gun was ready for immediate use, Kirov transferred it discreetly to his jacket pocket before turning and walking towards the waiting figure of Ybreska.

A loose end, Kirov reminded himself as he came close to the man. Nothing more. Identity did not matter, humanity was a side-issue, with no real relevance to the matter at hand. Nevertheless, Kirov could not stop himself staring at Ybreska's face and feeling the sense of overwhelming pity once again. He did not enjoy killing.

The gap between the two men had closed to a matter of a few yards. Kirov's eyes continued to scan Ybreska's face, trying to probe the strange mixture of expressions which it displayed openly. Ybreska seemed both excited and worried at the same time. He appeared jumpy and ill at ease, ready to blurt something out at any moment.

Perhaps the man was excited because he saw the chance of making more money, Kirov reflected, in the hope that reminding himself of the mercenary side of the Jew's character might make his job a little easier. Casually, Kirov dipped his hand into the pocket, encountering the cold hardness of the gun.

They were face to face now. Ybreska's lips trembled. He stuttered out what he had to say.

"Forgive me, Georgi Kirov . . . but I think I must disappoint you. I can undertake no little errands for you."

"No, you cannot undertake any more errands," Kirov repeated, in a cold, dull voice. His fingers curled around the butt of the gun, taking up a gentle purchase on the trigger. "Still, it is of no consequence now."

The decision expressed, Ybreska could no longer restrain the happiness and excitement which welled up inside him. The small obstacle which he had feared appeared to have been a groundless worry. Kirov did not seem unduly disappointed that he could no longer help him. Ybreska reached out with both arms to embrace Kirov by the shoulders, his face wreathed in a rapturous smile.

Kirov stepped back smartly, his senses alerted. His finger tightened on the trigger. His hand began to lift gently and slowly from his pocket.

Ybreska's extended hands embraced only empty air as Kirov moved back out of his reach, but it didn't matter. His news was too important, too wonderful to be contained for a single instant longer.

"It came, Kirov, it finally came," he screamed out exultantly. "My exit visa. In only three days I shall be free to leave for Israel."

Compassion hit Kirov in the gut, a cold, sharp feel of twisting steel. It mingled, clashed with the equally cold sense of duty, the detached knowledge of what had to be done. Kirov's eyes bored into the bright, expanded pupils of his comrade, seeing the joy of life and living which they reflected, and feeling the icy coldness of death which he bore to extinguish it. There was a moment of terrible confusion and doubt, in which Kirov's body was frozen and immobile. Then his hand began to move again, clearing his pocket.

It emerged empty, to dangle listlessly at his side. Knowing nothing. Ybreska continued to babble on excitedly. "Just imagine, Kirov, after all these years. I can hardly believe my luck!"

Kirov exhaled a long, shuddering breath. "You are lucky indeed, Ybreska. How lucky, you will never know."

"So you see, I am happy, yet I regret that I can no longer be of any assistance to you," Ybreska murmured, deferentially.

"I told you . . . it is of no consequence. You will be leaving Tbilisi soon?"

Ybreska nodded happily. "I leave for Odessa this very night. My ship will sail in two or three days."

Kirov found the speed of the man's departure something of a consolation. He appeared to risk very little by letting him live. "I wish you every happiness in your new homeland, Alexai Ybreska," he murmured, with genuine warmth. With that, he turned away and walked towards the waiting van.

Ybreska watched it depart in a swirling dust-cloud. There was only one small patch of disappointment in his vista of happiness. He had expected some final pay-off, a terminal settling of accounts for services rendered.

Kirov the tailor put a last quick tuck in position and stepped back to appraise his workmanship. He spoke through a mouthful of pins. "What do you think, Major?"

Major Tzann posed like a peacock, inspecting himself in a nearby mirror. "A little more shaping at the waist, perhaps?" He could not fault the appearance of the almost-finished uniform, and he understood nothing of the tailor's craft. Still, it kept civilians and lower ratings in their place to affect a certain degree of criticism.

Kirov nodded humbly, used to such posturings. "Perhaps you are right," he muttered. "It is not easy to hang a fine suit from shoulders so broad and straight as yours, Major."

A slight smile of pride crossed Tzann's face at the discreet flattery. "It is a problem which has been remarked upon before," he lied.

Kirov crouched at his side, removing a couple of pins and replacing them in exactly the same position. "There now, is that better?"

"Yes, much," Tzann retorted. "I think you have it now."

"Good." Kirov stood, moving back a couple of paces. "Perhaps if you could be so good as to slip the jacket off, Major, we might complete the hanging of the trousers?"

"Of course." Tzann divested himself of the jacket. "And then? You can complete the uniform quickly?"

Kirov spread his hands, affecting a faint shrug. "A matter of two days at most. Then I can deliver the finished uniform when I come this way again . . . perhaps in a week or so?"

Tzann clucked his tongue with mild exasperation. "It is not possible before then?"

"The Major is in a hurry?" Kirov enquired.

Tzann saw another opportunity to assert himself. "It is simply that I expected better service," he snapped. "I have an important function to attend in a few days' time. A matter of the utmost importance, you understand?"

"Of course, Major," Kirov murmured deferentially. "Then perhaps you could make a small room available to me for a few hours? I have with me everything I require. I would be happy to finish the uniform here before returning to Tbilisi."

Major Tzann thought for a few seconds. "Yes, that would be possible. I will arrange for a spare office to be placed at your disposal."

"Thank you," Kirov said. He dropped to his knees, busying himself with adjusting the drop of the trousers from Tzann's inside leg and fighting the irrational and childish desire to jab a pin into his testicles. "Do you know Tbilisi, Major?" he inquired, conversationally.

"I have been there," Tzann said, off-hand. He was a Muscovite. "A dreary little place, if I remember correctly. Typically Georgian, like the people. Surly, and far too fond of their drink."

"But fine pilots sometimes, eh?" Kirov inquired, slyly.

Tzann took the bait. "Pilots?"

Kirov chuckled. "I am proud to say that one of our comrades is in this very squadron. Mikhail Vologsky . . . you would know him, of course? He is a fine young officer, I understand? A lieutenant, I believe, unless he has been promoted. It is some time since I heard news of him. I was a close friend of his parents, you know. Both dead now, alas. A tragic accident some years ago."

"Vologsky?" Tzann appeared to ponder, as though the name of a junior officer meant little to him. Actually, he knew Lt. Vologsky well. A typical Georgian, and no mistake. Strange fellow, quite disliked by his comrades. "Yes, I have heard of him. He is still a lieutenant, and quite unlikely to rise much higher." A sudden joke, at Vologsky's expense, occurred to Major Tzann, and he voiced it. "A great tragedy, in his case. He had great dreams of rising very much higher indeed. Into space, in fact." Tzann laughed nastily at the bitter witticism, inviting Kirov to join in, maneuvering him into a betrayal of his countryman.

Kirov went along with it, laughing with apparent gusto. "Hopelessly ambitious, obviously," he put in. "It is only the cream of our young manhood who can aspire to be one of our glorious cosmonauts. That is why we lead the world."

"Indeed," Tzann murmured. "No, I'm afraid your Lt. Vologsky did not measure up at all. Odd fellow altogether."

"Ah, well," Kirov sighed. "It is so often the case, Major. Parents have such high hopes for their offspring and then they grow up to be a big disappointment. Still, perhaps I shall get a chance to at least pass my regards to young Mikhail while I am here."

"I doubt it," Tzann said. "He is due for immediate leave, I seem to remember." He cut off sharply, aware that the statement had negated his earlier pretense of hardly knowing the young pilot.

"Really?" Kirov was not going to let go now. He had

learned some very important new facts, and it was now even more imperative that he make contact with Vologsky while the chance presented itself. "Then it is possible that he will be planning to spend some time in Tbilisi. I might be able to offer him a lift. The journey by train is not a pleasant one." He paused, allowing a slightly abject look to creep into his eyes. "I wonder . . . if I could presume, Major . . . to ask if you might ask one of his fellow officers if he is still on the base? Perhaps they could tell him where I will be working."

"I'll see what I can do," Tzann grunted.

Kirov straightened, smiling slightly. "Well, that seems to take care of that," he said, regarding the superb hang of the trousers. "Now if the Major would be so good as to arrange a workroom, I can have the suit finished in a couple of hours."

"Yes, of course. Wait outside please," Tzann snapped. It would not be dignified to remove his trousers in front of the tailor. He gestured abruptly to the door, dismissing the man.

Kirov moved towards it, smiling deferentially. "Thank you, Major Tzann. You have been most considerate and co-operative," he muttered. "Most co-operative."

There was a gentle tap on the door. Kirov glanced up from his sewing, calling softly: "Come in."

The door opened. Kirov looked at the young Lieutenant who stood framed in the portal, regarding him uncertainly. "There was some kind of message . . . something about a man from Tbilisi. . .?"

It was time for direct, positive action. Kirov ran across the room, beaming with pleasure. He embraced Vologsky in a bear-hug, then stepped back, as though admiring him. "Can it possibly be young Mikhail? Such a strong, fine young man. The years have been kind to you."

Vologsky's dark eyes reflected his puzzlement. He could not understand the familiarity of the elderly stranger, who gazed at him with the pride of a long-lost brother.

Kirov left no time for the surprise to breed doubt, and then mistrust. Acting with the flair of a seasoned thespian, he forced tears into his eyes as he spoke again, in a quavering voice. "I would have hardly recognized you, Mikhail... such a man you have become. God knows, dear Kataya would have been so proud of you."

Vologsky flinched visibly at the mention of his dead

79

mother's name. His lips trembled. "You speak of my mother
. . . yet I do not know you . . ."

Kirov allowed his face to fall, smitten with hurt and disappointment. "Can it be that you do not remember me,
Mikhail?" he pleaded. "I who used to push you upon the
swings in the Lenin Plaza?" Kirov took a couple steps back,
keeping up the look of rejection before allowing his face to
clear. "But of course, it is a long time. I have grown old . . .
these time-ravaged features of mine are lined and disfigured
with the years. You were no more than a boy the last time I
saw you . . . twelve, thirteen at the most. Leonid never
brought you to the house after the troubles began."

The dropping of his father's christian name rocked Vologsky anew. He spoke in a hushed, awed whisper. "You were a
friend of my parents?"

The tears pricked in Kirov's eyes again. He laughed bitterly. "A friend, Mikhail? Ah yes, a friend indeed. Can it
really be that you do not remember?"

Vologsky was tormented beyond endurance. He struggled
to remember the sad old man, picture him as a part of his
half-forgotten childhood. It seemed callous to hurt him so,
and a terrible rejection of his dead parents to have forgotten
a friend who had obviously loved them both very much. His
mouth twitched uncontrollably, torn by conflicting emotions.
"Forgive me," he managed to mutter weakly. "As you say
. . . the years make strange changes in us all."

Kirov nodded weakly. "But never mind, Mikhail. It is so
good to see you anyway." He fell silent, continuing to regard
the young pilot with deep fondness.

Vologsky spoke again, uncertainly. "You spoke of my father . . . before the troubles began. I do not understand."

A look of terror flashed across Kirov's face, the terror of
having committed an indiscretion. He pressed a finger to his
lips urgently, shaking his head. "A slip of the tongue," he
blurted out, in a shaken voice. "It was the excitement of
seeing you again so unexpectedly."

Vologsky was puzzled even more, but he took the hint.
Somehow, the old man had let out a dangerous secret, one
which could not be discussed in a room on an Air Force
base. It seemed to concern his father and the stranger, and as
such, must be of the most terrible importance. Containing his
curiosity for the moment, Vologsky smiled and adopted a

more casual tone of voice. "You are busy. Perhaps I should come back later, when you have finished your work. We might take a walk together."

Kirov nodded, smiling. To any Russian, the phrase "taking a walk" had a second, more important meaning. It meant the freedom to talk freely, discuss matters which could not be voiced within four walls. In Russia, most walls had ears. On a military base, they could have eyes as well.

"I will be finished in a matter of half an hour, Mikhail," Kirov murmured. "Then I shall be driving back to Tbisili. I thought you might care to join me, spend your precious leave in the place of your birth."

Vologsky did not hesitate to even consider the matter. He nodded enthusiastically. "That would be a wonderful idea." he said. "It will take me a while to get my travel permit stamped. Then I will be free to go. Perhaps I should rejoin you here when you have finished?"

"These troubles you spoke of . . . what did you mean?" Vologsky asked, when the Kharkov air-base was many miles behind them.

Kirov looked across at his passenger, an uncertain flicker in his eyes. "It is not easy for me to talk of such things to you," he murmured, a trifle hesitantly. "I do not know what sort of a man you have become, Mikhail, and you say that you do not remember me. The matter crosses delicate and dangerous ground, and it might be better for us both if it remained unexplored."

Vologsky hastened to reassure him. "Please forgive me for not remembering you, Georgi Kirov. As you say, I was little more than a boy. But the fact that you were a close and dear friend to my parents gives us a close bond, nevertheless. I give you my sworn word as my father's son that I would never betray any trust you placed in me."

"Ah." Kirov nodded abstractedly. "I trusted Leonid with my life, Mikhail. I can do no more for his memory than to extend that same faith to his son." Kirov broke off to slip the Moskvich out of gear, allowing the van to cruise to a halt by the roadside. He switched off the engine, then turned in the driving seat to face Vologsky. "Do you know how and why your parents died, Mikhail?"

Vologsky shrugged. "It was always a little vague. An acci-

81

dent . . . a factory explosion," he murmured. "There were many deaths."

Kirov smiled wistfully. "Yes, it is as I thought," he mused. "The truth was kept from you . . . perhaps for your own protection. Maybe it would do you no service to face it now."

Vologsky reached out, gripping his arm. "I have the right to know how my mother and father died."

Kirov paused for a while, appearing to think deeply. Finally, he sighed heavily and continued speaking. "Your parents' death was no accident, Mikhail. They were shot down in cold blood with their friends, by the KGB."

Vologsky was stunned. "Murdered? Why?"

"Your father was a brave man," Kirov went on. "He dared to feel, as many of us did, that the people of Georgia were receiving a bad deal from the Kremlin. We produced much wealth, a great deal of food . . . yet the peasants starved, the State coffers were poured upon the people of Moscow, Leningrad, the Siberian wastelands. We were a group . . . I suppose you would call us dissidents. We had vague, idealistic dreams of obtaining strength and prosperity for our Georgian homeland. Alas, the Kremlin did not like it. We were marked for extermination, like so many rats. They hunted us, infiltrated us, and turned friend against friend. Finally, the KGB assassinated a dozen members of our group as a warning to the others. Your mother and father were among them."

Vologsky sat, shaking, in silence. Several minutes passed. Kirov said nothing, content to sit back and let the full impact of his well-constructed lie sink in.

Finally, Vologsky spoke, with a quaver in his voice. "Were you there, Georgi Kirov? Did you see my parents die?"

Kirov nodded sadly. "Yes, I saw them die, Mikhail. More than that . . . I buried them."

Vologsky suddenly exploded into action. He almost threw himself across the van, grasping Kirov firmly by both shoulders. His voice rose in a shout. "You know where my parents are buried?"

Kirov nodded. "An unmarked grave, I'm afraid. It had to be that way. But in consecrated ground, at least," he added, as a consolation.

"They had a priest?" Vologsky queried. "They received the last rites and a blessing?"

Kirov smiled thinly, nodding gently. "They went to their

maker blessed," he murmured. "It was the least I could do for them."

Vologsky's turbulent emotions broke at last. He hugged the old tailor to him, kissing his cheek while the tears rolled from his eyes. "God bless you in turn, Georgi Kirov," he sobbed. "I am forever in your debt."

Kirov detached Vologsky's arms from around his neck. He shook his head slowly. "You owe me nothing, Mikhail. It is I who owed them everything. Your mother and father died without betraying me. Doing so might well have saved them."

"Will you take me . . . to the grave?" Vologsky asked.

"Of course," Kirov murmured gently. "It is only a few miles outside Tbilisi. We will stop there on the way and I will leave you for a while to pay your respects."

He started the van's engine again. Vologsky fell back weakly into his seat as the vehicle lurched into motion. He felt drained, absolutely shattered by the enormity of all he had learned. He could not talk any more. There was already too much to be assimilated, considered.

Kirov was happy with the silence. It gave him relief from the tension of sharing the young man's terrible anguish. He felt some shame in digging up long-dead ghosts to torment Vologsky, and a sense of moral wrong in telling him such a bundle of blasphemous untruths. But Kirov felt a certain pride in the efficiency of his work, and the end it would achieve. The entire plot had worked even better than he had dared to hope. It was lucky for him that Vologsky was such a sensitive, highly emotional individual.

Confident that he was well on the way to final success, Kirov drove silently towards the abandoned churchyard.

CHAPTER ELEVEN

LEVITT ELEC CO PERSONAL MANVILLE
  CUCKOO LP 86003
  ORIGIN BRUSSELS STOP RANELEIGH
  MESSAGE BEGINS STOP BIRD IN HAND STOP AVIARY
CONFIRMS SPECIMEN IDEAL BUT WILL REQUIRE SOME
WEEKS FOR TRAINING PRIOR TO MIGRATION STOP SUGGEST
YOU BEGIN FEATHERING NEST IN SUITABLE HABITAT TO
FACILITATE LAYING OF EGG STOP SPECIES OBSERVED TO
LIMIT MIGRATORY FLIGHTS TO 2000 MILES WITHOUT REST
FOR FEEDING STOP THIS FIGURE NOT ALLOWING FOR
ATTACKS FROM PREDATORS SO MUST BE CONSIDERED
ABSOLUTE MAXIMUM STOP PLEASE ADVISE SOONEST STOP
MESSAGE ENDS STOP
WED 0900 GMT

LEVITT ELEC CO PERSONAL MANVILLE
  CUCKOO LP 86003
  ORIGIN ANKARA TURKEY STOP ANDERSEN
  MESSAGE BEGINS STOP ORNITHOLOGY REPORT SUGGESTS
SWEDEN DENMARK AND FINLAND TOO COLD AT PRESENT
TO OFFER SAFE REFUSE FOR MIGRATING SPECIMEN STOP
THERE COULD BE A WARM NEST HERE HOWEVER AND AM
INVESTIGATING STOP HOWEVER NESTING MATERIALS

Manville put the contents of the two messages together and
congratulated himself that things seemed to be going so well.
Georgi Kirov was not a man to be overtly optimistic. If he
considered Vologsky to be an ideal choice, then he could
have few doubts about his ability to persuade the pilot to defect.

Manville opened his desk drawer and pulled out a large-
scale world map and spread it out. Setting a pair of compas-
ses to measure a distance of exactly 2000 miles, he fixed the
point squarely on the Russian township of Kharkov and in-
scribed a full circle. Within that penciled circle lay the
theater of operations. Allowing for a margin of error in fuel
reserves, and for a certain degree of defensive maneuvering
to avoid missile sites and aircraft intercepts, 2000 miles was
the maximum distance the Foxbat could cover without refuel-
ling. The eventual landfall of the aircraft could only be
within that limited area.

It was a pity that none of the Scandinavian allies were
willing to co-operate with the scheme. Finland would have
been an ideal landing site. Still, Manville could easily understand the unwillingness. The Finns were not the most adven-
turous of people under any circumstances, and courting
trouble with the Russians was a highly dubious enterprise.
When an ant shares a common border with an elephant, it
makes a lot of sense for the insect to stay well clear of the
animal's footsteps.

Turkey would do as an alternative. In some respects, it was
a safer bet. The fugitive plane would be headed directly away
from the massive missile defense systems which ringed Moscow and Leningrad. Once over the Black Sea, the aircraft
would hopefully quickly get out of range of most of the
land-based missile sites, and the only danger would come
from the Soviet Navy. Current intelligence suggested that
there were only two missile-bearing submarines of the *Juliette*
class operating in the area, although there was no information as to their exact complement of SAMs. As far as surface
craft went, upwards of five *Kara* or *Kresta II* cruisers could

be deployed, armed with SA-N-3 systems for Goblet missiles. It was a formidable threat, but not insurmountable. If the reports on the Foxbat's speed and defense capabilities were anywhere near correct, the aircraft should be able to evade any naval attempts to bring it down without much trouble.

The more he considered all the aspects of the matter, the more Manville came around to the view that Turkey was the best possible choice of all. The fact that certain palms would have to be greased to the tune of $250,000 was a minor matter. The sum was chickenfeed, and the more governmental corruption that went on there, the better. It kept them busy.

Turkey it would be, then. The word was go. Manville unlocked his security drawer, took out the master file for Operation Cuckoo and stamped CONDITION RED on its cover. The single, simple action was all it took to move what had once been just a concept into the final stage of action. All that remained was to issue specific orders for action to Kirov in Russia and Phil Andersen in Turkey. Manville busied himself preparing the messages for dispatch.

ORIGIN PAUL MANVILLE, LEVITT ELECTRICAL. DESTINATION BRUSSELS FOR EYES OF ALEX RANELEIGH ONLY. OPERATION CUCKOO CONFIRMED ACTIVE. FORWARD OFFICIAL CLEARANCE TO AVIARY. EXACT NESTING SITE TO BE CONFIRMED LATER THROUGH EMERGENCY RADIO CHANNEL. CONFIRM IN CODE SIX.

ORIGIN PAUL MANVILLE, LEVITT ELECTRICAL. DESTINATION TELEFAX COMPONENTS LTD, ANKARA, TURKEY. PERSONAL PHIL ANDERSEN, CONFIRM NEST BUILDING PROJECT. FUNDS BEING TRANSFERRED FROM SPECIAL SERVICES DEPT. CONFIRM WHEN AGREED YOUR END. TIMING TO BE FIXED LATER.

They were ready.

CHAPTER TWELVE

"Space, Mikhail? That is a very strange ambition for a young man. Cold, lonely, unknown. When I was your age, the moon and the stars were things to kiss a sweetheart under, not crawl about on in cumbersome suits and strange machinery."

"You mock me, Georgi Kirov," Vologsky muttered, but it was said in a friendly, chiding voice rather than as a rebuke.

It was their third meeting. Major Tzann had been highly impressed with his new uniform. He had persuaded two fellow-officers to follow his example and take Kirov as their personal tailor. It gave Kirov the ideal opportunity to return to the Kharkov air-base and, of course, to see Vologsky.

Vologsky had never seen a need to question Kirov's authenticity, or to probe him for details of his mother and father. Almost without question, he had accepted Kirov as something like an uncle. Vologsky's need to feel that he was not alone in the world had lain dormant for a long time.

Nevertheless, Kirov had discreetly continued to drop vague references, recall some fictitious anecdote concerning Vologsky's parents. Kirov played a subtle, but insidious game, never heavy-handed. The bond between the two men had been established quickly, but was being strengthened with slow, deliberate precision. Now, Kirov had moved into a secondary stage, manipulating every conversation so that apparently casual words left just the subtlest hint of something else unsaid, yet implicitly suggested.

The current discussion of Vologsky's ambition was no exception. Kirov took up the conversation again.

"You're living in the wrong country, that's the trouble," he said, grinning broadly as he spoke.

Vologsky's face clouded for a second. Even as a joke, such a slur was indelicate, to say the least.

"To go into space," Kirov added, quickly. "It is only the Americans who continue to waste their time and money sending their expensive toys beyond the stars, collecting useless rocks from the moon. We Russians have our feet firmly on the ground. We chose to opt out of that pointless race to nowhere."

Vologsky shrugged. "Perhaps you are right. I still think that there are valid scientific reasons for continued exploration, however."

Kirov laughed. "You seek to justify, Mikhail. I think all you would-be spacemen are just little boys at heart, wanting to play an elaborate game. Perhaps you should go to America. There all the men remain little boys until their dying day."

"Now you *are* mocking me," Vologsky murmured, with a slightly embarrassed smile.

"No." Kirov became serious, adroitly changing the course of the conversation. "Perhaps I mock the world in general, if I mock at all. Often I reflect that we live in crazy times, Mikhail, under crazy circumstances."

"Crazy?" Vologsky prompted.

Kirov smiled sadly. "Do you not think it insane that Man shrinks from his Maker? That now, when perhaps we need Him most of all, we allow ourselves to be weaned away from He who gave us life? Our churches and cathedrals rot while we build dams and factories to worship as objects. Instead of the inspired word of priests, we listed to the advice of party leaders, masters of war. It is not right, Mikhail, that we should be driven from our roots in this way. A man should be free to believe in what he knows to be good, or right. How can there be freedom, when people such as your father and mother are murdered for believing in something?"

Vologsky was stunned. He could only murmur, weakly. "I had no idea . . ."

Kirov laughed, a little bitterly. "That I was a dissident? A heretic? Ah, well, if that is a label they have to place upon me, then perhaps I should wear it with pride. I feel only that we have taken a wrong direction somewhere, and are blindly stumbling on because our leaders blindfold us. I do not think it wrong for a man to open his eyes, look around him and consider that there might be other roads upon which to travel." He broke off, squinting at Vologsky. "I shock you?"

Vologsky shook his head slowly. "Surprise me, perhaps. But no, I am not shocked. Since I learned about my parents, my thoughts have been troubled also. It is easy to hate the blind arrogance of power, when it destroys that which is loved."

As he spoke, Vologsky glanced about him nervously, yet with a strange, enigmatic smile on his lips. It was as if he had released some dark and terrible secret which had been boiling within him. By releasing it into the world, he relieved himself and taunted the fates to punish him. It was, essentially, the delight of a child exercising his powers of defiance, flexing his latent powers of adulthood.

Kirov noticed it, and he had to control his elation. His calculated gamble had paid off. By opening himself, he had forged another bond, which drew Vologsky out of his safe, ordered shell and exposed him to the ravages of unrestrained speculation. By forcing the man to admit hate for one tiny part of the system, Kirov opened the mental floodgates for doubts about the whole to pour in.

Kirov fell silent, knowing that he had said enough for the time being. The two men continued to stroll leisurely around the perimeter fence which separated the living quarters and parade grounds of the air-base from the restricted areas of the hangars and control tower.

After a while, Vologsky spoke again, hesitantly. "Can I ask you a personal question?" he said to his companion.

Kirov's eyes twinkled. "You can ask, but I might not be free to give you a truthful answer."

"This Georgian movement . . . which my father and mother died for . . . is it still active?"

"Perhaps. Who knows?" Kirov answered, defensively. Again, he aimed to draw Vologsky further out into dangerous territory.

"I think you know." Vologsky committed himself with the flat statement.

91

"Ah." It was Kirov's turn to be enigmatic. He nodded to himself, saying nothing.

"You refuse to answer me?" Vologsky pressed.

Kirov shrugged. "I told you, I might be free to answer you truthfully. As I said earlier, under the circumstances which prevail, no one is really free."

Vologsky was too deeply enmeshed now to be put off by Kirov's vague evasions. Doggedly, he pursued the matter. "But surely, if the movement still exists, I ought to know more about it? I would owe that to my father . . . to try and understand something which he believed in enough to die for?"

Kirov regarded him sadly. "It is not enough, Mikhail. A sense of guilt, of filial duty, that is a whim, not a commitment."

Vologsky bristled with indignation. "You insult me, Georgi Kirov."

Kirov looked apologetic. "I am sorry, Mikhail. It was not intended." He stopped dead in his stride, regarding the younger man closely. "Surely you must realize that I have placed myself in a difficult position? I have said far more than I should have already today. I embarrass us both."

"Yes." Vologsky's brief anger subsided. "I also realize that I am presuming upon you. I have no right to tax you with such indelicate questions."

Kirov spread his hands in a gesture of frustration. "Right, Mikhail? Every man has the right to question, to demand truths. In this case, you perhaps have more right than anyone. If it were purely up to me, I might well feel disposed to tell you everything you wanted to know."

Vologsky stared at Kirov in puzzlement, thinking deeply. Finally, he spoke. "I cannot quite understand, Georgi Kirov. You seem oddly ambivalent in your attitude. I sense that you neither wish to drop this matter, or to pursue it. If I persist in pressing it, I am not sure whether I anger or please you."

Kirov smiled. "You are a very perceptive young man, Mikhail. I am only too well aware of this ambivalence. Unfortunately, there is little I can do about it. It is not a question of you and I. Others are involved. I cannot speak for them."

The answer failed to satisfy Vologsky. He became increasingly agitated. "Which, then?" he demanded petulantly. "Do you play with my feelings?"

Kirov's face was a study in sympathy. He played his difficult role superbly. "Mikhail . . . we are still comparative strangers, but I would have hoped you already knew me better than that. I would not dream of toying with you. It is not my way. It is just that, for a normally cautious man, I feel dangerously out of my depth in this situation. You make me say things which should remain unsaid, you pressure me on an emotional level which I find difficult to control. There is so much of your father in you, Mikhail . . . it's like finding an old and dusty mirror in the attic and finding that it reflects only the past."

"Words. Meaningless images clothed in words. I am my father's son yet you will not trust me. I ask only a simple question, which does not entrap you in any way. Does the movement still exist?"

Kirov sighed deeply, appearing to give in against his will. "Yes, it exists," he murmured. "Now, are you satisfied?"

"For the moment," Vologsky answered. "I thank you, Georgi Kirov, for your help. I will not presume upon your friendship any further. The subject is closed."

"Is it?" Kirov had the look of a man hopelessly trapped in a maze. "I read your thoughts, Mikhail. You intend to investigate further on your own."

Vologsky did not attempt to deny it. He merely retreated to a defensive, defiant position. "And if I did?"

Desperation showed in Kirov's expression. "It would be dangerous. You could well place us both in peril." He broke off to gesticulate hopelessly with his hands, expressing final despair. "There, you see. You have trapped me completely. Yes, I am still deeply concerned with the movement. I am still an activist. Now you know."

Vologsky spoke slowly and thoughtfully. "I do wish to know more about it. Will you help?"

The reply came as a whisper. "Yes, I will do what I can. For your father's sake. But it will not be up to me alone. You may have to do something to help yourself."

"Such as?"

"A gesture. A token . . . of commitment," Kirov murmured vaguely. "Those involved have needed to become secretive, for protection. No stranger, even the son of a dead leader, would not be admitted to a meeting without some tangible proof of his loyalty."

Vologsky was puzzled. "Proof? What proof can there be of

93

a man's feelings? Loyalty, belief—it is all in a man's own mind. There is no way to display it."

Kirov shook his head. "There are ways," he said, mysteriously.

There was no going back now. "Explain," Vologsky demanded. He failed to recognize, or understand, the subtle change in emphasis which had taken place. Now he danced to Kirov's tune, without knowing the steps.

Kirov was brutally frank now. A man who has given away his greatest secret cannot afford further pretense. "A man would have to supply some sort of evidence that he was not a slave to the State, a spy of the KGB. To gain admittance to the movement, he would have to commit some act which would make him as vulnerable as those already involved. A guilt shared is a mutual bond of trust—or mistrust. Each party has a weapon against the other, so that betrayal invokes immediate revenge. Thus both are protected. Do you understand?"

Vologsky nodded. "Yes, of course. But what could I provide? I know nothing of the movement, I have no guilty secrets to reveal."

Kirov shrugged. "Some information, perhaps?" he suggested casually. "The movement can always use secret information, to bring pressures to bear, to embarrass the authorities. Military information is always particularly valuable."

Vologsky's face fell. Up to that point, he had hardly realized just how deeply he was involving himself. "Treason?" he breathed, his lips trembling slightly.

Kirov shrugged the fear off. "Oh, nothing serious of course," he murmured. "We are all working for the same country, after all. It is *not* treason we are involved in. It is working for Russia, a better Russia, in which the state of Georgia plays a rich and useful part. Anyway, it was just a suggestion. Foolish, perhaps."

"No." Vologsky rallied himself. "What sort of information do you suppose might be acceptable?"

"Something not terribly important? Something that you just happen to know because of your profession?" Kirov suggested. "For instance, you fly regular missions near the border, do you not?"

Vologsky tensed up again. To confirm the fact was a serious security breach in itself.

Kirov stepped up the pressure. "Now see how our roles are

reversed, Mikhail. You pressed me to condemn myself, yet you fear to confirm something which we both know."

"Yes, I'm sorry. We all overfly the border at regular intervals. But if that is generally known, surely it has no value?"

"There are many rumors in the cities," Kirov went on. "Stories of vast Chinese armament build-ups. If they are true, some details would be very valuable indeed. Do you not think that the people deserve to know what threatens them on their very doorstep? Have we not the right to fear for our homeland as well as to fight and die for it?"

Vologsky considered this for several minutes. Finally, he nodded. "I will do it. My next mission is in four days time. I will make notes, and pass them on to you."

Kirov smiled, again seeming to dismiss the entire thing as a silly, childish game. "There, you see, it is as easy as that. Just an exchange of trusts, a gesture . . . nothing more. I will make contact with the movement and get permission for you to attend the next meeting."

"Thank you, Georgi Kirov," Vologsky said quietly.

It was like complimenting an assassin for the professional way in which he slides a stiletto under one's ribs and into the heart.

CHAPTER THIRTEEN

"Ah, Paul. Come in and sit down." Hayman welcomed Manville into his office, crossing it to the drinks cabinet. "Drink?"

Manville nodded. "Rye, on the rocks."

Hayman fixed the drink, handed it to Manville and then sat down behind his desk with a chunky tumbler half-filled with Scotch. He raised it in the air. "Cheers."

"Down the hatch." Manville took a good gulp and appraised his superior over the rim of the glass. Hayman was beaming. To Manville, it meant only one thing. Something was up. He waited, silently, to find out what it was.

"Thought it might be as good a time as any to chew the fat, talk over the current status of Cuckoo," Hayman started casually enough. "How is friend Kirov making out?"

Manville permitted himself a smile. "Fine, couldn't be better," he enthused. "No hitches so far, and he's even come up with a little bonus on the side. The crafty old devil has not only got his bird eating out of his hand, he's managed to dig some up-to-date data on the border build-up out of him. I take it you've studied that report?"

Hayman nodded, and his smile began to fade. This is it, Manville thought. Here comes the cruncher.

"It ties in pretty well with our own satellite observation reports," Hayman muttered. "Taken all together, it gives us a pretty good overall picture." His face was grave now. "It looks like one hell of a mess, Paul."

Manville was surprised. "You think it's serious this time?"

Hayman nodded. "This could be the big one. The Chinks have got everything bar pea-shooters piled up. If this thing breaks, it isn't going to be one of those simple little border clashes. This could be a full-scale offensive. The works."

Manville grinned. "Why sound so grim about it? Best thing that could happen, the way I see it. Let the bastards shoot it out. With a bit of luck they'll wipe each other off the face of Asia."

"Oh, sure," Hayman agreed. "It's our little party I'm worried about."

It struck Manville with no irony that Hayman had dismissed the two largest nations on the face of the earth to focus his attentions on just one man and an airplane. He was used to such priorities. "I don't see the problem," he said quietly. "How does it affect Operation Cuckoo?"

Hayman's monkey-like face screwed into a frown. "We've got to get our bird out of there before the balloon goes up. If we want that Foxbat, we have to have it before the Chinks blow the last one out of the sky. These reports indicate they've got more bloody AAMs than we ever dreamed of. They've been bloody inscrutable alright. Jesus Christ, those bastards have been busy in the armaments factories."

Manville whistled through his teeth. "That bad, eh?"

"That bad," Hayman confessed with a curt nod. "The damned Soviets won't know what the hell hit them. They could be fighting a ground war within a month."

Manville shrugged. "Kinda sorts out our problem anyway, doesn't it? Their air-strike capability would be knocked out for years. We'd have more than enough time to catch up, even overtake them."

"That's hardly the point." The statement was a veiled reprimand. "I promised to deliver the goods. I don't like to renege on a contract. How soon could Kirov get his bird off the ground, do you think?"

"One month. Two, perhaps. It might even be less. Without any direct contact, it's difficult to know what state the negotiations are in."

Hayman thumped his clenched fist down on the desk. "It's too long, dammit. This bloody border war could flare up any day now. Get through to Kirov, ask him if he can advance the project. I want that bird flying in a couple of weeks or less."

"All right." Manville agreed without real conviction. "While we're on the subject . . . what about Kirov, after this operation? He'll be finished, you realize that? He's had too much contact with the pilot to stay under cover. The KGB will be on to him like a shot."

Hayman didn't seem unduly worried. "It'll be worth it—if we get that plane. Kirov's done his best work for us, anyway."

"That's not what I meant," Manville said flatly. "Do we have any contingency plans to get him out?"

"What do you suggest—we send a taxi?" Hayman asked sarcastically. "Kirov's a pro, he knows the risks. If he can get clear of Russia, maybe we can pick him up. Prague, maybe, or preferably Berlin. Short of that, there's not much we can do."

"No, I guess not." Manville's brief concern for the Russian agent evaporated. He stood, pushing his chair back. "OK, I'll get on to it straight away, see what I can do." He began to move towards the door.

"Keep me informed," Hayman barked after him.

"Sure." Manville walked out, closing the door behind him.

ORIGIN PAUL MANVILLE, LEVITT ELECTRICAL. DESTINATION
BRUSSELS FOR EYES OF ALEX RANELEIGH ONLY. CUCKOO
NOW ON PRIORITY ADVANCE. INFORM AVIARY MIGRATION
NOW IMPERATIVE IN THREE WEEKS. ALSO INSTRUCT
AVIARY TO LISTEN FOR BIRDSONG ON REGULAR CHANNEL.
AVIARY TO CLOSE IMMEDIATELY BIRD TAKES WING.
SUGGEST TRANSFER TO WILDLIFE SANCTUARY PENDING
COLLECTION. AFTER BIRDSONG DISMANTLE EXISTING
COMMUNICATIONS CHANNEL AND RETURN TO HOME NEST
IMMEDIATELY. CONFIRM IN CODE SIX

Manville perused the cryptic message with satisfaction. It said all that needed to be said in a clear enough manner. Kirov was to advance Vologsky's flight to early July. His exact instructions would be fed direct to him through the disc-jockey on Voice of America. Then all Kirov had to do was run for cover and wait. Alex Raneleigh's job was also terminated. With Operation Cuckoo brought to a conclusion, the entire three-man link to Georgi Kirov was as useless and obsolete as the old agent himself. It would be severed at once, leaving no trail for the KGB to follow.

Returning from the dispatch room, Manville started the second half of his emergency plan. Using the scrambled security telephone, he dialed the program controller at the Voice of America broadcasting headquarters.

"Hello, Felix? It's Paul Manville, from Levitt Electrical. Listen, Felix . . . I want to get a dedication on your overseas channel. Next Thursday . . ."

CHAPTER FOURTEEN

Kirov's fingers trembled as he adjusted the fine-tuning dial of his radio set. They trembled not from fear, but from anger and resentment which had built up rapidly in the 24 hours since he had heard the ridiculous order from Washington. They had absolutely no right to meddle with his plans in this way. They must be mad that they should expect such a delicate business as his preparation of Vologsky to be speeded up as though it was a crude operation on a factory bench. There was no way in which he could turn a young man's allegiance completely against his motherland in just three weeks. It was senseless.

Kirov checked his watch carefully as he tuned the set to Voice of America. It was about two minutes before 2100 hours. The message would be contained in the dedication which the announcer read out before playing his first record, with perhaps some added information in the words of the song itself.

The brief jingle of the station's call-sign sounded, quickly interrupted by the announcer's voice. Kirov placed his ear close to the loudspeaker.

"This is Voice of America, broadcasting to the world. It's Lovers Overseas . . . your chance to send your love, and a song, to those dear ones who are far away. And our first request tonight is for Mr. and Mrs. Levitt, whose son is serving overseas in the Air Force. They say they are looking forward to seeing him soon, and that he will be safely with them to sit down at the table and enjoy the feast of the next Thanksgiving dinner. The request is for a real blast from the past . . . that lovely old Peter, Paul and Mary folk song . . . The Cuckoo."

Kirov listened attentively to the first few bars.

"Oh the cuckoo . . . she's a pretty bird . . . she warbles as she flies. She never . . . says cuckoo . . . 'til the fourth day in July. Now I've played cards . . . In England . . . I've played cards, in Spain . . ."

Kirov snapped the radio off. What message there was had already been delivered. He spun the radio tuner at random, to leave no evidence for prying eyes that he had been listening to a foreign station. Then he turned his attention to the small tape-recorder, which had faithfully copied the brief transmission.

Kirov's anger dissipated somewhat as he played the recording over a couple of times. He could not resist a faint smile creeping over his face. Paul Manville had to be given his due—he could not have chosen a more apt record to convey his message. It was clear enough. Vologsky was to be ready to fly on or about July the fourth. As far as his destination was concerned, the clue had to be in the dedication. The thanksgiving dinner, the feast . . . that was it, of course. What did the Americans have as the main part of a thanksgiving dinner? A turkey. So that was to be the landing place, on July 4th.

Korov stripped the tape from its spool and carefully incinerated it. He sat down to concentrate. Was it possible, after all, that Vologsky could be primed to defect in less than a month? It was not likely that he could be enticed in that time, that was for sure. Therefore, he had to be driven. But what could be strong enough to drive a man from his homeland, to face terrible dangers in the skies? Maybe not even the fear of death itself.

Kirov mulled over what he knew of the man thus far. Vologsky did not appear to be a strong individual—yet he wanted to go into space, so he could not be a physical coward.

Then what *would* motivate him? Fear of disgrace, shame, ridicule? The bleak prospect of the labor camps, slavery in

Siberia? Torture, perhaps, either physical or mental? The KGB were masters in both, from the crude use of the rubber hose to the sophisticated and mind-shattering techniques of the Black Room, the Sonic Disorientation Chamber, or a half-dozen other brain-washing methods.

Kirov turned the brief list over in his mind, and a degree of optimism returned. There was enough in the way of threats to drive even the strongest, bravest man. Given the right crime to answer for, Vologsky might well not fear death itself, but he would certainly fear to continue living. In Russia, at least.

But that could wait until the following day. Kirov had other problems on his mind. His own survival, mainly. He had still to plan his own escape route, find a way to get out of the country himself. It might not be as easy as plotting Vologsky's defection—and Kirov had only just reminded himself of a few of the terrors which he could face if he failed.

In the cold, objective light of morning, the issues were even clearer. The main thing was, purely and simply, the matter of survival. Kirov understood that fully now, along with all the implications.

Already, he knew that his chances of living through the next four or five weeks had been severely curtailed. Fate was strongly biased against him. Only with incredible luck, against all the odds, could he reasonably hope to make a safe exit from Russian soil and reach safe ground from which the Americans might be able to extricate him in one piece. That slim chance in itself depended wholly upon his persuading Vologsky to fly the Foxbat out of Russia. Failure to bring about the defection would mean certain imprisonment, possibly death, for if he did not bring matters to a successful conclusion, Manville and his colleagues would not make the slightest attempt to help him. They might, conceivably, even speed up his demise by informing upon him, for the CIA had little use for a failed agent whose cover was blown.

There was a third possibility, which also promised only death. If Kirov chose, he could drop Vologsky, and Operation Cuckoo, like a hot brick. Then it would be purely a matter of waiting for the assassin's bullet to strike home, or a carefully planned accident to take place.

Kirov was under no illusions about his Western puppet-masters. They dealt in results, and nothing else. Positive or negative—results were all that mattered. Kirov was a rat caught in a trap of his own making, and time was running out. He needed to summon all the devious cunning with which nature had endowed him if he were to escape.

He considered the matter coldly. His original plan had been largely dependent on much more time to play with, and involved a much closer personal interplay between himself and the young pilot. Within the confines of a shorter time-scale, it lost much of its effectiveness. Still, it was not quite valueless. It could still be modified for use, provided it was backed up with some new, stronger coercion. Kirov racked his brains, plunging to the bottom of his mental barrel without squeamishness. It was no time for niceties.

The answer came, finally. Kirov could not repress a slightly bitter, ironic smile as he thought about it. One of the oldest ploys in the business. Techniques of interrogation and espionage improved and became more sophisticated every day—yet still the old methods remained as effective as they ever had.

He took out the slim dossier on Mikhail Vologsky which he had been able to put together over the past few weeks. From it, Kirov drew out a slim sheaf of black and white photographs of the young pilot, and a single sheet of personal notes which he had compiled from their conversations.

They had conversed intimately. Kirov had opened himself up so that the younger man would trust him enough to confide his deepest thoughts. He had provided a father-confessor figure to absolve the youngster's sins and absorb his phobias. From the many small things he had learned, one above all now seemed important. Vologsky feared that there were certain unfounded and unsavory rumors circulating about his sexual proclivities. It would be Kirov's job to turn those rumors into reality, provide evidence which would damn him forever.

Kirov sorted through the photographs, choosing two or three which seemed to most suit his purpose. There was one posed beside the grave, offering a clear full-face shot of the young man. Kirov stared at it carefully before finally rejecting it. The expression on Vologsky's face was too serious and pensive for what he had in mind. Kirov chose another snap which he had taken at a pavement cafe in Tbilisi, bringing his final selection to four. Slipping them into a plain buff envelope, he transferred it to the inside pocket of his jacket and prepared to go out.

Boris Zhukov's photographic studio was a converted attic on the fourth floor of a cycle repair factory on Chukovsky Avenue. Kirov glanced about him cautiously. No one appeared to be observing him. Quickly, he ducked through the unadorned side door of the building and began climbing the four flights of rickety wooden stairs. At the top was a faded blue-painted door with the single word, Studio, emblazoned upon it in plain black lettering. Kirov rapped gently.

"A few moments, please. I am in the darkroom," called a voice from inside. Kirov waited patiently for several minutes before the door creaked open and Zhukov's bearded face peered around the jamb.

Underneath the black hair, the man's fleshy lips curled into a grimace which passed for a smile. "Kirov! You have come on business, I hope?"

"Of course," Kirov snapped, vaguely resenting the implication that he might make a purely social call upon the photographer. Considering his own, highly dubious profession, Kirov had his own set of moral values. He found aspects of Zhukov's business highly distasteful, even though he had come expressly to use them.

"You'd better come in," Zhukov murmured. He opened the door, peering out over Kirov's shoulder and glancing furtively down the empty stairway. Satisfied that Kirov was alone, Zhukov led the way into his tiny studio.

Kirov glanced casually at a pair of tripod cameras and an umbrella floodlight. It was doubtful if the equipment had been used for years. Zhukov had long since realized that there was little money in photographic portraiture and had turned his talents to other, more profitable sidelines. Kirov had used his services before, to produce false papers, touch up prints or produce blow-ups from microfilm. Besides these nefarious activities, however, Zhukov was also a pornographer. Today, Kirov intended to call upon this facility for the first time.

Zhukov pulled a bottle of Polish White Spirit from a shelf. "A drink, comrade?"

Kirov shook his head. "I would rather you did not indulge yourself either, Zhukov. The job I have for you will entail a clear eye and a steady hand."

"Ah." Zhukov clucked his tongue in a gesture of regret and replaced the cork in the bottle, returning it to the shelf. His brown eyes twinkled excitedly. "A faked exit visa? A change of identity card?"

"Nothing so simple. I want you to doctor a photograph for me," Kirov said.

Zhukov nodded. "That could be tricky . . . and expensive, of course."

"Of course. If you produce what I want, you will not find me ungenerous," Kirov assured the man. He produced the snapshots of Vologsky and held them under Zhukov's nose. "I want this man in a very special kind of photograph," he muttered.

Zhukov took the four snaps, examining them closely. A crafty grin spread across his face. Suggestively, he tapped his forefinger on Vologsky's torso. In each photograph, the pilot was in uniform. "This might be a lot more tricky than I had first supposed. And very, very expensive. As you know, comrade, I usually cater to a civilian clientele."

Kirov suppressed his growing disgust. "Name your price," he snapped curtly.

Zhukov fenced with him. "That will depend . . . on what exactly it is you want," he muttered vaguely.

Kirov explained in detail. When he had finished, an obscene leer lurked beneath the black beard.

"I could not possibly consider such a commission for less than five hundred roubles."

Kirov was not disposed to haggle. "You shall have it."

"In advance," Zhukov added, extending his palm. "Plus another hundred roubles for expenses. I shall have to hire models, purchase some special materials."

Silently, Kirov peeled off six hundred roubles and placed the money in Zhukov's hand. "How soon can you deliver?"

Zhukov considered for a moment. "Say three days?" he suggested.

"Say two," Kirov said.

The photographer nodded. "Two days, then." He chuckled. "You will call for the photograph, of course? Not quite the thing to send through the mail, is it?"

Stony-faced, Kirov replied. "I will call, Zhukov. In two days. I expect your very best work."

Zhukov waved the money in the air. "You shall have it.

106

Here the customer always gets exactly what he pays for." He gestured towards the bottle once again. "That drink, now?"

"No, thank you," Kirov said, firmly but politely. He turned smartly on his heel and walked to the door.

CHAPTER FIFTEEN

"There, what do you think?" Zhukov said proudly, handing a postcard-sized photograph to Kirov. "It's a splendid fake. You couldn't tell it from the real thing."

Kirov looked at the photo, his nose wrinkling slightly in disgust.

"Well, well? Is it not worth every kopeck?" Zhukov demanded excitedly. "Did I not tell you it would be my very best work?"

Kirov found it difficult to enthuse over the photograph, mainly because of the subject matter. However, the technique was undeniably first-class. "Not bad," he murmured.

"Not bad?" Zhukov snorted in annoyance. "It is a masterpiece, I tell you. I am an artist. No other photographer in Georgia could produce a fake as good as that."

"Yes, you have done well." Kirov realized that he was going to be pestered by the man until he made some sort of complimentary comment. The concession did not have the desired effect, however.

"It was not easy, I can tell you that," Zhukov went on. "Those snaps you gave me—they were not much good, very difficult to work with. I had to get the angles just right, fiddle about with the perspective and the reduction to get a perfect match. And the hours I spent with the airbrush . . . ah, five hundred roubles was chickenfeed for the work I put in."

Kirov forced himself to examine the faked photograph in detail, his keen eye searching for the slightest flaw. He had to admit to himself that Zhukov had executed a most professional job. Even knowing what he did, Kirov found it difficult to see how the optical illusion had been managed.

The photograph depicted two naked men, engaged in one of the most nauseating of homosexual acts. One of them was unmistakeably Mikhail Vologsky. Zhukov had posed the photograph with two of his "models", then meticulously superimposed the face of Mikhail Vologsky upon one of them before touching up and re-photographing the composite. More judicious air-brushing, and a slightly blurring effect, and the fake was complete. Pictorial evidence that Vologsky was a sexual pervert—enough to get him court-martialed, out of the Service, reviled by his fellows, and possibly imprisoned. To add an even more damning touch, Zhukov had draped an airforce uniform over the edge of the bed, and superimposed Vologsky's personal insignia upon it. It was a job of the utmost precision, and even a large-scale blow-up might not reveal that it was not genuine.

Kirov averted his eyes from the photograph abruptly. Thinking of the young man, and his quiet, idealistic manner, he felt a slight twinge of shame. Fighting it, Kirov reminded himself that he was involved in a matter of life and death. *His* life and death. He turned back to face Zhukov. "You have a negative, I take it?"

A slight frown of disappointment passed over the photographer's face. He had been hoping that Kirov would not demand the negative of the composite. As an exercise in pornography, Zhukov had been rather pleased with the original pose. He had been expecting to sell quite a few additional copies of it to those customers of his who appreciated such things.

Kirov noted the look, and correctly identified the thoughts behind it. He held out his hand. Scowling, Zhukov produced a strip of film negative and handed it to him.

Kirov held it up to the light, studying it. It was the correct negative. It would not be past Zhukov's greed and cunning to try and fob him off with the wrong piece of film. As Kirov transferred it to his pocket, a further thought struck him. It was more than possible that Zhukov had already taken off more prints for himself. He could not risk having such highly dangerous spares in circulation.

This worry strengthened Kirov's earlier misgivings about Zhukov. The man was another one of those loose ends, potentially a direct link to himself. Unlike Alexai Ybreska, Zhukov was not disappearing out of the country in a hurry.

Kirov studied the photographic print again, suddenly muttering a faint curse. "Damn it, Zhukov, there's a flaw in this picture."

"A flaw? Never," Zhukov said vehemently. "Boris Zhukov never produces work with flaws." Despite his protestation, he moved across the studio to inspect the photograph closely.

"There, you see?" Kirov said quietly, pointing to the face of Vologsky. "Can you see that slight join?"

Zhukov snatched the photograph, bringing it close to his eyes. Kirov stepped back a pace, and in one swift movement delivered a vicious chop to the back of the photographer's neck. Zhukov dropped like a stone.

Kirov stooped over his crumpled form, retrieving the photograph from between his fingers and tucking it safely into his inside pocket. Checking Zhukov's pulse, he satisfied himself that the man would be senseless for at least another five minutes, then walked smartly into the darkroom, switching on the red safety light. In the hellish glow, Kirov's eyes roamed the shelves, seeking out a bottle of chemical poison with which to arrange a fatal accident.

There was nothing. The bottles of developing fluid and fixer were harmless enough, treated with the care that a trained photographer would be sure to take.

Something else then. Kirov scanned the small darkroom from floor to ceiling. His eyes finally settled on the old stoneware sink in which Zhukov did his fixing. The edge of it was chipped and scratched with years of wear and misuse. At one corner, a large chunk had been knocked out completely, leaving a nasty, jagged edge. Kirov felt it with his fingertips and rapped his knuckles against the main body of the sink unit. It was as solid as rock.

He returned outside and began to drag the unconscious Zhukov into the darkroom. With considerable difficulty, Kirov managed to hoist the photographer to his feet, supporting his dead-weight by his arm-pits.

Carefully, Kirov adjusted his position, his eyes focused on

111

that cracked sink-edge. When he was sure that Zhukov was in the right position, Kirov let him go.

His aim was perfect. The limp body collapsed backwards, the base of Zhukov's skull striking the edge of the sink with a vicious crack. Kirov dropped to his knees, gingerly placing his ear over the man's heart. It was still beating, but with a fluttery, irregular rhythm. From the back of his head, blood flowed copiously, appearing a deep maroon color under the glow of the red light.

Kirov straightened, nodding to himself. From the rate of flow, Zhukov would be dead from loss of blood long before he regained consciousness. Returning his attention to the shelves, Kirov chose a large glass bottle of hypo and, skirting Zhukov's body, retreated to the door. From there, he lobbed the bottle to the tiled floor beneath the sink unit, where it smashed into pieces, releasing its contents to flow over the floor.

The accident was set. When Zhukov's body was eventually found, the cause of his death would be obvious. He had dropped the bottle of liquid, and then his feet had slipped on the treacherous tiled floor. He had fallen badly, his head smashing against the chipped sink with enough force to crack his skull like a breakfast egg.

Kirov took only a few more minutes to search the small studio from top to bottom. There were no prints of the compromising fake photograph. When he had convinced himself of this, and made sure that there was no other evidence which could lead the authorities to him, Kirov made his discreet departure.

CHAPTER SIXTEEN

Kirov arrived at the agreed meeting place as he always did, at the exact specified time. He ran his eyes over the figures seated at the tables outside the pavement café and a twinge of fear ran through him.

Vologsky was not there. He had failed to keep the appointment. Something had gone terribly wrong.

Kirov steeled his body against the rush of adrenalin which pumped into it, reminding himself that the trains into Tbilisi were notoriously unpunctual. Perhaps the pilot had been delayed, or had experienced some difficulty in finding a taxi at the station.

Calmer now, Kirov searched the tables again. Vologsky was seated near the café door, at a small table for three. Kirov had missed him at first glance, understandably, for the young pilot was clad in a pair of light grey slacks and a faintly-patterned blue sports shirt. It was the first time that Kirov had ever seen him out of uniform.

Kirov walked straight toward the table. Glancing up, Vologsky recognized him and his handsome, olive-skinned face creased into a welcoming smile. He lifted his glass of rich, red Georgian wine from the table, raising it in the air in a gesture of greeting.

"Georgi! You'll join me in a glass of wine? Just the thing for a glorious day like this."

Kirov's face was grim and impassive. He refused the offer with a curt shake of his head, speaking in a clipped whisper. "Drink up, Mikhail. We must walk, and talk privately."

A slight flicker of uncertainty showed in Vologsky's brown eyes. He had been in an ebullient mood, enjoying the superb weather and the lazy, carefree atmosphere which pervaded the busy café. Now, Kirov had suddenly injected a chilling air of despondency into that pleasant ambience. He lifted his glass to his lips, draining it at a gulp. Dropping a handful of loose coins on to the table, he set the empty glass down and rose to his feet.

Silently, Kirov moved away from the table and began to walk slowly down the street. Vologsky fell into step beside him, the residue of his good mood still urging him to draw Kirov into it, share its benefits.

"I was very fortunate to get away. For some reason, all leave is being cancelled in three days from now. It was only because mine was overdue that they did not cancel my pass."

Vologsky talked openly, not even realizing any more that he was breaking security by such talk. Having committed himself by revealing defense secrets, such freedom of speech seemed a trivial matter.

Kirov remained silent. Vologsky increased his pace, momentarily, gaining a few feet so that he could look back at Kirov's grim face. Falling back into step beside him, Vologsky threw his arm around Kirov's shoulder, hugging him gently. He spoke in a sympathetic, yet cheering voice.

"Hey, old friend. You seem unusually morose today. Is something troubling you? Tell me about it, get if off your chest. It will make you feel better."

Kirov stopped, suddenly, turning to face across the street. "Yes, we must talk. But not yet, not here." Kirov stepped into the street and began crossing toward the open park on the opposite side.

Vologsky followed him across the street and into the park. Silently, they walked past dozens of sprawled figures basking in the early afternoon sun until they came to a fairly quiet and deserted stretch of grass, beneath a plane tree.

"Now, old friend. What is on your mind? What is the trouble?" Vologsky urged, still only slightly concerned. He could not conceive that anything really serious could be worrying his friend.

Kirov half-turned, so that he faced Vologsky squarely. The icy fear which showed in the older man's eyes cut through Vologsky's mild concern like a knife, chilling him to the bone.

Kirov's voice trembled as he spoke. "Mikhail . . . I feel like an assassin. I could tear my own heart out."

Vologsky's mouth dropped open. "What is this talk, Georgi? What has happened?"

Kirov buried his face in his hands, as though he were about to burst into uncontrollable tears. In a muffled voice, he said: "It is terrible, Mikhail, unthinkable. I have placed you in the gravest danger. I feel so wretched, so helpless . . ." His anguished voice tailed off, to intensify the effect.

Vologsky felt the first tremblings of real fear creeping into his own body. In a dead, flat voice, he said: "What has happened?"

Kirov took in breath, waving his hands wildly in the air, gesturing utter distraction. "There was a meeting, of the movement . . . four nights ago. Someone must have betrayed us. There was a raid by the KGB . . . it was terrible, tragic." He paused again.

The tension snapped Vologsky's last reserves. With something fast approaching anger, he gripped Kirov by the shoulders, shaking him. "Go on."

Kirov's head was bowed in shame and despondency. Collecting himself a little, he continued in a quiet voice. "It happened after I had left. They came in with guns at the ready, expecting trouble. Two of our people were shot and killed outright, five more wounded. Only a couple escaped, the rest were herded up like pigs and dragged to headquarters for interrogation. God only knows what the KGB will do to them, poor wretches."

"You spoke of my being in danger—what has all this to do with me?" Vologsky demanded.

"Your notes—those you made of your last reconnaissance flight . . . I had taken them to the meeting. Everything was seized . . . they are in the hands of the KGB."

"Oh my God." Vologsky's whole body shuddered. The spectre of the Lubyanka Prison loomed up, closely followed by even more terrifying images. The labor camps, temperatures of 50 degrees below zero, a lifetime condemned to stare out over thousands of miles of the bleak, barren permafrost, where blindness eventually came as a minor blessing. These were the alternatives to a quick, merciful death.

Against such chilling prospects, Vologsky's mind rebelled in a frenetic search for hope. "Those notes—they did not bear my name. They could have come from anyone, anywhere."

Kirov shook his bowed head. "You underestimate the efficiency of the KGB, Mikhail. They will scratch at scabs, pick them until they bleed. They do not give up. They investigate, interrogate, sift every scrap of evidence until they narrow down the field. It might take them weeks, maybe months, but they will eventually track those notes back to you, somehow."

Vologsky could not, would not, accept his fate. "But there would be no proof," he protested. "I was careful. I made those notes in crude capital letters. They could not identify my writing. They might suspect—but they could prove nothing."

Even as he spoke, Vologsky was well aware of the hollow ring to his words. The KGB did not need proof; suspicion was more than enough. He fell silent, brooding, trying to come to terms with his fear.

Kirov spoke quietly, his voice choked by irregular sobs. "Try to forgive me, Mikhail. It is all my fault. I wish now that I had never spoken to you."

Even in his own troubled mind, Vologsky dredged up sympathy for the old man. "There is nothing to forgive. It is done. No one is to blame except myself. I chose to involve myself in matters best left alone. I forced you to help me."

"Help you?" Kirov laughed bitterly. "That was the last thing I did for you, Mikhail. But perhaps I can help you now. There is a way out for you, an escape."

"Escape? How?" Vologsky grasped desperately at the floating straw.

"You can get out of the country before they come for you. You have the means at your disposal. You are lucky, Mikhail . . . you have the skill, and the aircraft, to fly to freedom and safety."

Vologsky could only stare blankly at his companion, his mind reeling from this new and unexpected shock. "Defect, you mean?" he hissed, finally.

Kirov shrugged. "A word," he muttered. "A meaningless word. Freedom . . . safety . . . those are the words you must bear in mind now, Mikhail. All other thoughts are negative, self-destructive."

Vologsky's brain swam in total confusion and turmoil. He could not even begin to believe the conversation his mouth indulged in, independent of his mind. "This is impossible," he muttered under his breath.

"No, not impossible," Kirov urged. "Unusual, perhaps. Unlikely—but not impossible. You can do it, Mikhail, and I can help you."

"You? How?" Vologsky was like a mindless simpleton, hearing without understanding, open to suggestion.

"I have friends, important friends," Kirov went on. "I can arrange for you to fly to Turkey, where the Americans will meet you and take you to safety. They will grant you asylum, Mikhail—in exchange for your aircraft and your knowledge of it. The Americans need the Foxbat. They will pay any price to get it. You could be a free man—rich, admired."

"Admired?" Vologsky seized on the last word, his brain snapping awake again. "Who can admire a traitor?" His eyes opened wide, and suddenly he could see Kirov in a new light. Realization dawned suddenly. He fell back a step, as though Kirov carried some terrible contagious disease. "You! . . . you are a spy . . ."

The pretense was over. There was no longer any need for Kirov to keep up his act, play the elaborate game. Kirov shrugged, carelessly. "Another meaningless word. I am a man, like yourself, Mikhail. A man who believes in life, liberty and the pursuit of happiness . . . you recognize those words?"

Still numbed, Vologsky could only shake his head dumbly.

"American declaration of Independence," Kirov murmured. "Now *there* is a word I savor. Independence. Men living free to make the best of their lives on their own initiative. Without harassment, without secret police, faceless bureaucrats, permits and papers, forms, prohibitions, repressions. So I believe in all that, Mikhail Vologsky, and I see a Russia which has none of it. Yes then, if you wish to call me a spy, then that is what I am. But not a traitor. It is not possible to be a traitor to the human spirit."

Vologsky stood stiffly, still keeping his distance. "You have what you believe in, Georgi Kirov. I will not presume to deny your right to feel as you do. But do not expect me to understand, let alone share, your views. I will take my leave of you now."

Vologsky began to move away. Kirov's arm snaked out, grasping the young man's elbow. "Think, Mikhail," he urged. "Think of what you have to lose. All you have to do is to fly that aircraft to Turkey. There, freedom awaits you; perhaps even more. You could achieve your greatest ambition, Mikhail—space, the stars. The Americans would welcome a pilot of your skill and experience. They would find a place for you in the Space program. I have already mentioned it to my American contacts, and received assurances . . ."

"I need no more assurances from you," Vologsky said coldly. "Now please let me go."

Kirov only gripped his arm even more tightly. "Why will you not consider it?" he pleaded.

Vologsky tensed himself, then jerked his arm free. He took a deep breath and gazed squarely into Kirov's eyes. "A man has one God, and one country. He can do no more than to respect and serve them both."

"You are a fool, Vologsky," Kirov spat, his patience suddenly exhausted. "Your God would not thank you for throwing away your life. Your country will destroy you without a qualm."

The insult, and the reversion to Vologsky's surname, snapped the last thread of the bond which had existed between the two men. Strangely, it also sliced through the air of unreality which had been preventing Vologsky from facing the real issues. He was suddenly much calmer, coldly aware of his true position. There was no need to leave now; he could stay and talk the matter out. He took a few moments to arrange his thoughts, make a few educated guesses and assess the full extent of the plot which had been built around him.

"You have spun me a whole tissue of lies, of course," Vologsky said finally. There was no anger in his voice, only a detached and impassive acceptance of the facts. "You did not know my parents . . . there was no Georgian movement. This entire charade was designed to entice me to defect?"

Kirov nodded silently, sensing that, after all, there might be a point of breakthrough.

"Very well," Vologsky went on. "Now let me see if I have an accurate picture of the situation to date. If I am to live, I must defect with my aircraft. If I refuse, you and your colleagues will make sure that those notes of mine find their way to the KGB, and I will be exposed as a traitor. Is that a reasonable assessment of the facts?"

Kirov nodded again. "There is more," he murmured. "Tape recordings of our conversation—and this, of course." He produced the pornographic photo, handing it to Vologsky. "There are several copies. If you fail to do what is required of you, prints will be sent to the KGB, to Major Tzann and one of your co-pilots at the base. There is no way out for you, other than to take the course we offer."

Vologsky glanced at the photograph, his features stiffening into a mask as he tried to repress his disgust. "I see," he muttered through clenched teeth, handing the photograph back to Kirov. "It is simple then. I must choose whether to live or die?"

"Essentially, yes," Kirov agreed.

Vologsky was silent and thoughtful for a long while. Finally, a sad, resigned smile curled his lips. "I am 28 years of age. There is a lot of living ahead of me. I do not wish to be a martyr. I choose to live, of course. You seem to have what you want, Comrade Kirov."

"Good. It is settled then." Kirov appeared a little surprised that it had all gone so smoothly. "You must make your move at the first available opportunity. Exactly when you fly will be up to you, but it must be before July the fourth. Here are the instructions you will need, a suggested flightpath, and your radio signal to contact Ankara landing control. You must not make contact until you are over your border." Kirov produced a small sealed envelope, handing it to the pilot. "Good luck," he added, hesitantly.

Vologsky sucked up a mouthful of saliva, and spat full in Kirov's face. "For everything you have done for me," he said contemptuously, spinning on one heel and striding away, without looking back.

Kirov stood and watched Vologsky depart, the spittle running slowly down the side of his face to drip from his chin. It was a long time before he pulled out his handkerchief and wiped his face. It did not make him feel any cleaner.

CHAPTER SEVENTEEN

It was a little after ten-forty-five as Manville walked in to his office, in a foul mood. It had been one of those bloody-minded mornings, when everything went wrong and even inanimate objects seemed to have banded together in a conspiracy against him. Firstly the electric alarm clock had fused sometime during the night, failing to arouse him at his usual eight am. Hurrying to make up time, Manville had cut himself shaving, and the cluttered bathroom medicine cabinet had stubbornly refused to yield up the secret whereabouts of the styptic pencil. The wound had been deep, and resisted all efforts to stop it bleeding. It was nearly fifteen minutes before Manville dared put on his clean shirt. The coffee percolator appeared to be on a go-slow, and the grill had incinerated his toast with a savage glee.

With a bloody chin and an empty stomach, Manville had left his apartment already fuming, only to discover that vandals had been at work on his car during the night. With a sinking knowledge of the inevitable, Manville accepted the fact that one spare wheel and a set of spanners would not cope with three slashed tires and a shattered windshield. Even if he had been able to fix the damage, Manville had no desire to drive through the streets of Washington with the slogan

"Fuck U Honkies" sprayed in bright red aerosol paint on the ice-blue hood of the Ford.

Entering his office, Manville saw that the tribulations of the morning were still not over. Propped up against his telephone was a fresh inter-departmental memo. It read, simply: "REPORT TO ME FIRST THING—HAYMAN."

Hayman glanced up as Manville walked in. "You're late," he muttered peevishly.

Manville's pent-up anger got the better of him. "I didn't know I was supposed to be keeping office-boy hours."

Hayman let it pass with a stony glare. "Seen the morning papers?"

Manville shook his head. "I was in a rush."

"Here." Hayman tossed a copy of the *Washington Post* across his desk.

Manville looked at the headline. "KREMLIN ON THE HOT LINE—President Leaves for Moscow Immediately."

He dropped the newspaper without reading further. "Well?" What does it mean?"

"It means we got trouble, that's what it means," Hayman grunted. "I had a Q-notice in by this morning's mail. There's an immediate freeze on all anti-USSR activities, retroactive to 2400 hours last night. Complete shut-down, pending new diplomatic moves."

"Cuckoo?" Manville asked.

Hayman nodded. "Cuckoo. It's dead. Overnight, our little bird has joined the goddamned dodo."

Manville flopped down in a chair without being asked. "Christ! What's up?"

"The Russians seem to be over-reacting to the yellow peril," Hayman observed laconically. "If it's possible to put the fear of God into a nation of atheistic bastards, then the Chinks appear to have done it. Suddenly, the Kremlin is falling over itself to get close to Uncle Sam. Trade missions, diplomatic niceties, hurried journeys between here and Moscow, the lot. It's all hands across the waters and let's be buddies. Most of the NATO countries are getting the same treatment."

"Great," Manville muttered without enthusiasm. "So we get a complete shut-down?"

Hayman shrugged. "The gist of the message seems to be "don't rock the boat." Operation Cuckoo was a bit on the

122

hairy side to start with. Now it's positively provocative. Get the lid slammed on it as quick as you like."

Manville was silent for several moments. When he spoke again, it was in little more than a whisper. "I'm afraid it's not possible."

"What the hell do you mean, it's not possible?" Hayman demanded angrily. "That's a direct order, for Chrissakes. From the top. So cut the bullshit, Manville, just get on with it."

I meant what I said. It's not possible," Manville repeated. "I followed your specific orders and advanced the schedule by several weeks. For safety, I dismantled the link to Kirov and gave the final go-ahead. Operation Cuckoo is happening, right now . . . and there's no way it can be stopped."

Hayman's voice was cold. "Are you telling me that you relinquished all control over the project?"

"On your specific orders," Manville repeated, knowing what was coming but trying to wriggle out anyway.

Hayman stood, slowly. He waved a shaking finger in Manville's direction. "Now you just hold it right there, Manville. I told you before, the buck stops firmly with you. You asked for Operation Cuckoo to be your personal responsibility and I gave it to you. So don't come back at me with any crap about my specific orders. I gave you guidelines, and that's all. If you've fouled up, you're on your own."

Manville fought against a rising anger. Hayman was right, despite the apparent unfairness of the situation. That was the system. When you were at the top, it was known as delegation of responsibility. Lower down the chain it was plain and simple buck-passing.

"All right, so it's my head on the block," Manville conceded. "How hard is the chopper likely to fall?"

"Bloody hard," Hayman assured him. "You're going to have to bloody jump to get yourself clear of this one."

"Suggestions?"

Hayman paused before answering. With a very deliberate gesture, he switched off the recording system which taped all normal office conversations. "Off the record?"

Manville nodded. "Of course."

"Have you got anyone on the spot who could hit Kirov? Take him out before he makes a run for safe ground?"

Manville shook his head. "Nobody big enough, and anyway, it might already be too late for that."

"A leak to the Soviet authorities, then," Hayman suggested. "Arrange for Kirov to be pulled in by the KGB. Would he keep his mouth shut under interrogation, do you think?"

Manville shrugged. "Who knows? Kirov's a good man, but how good would he have to be? God only knows what those bastards would do to him. The chances that he would blow everything are too high to risk."

"We'd deny any part in it, of course," Hayman added. "You've already dismantled the link to Kirov, so there's no way the authorities could prove he hadn't acted on his own initiative. I'd give you all the cover I could, of course."

It was the last few words which tipped the balance. Quite suddenly, Manville recognized the conversational charade for what it was. Both Hayman's suggestions were too loose and half-baked for a man of his devious cunning to consider seriously for a moment. So it was a snow-job, a cover-up. An attempt to lull him into a false sense of security. Manville stood up, abruptly. "You're being too bloody helpful, Hayman," he snapped.

Hayman flashed him a cold glance, nodding thoughtfully. "Yeah," he muttered. They both knew the score.

"How long?" Manville asked.

"Forty-eight hours. That's all I can give you."

"Then I'd better get my ass into gear. It might not be too late to get a direct order through to Kirov on the radio. I'll try that first."

"You do that," Hayman said. There seemed no point in affecting friendliness any longer.

Hayman listened to Manville's footsteps fading away down the corridor outside. As silence fell, he snatched up the green telephone and stabbed out the number of the Internal Security department.

"Collins? Got a priority one for you. Paul Manville. He's a potential embarrassment. Remove him . . . at once."

"Yes sir." The reply was coldly efficient. The line clicked, and went dead.

Hayman dropped the receiver back into its cradle and lolled back in his chair, sighing to himself. It was a bloody business, but the rules were the rules. Everything in strict priority; the country first and personal survival second. The country dictated that Operation Cuckoo be abandoned. Personal survival entailed preparing for the possibility that it couldn't be stopped. Manville had to be the fall guy. Hayman knew he couldn't afford to have the man around to answer to a Congressional enquiry if the shit hit the fan. End of story. Lying to Manville about the 48 hours grace hardly seemed to matter, in that context.

There was Voice of America, and there was Leon Phasenko, based in Moscow. Manville tried both, hopeful countermeasures rather than effective action. Even if Kirov was still listening out for radio contact, he was unlikely still to be in direct touch with the pilot. Phasenko was a cell-link, a contact man only. He had never been used for a hit, and it was unlikely that he could get from Moscow to Tbilisi anyway. With those last two straws cast upon the water, there was nothing more Manville could do except wait and hope. Operation Cuckoo might already be a non-runner; diplomacy could break down suddenly, restoring the status quo.

At five pm, still counting on over 40 safe hours, Manville left his office. The condemned man had failed to eat a hearty breakfast, and lunch had consisted of two tacos and three cups of coffee. There was little point, Manville decided, on a man eating on an empty stomach. He went straight to the nearest bar, where he remained until just after midnight.

Through an alcoholic haze, Manville saw the dark blue Dodge pull away from the opposite curb and cruise toward him. It moved slowly, its headlights dimmed.

Like a cat, Manville thought, his mind only half-awake. A big, fat alley-cat, prowling, on the hunt.

The realization that he was the mouse came instinctively, quickly followed by the slightly ludicrous observation that someone had made a gigantic balls-up. Hayman had given him 48 hours. Some bloody fool had slipped up on orders, taken off half-cocked.

"Oh Jesus! Sweet fucking Jesus Christ!" A cold shiver rose up from Manville's feet to his head, jerking the blasphemy from his mouth. A sob rose in his throat, blending with an incredulous, nervous giggle framed by his lips.

Self-pity had no place in his predicament. Anger and sheer instinct took over as Manville suddenly *knew*, deep inside himself, the exact name and nature of the game. It was survival. He was sober in an instant, his years of training coming back to him as though no time had passed at all.

Survival, at all costs. It *was* possible. It had to be possible. Manville's mind raced, running over the possibilities. So Hayman had betrayed him, sent the liquidators in. What else? The answer came quickly, from Manville's deep knowledge of his adversary. Nothing. Hayman had implicit trust in his hit-men, especially against someone he regarded as an old, rusty, washed-up veteran. Hayman would have sent out the single team, confident that they would handle the job quickly and efficiently.

All Paul Manville had to do was to get out of this immediate mess. Then further possibilities for his continued survival would be open to him. His security status would guarantee him a priority flight on virtually any civil or military aircraft. He could be out of the country in less than an hour, headed anywhere in the world. Then one day, soon, he would be back.

"You bastard, Hayman," Manville screamed out to the empty, darkened streets. Then he was down on the sidewalk, rolling into the shadows for cover and tugging his automatic from its shoulder holster at the same time.

The Dodge mounted the curb, headlights suddenly stabbing out on full beam. The car stopped, and all four doors flew open simultaneously. Half-blinded by the glare, Manville picked out two black shapes moving toward him and brought his gun up quickly, thumbing off the safety catch. He squeezed off three shots at the nearest. Above the crack of the automatic, he heard a thin squeal of pain and sensed, rather than actually saw, a man topple sideways into the gutter.

A searing fire of elation bathed him suddenly, driving away the last vestiges of fear. Manville remembered now, what it had all been about, why he had needed so desperately to return to this, at least once before he died. It was all part of him again. Him against them, life against death . . . total commitment, both mental and physical. It was the supreme test.

Manville was aware of his back slamming against a wall. He curled his body up into a ball, presenting the smallest possible target. He was deep in shadow now, protected from the direct glare of the car headlights by the stone portal of a doorway. He held his automatic out sideways, away from his body so that they could not aim in on its flash, and fired two shots at the left-hand headlight of the Dodge. There was a crash of breaking glass and the car went blind in one eye. Rolling to a new position, Manville took the other headlight.

His position was already improved by at least a 100 per cent. He had the first kill, and everyone was equally handicapped. They had counted on the shadowy street to mask the approach of the car. Now the dim light gave Manville a very slight edge, for he was in cover and his adversaries were not. The only protection they had was the car itself.

Manville straightened slowly, keeping his back pressed flat against the wall. Gingerly, he began slipping his jacket off his left shoulder, then transferred the automatic to his left hand and pulled the coat off completely. Grasping it in his left hand again, he resumed a grip on his gun. Inching his way to the very corner of his protecting doorway, he tossed the jacket out toward the car, then moved out behind it.

Two flashes lit the air for a split second. Manville aimed directly below one of them. Before ducking back into cover, he was rewarded by a clear sight of a man falling back behind the Dodge, Manville's bullet buried in his stomach.

He pressed himself back once more against the wall, panting with excitement. Two down, then—and two to go. All four doors of the car had opened, so it was a four-man team. He was another 100 per cent up on the odds. It got better by the minute.

Manville held his breath, listening, waiting, thinking. They would try a rush next, he predicted. One man to come out of cover, to draw his fire, while the remaining operative pumped out enough shots to virtually guarantee a hit.

It was a good trick, but only if the victim didn't know how it worked. A smile sprang to Manville's lips. He had been performing that little number when these kids were wetting their diapers. As with everything, there was a solid countermeasure. You simply resisted your natural temptation to worry about the man breaking cover, and took the hit-man before he took you. Convinced that the ploy was about to be put into operation, Manville concentrated his attention on the hood of the Dodge, just above the offside wheel.

There came the faint scuffle of moving feet, and a dark shape moved out from the rear of the car. Manville resisted the temptation to shift focus. Exactly as expected, the shape of the second man emerged suddenly above the car's hood, ready to pump bullets toward Manville's gun-flashes.

He never had the chance. A micro-second after he saw the

first flash, the bullet which had come from it was embedding itself in his skull. Following through in a single smooth action, Manville threw himself to the ground and rolled out of the doorway on to the sidewalk. The fourth man, caught without cover, had no chance at all. Manville loosed three shots up at him, two of the slugs finding a mark in his chest. With a horrible gurgle, the man toppled backward to lay across the trunk of the car, finally slithering down it into the gutter.

Manville held his breath, listening intently for the faintest sound of life. There was nothing. Nevertheless, he remained crouched on the ground for several seconds before dragging himself to his feet. He stood upright, looking from side to side in wonder. He could hardly believe that he had done it. Against odds of four to one, he had come through alive. Jesus, that had to prove something about the old standards.

Now it was time to get the hell out of the area before half a dozen screaming squad cars came to find out what all the shooting was about. Manville tucked his automatic back into his shoulder holster and bent to the sidewalk to pick up his discarded jacket.

Too late, from the very top of his eyes, he saw the prone body laying in the gutter begin to move, and the black muzzle of the gun only a matter of inches from his face.

Manville knew then that Hayman had been right in writing him off as a washed-up veteran. One of the oldest tricks in the book and he had completely overlooked it. Standard night-fighting technique in group tactics. Right at the beginning of a gun-fight, one man feigns a hit, screams, and goes down. He stays down, just in case the target manages to take out all his colleagues. Then, when it is all over . . .

Out of the darkness there came a single brilliant flash. Manville hardly felt the entry of the .38 slug as it chewed into his body just below the bottom rib, burning upward at an angle through his lung.

Manville was dead long before the heavy iron chains fastened around his ankles dragged his body to the bottom of the Potomac River.

CHAPTER EIGHTEEN

Kirov's face bore the unmistakable look of a man who has deliberately walked into a cage of lions and emerged again unscathed. Surprise fought for supremacy over sheer relief, the final result hardly strong enough to chase away the last vestiges of fear. He leaned back against the wall of the KGB building, his knees weak and trembling. Two hours spent inside those drab grey walls had been like a life sentence.

Yet, the desperate ploy had worked. Kirov dipped his hand into his pocket, pulling out the freshly stamped papers and looking at them in amazement. The gamble had worked, when a dozen different things could have gone so terribly wrong. He could have failed to get a personal interview with the one man with whom he had some sort of contact. His request could have been investigated more thoroughly, his premises subjected to a search and inventory which would have revealed his blatant lie. Any one of thirty officials inside the building might have noticed his trembling body, or the tiny beads of sweat pricking his brow, and taken him aside for interrogation. But none of these things had happened. Kirov had found Pevrolensky with some free time, had put his case openly, and it had been treated sympathetically, without any detailed investigation.

Against all the odds, he carried freshly-stamped papers which enabled him to cross into Czechoslovakia to purchase some new rolls of cloth. The offer of a free suit to Pevrolensky clinched the deal, and a shared vodka had set the seal on their minor piece of *blat*. "*Ty mne i ya tebe*," people said, a knowing smile on their faces. You scratch my back and I'll scratch yours. It was the essential corruption of an underprivileged people. It worked on all levels.

Kirov kissed the papers before tucking them safely back in his pocket. Once in Prague, he would be comparatively safe. There were connections there, safe houses where he could hole up for a week or more, while his American friends made arrangements to get him out of the country and into free Europe.

There was no need to go back to the shop. Before leaving, Kirov had destroyed what little incriminating paperwork there was. It had seemed a natural precaution. The single remaining piece of evidence which linked Kirov the tailor to Kirov the dissident activist was in his pocket, sealed within a plain brown, un-addressed envelope. Soon, it too would be out of his hands, leaving no trail.

Pushing himself away from the walls of the KGB building, Kirov walked in the direction of the Post Office. He purchased a stamp from the counter clerk, licked it and affixed it to the envelope. Then, crossing to a quiet corner, he wrote Major Tzann's name and the address of the Kharkov airbase in crude block letters. Feeling the stiffness of the obscene photograph through the thin envelope. Kirov held it by one corner, wiped it with his sleeve, and dropped it into the post box. His last task was completed. Vologsky had no way to back out now. The cuckoo had to fly to a new nest, or perish.

Kirov walked down the street toward the car park with a renewed strength in his step. His knees were no longer weak, and his old legs felt like those of a 30-year-old once again. He was walking toward a new life, a kind of freedom which had only been an idealistic daydream for nearly sixty years. Long before the incriminating photograph turned up on Major Tzann's desk, he would be over the Czech border and awaiting the transport which would convey him to Germany, and thence to the United States.

Only retirement, and verdant Mid-Western pastures, lay in front of the old work-horse now.

CHAPTER NINETEEN

Vologsky sat in the cockpit of the Foxbat, vaguely aware that his mind and body were strangely uncoordinated. Physically, he was stiff and tense, the muscles in his back and shoulders resisting the comforting embrace of the padded flightcouch. There was a dull pain in his lower jaw, from hours of teeth-clenching, and the fingers of his right hand flexed and un-flexed spasmodically, like those of an elderly arthritic.

Despite all this, his mind was dull, dead, vacuous. His brain functioned, but on a detached, robotic level. The vital senses, sight, hearing, touch, responded perfectly. Yet all in-coming data was rejected as soon as it had been acted upon. Apart from pure reflex, there was no memory, no thought, no feeling. Vologsky was like a zombie, existing on the outer-most fringe of sentient life.

The state had persisted for over three days now. Ever since Kirov had dropped his bombshell, Vologsky had reeled from the shock, his brain free-wheeling in a limbo which offered no thread of reality to latch on to. At a single stroke of fate, Mikhail Vologsky was nothing, with only uncertainty to look forward to. He was, to all intents and purposes, homeless, stateless—a non-person. His entire past was cut away from him as though he, and the world he had known, had never even existed. Without the past, there could be no future, and

131

the present had absolutely no relevance. Life was a continuous thread; snap it, and mindless instinct remained, with no direction or purpose. There was not even a sense of anger, or regret. They were only too positive emotions, requiring far more depth of concentration than Vologsky was capable of summoning.

His eyes and ears picked out a flashing red light, an insistent warning bleep. Vologsky's inner robot acknowledged that the missile detection apparatus was functioning, and took the appropriate action. He leaned sideways, looking out of the opened perspex canopy of the plane. Below him, half-hidden by the bulging air-intake on the port side of the aircraft, a mechanic tinkered with the complicated electronic innards of the Foxbat, through a small inspection hatch.

He ducked down, looking up at Vologsky from a crouch. "Detection system?"

Vologsky gave him a thumbs-up sign. The mechanic gave a satisfied nod, and began screwing the inspection plate back into place. Finished, he stepped back from the aircraft. He called up to Vologsky. "That's it, then. All systems are functioning perfectly. You could fly this bucket to the moon and back." He flashed Vologsky a grin which was not returned, then shrugged, turned and walked back across the tarmac toward the administration buildings. Strange, moody bastard, Vologsky. Always had been.

Automatically, Vologsky completed his pre-flight check, finishing with a pre-programmed check-list on the on-board computer. Predictably, the program ran through cleanly. Vologsky erased the visual print-out and switched off all auxiliary power. The Foxbat was ready to fly.

Vologsky glanced at his watch. There was over an hour to go before the final briefing. Only then would he knew his destination. And maybe change it, if he got the chance.

Everything had happened without warning. The call for the entire squadron to scramble for a major transferral had come at 0.700 hours. Instantly, the Kharkov base had become a hive of frenetic activity, preparing to swarm. In the mess, speculation had buzzed about in hushed whispers, knowing, secretive nods. Most of it had passed over Vologsky's head. He neither knew, nor really cared, what was going on around him. He just went with it, unresisting and unquestioning. Nothing seemed to matter all that much. The scramble might be a training exercise or it might not. Either way, Vologsky had no choice but to obey blindly. It was all he had left to bind him to reality. He was still, for the moment, a military man. Therefore, he followed orders. He was a pilot. It was his simple function to fly aircraft.

Major Tzann followed orders too. His higher position in the chain of authority made very little difference, really. If the air-base were to be likened to a hive, then he was a drone rather than a worker. That was the only difference between him and the pilots and the mechanics below him. They all went about their duties mindlessly, vaguely aware of a higher power which directed their efforts, but largely in ignorance of its direction and purpose.

Tzann toyed with the sealed official envelope containing the briefing orders. Tentatively, he ran his thumbnail over the thick seal, exerting a careful pressure which made an identation in it without actually cracking it open. It was like a childish dare, a game of bravado. The orders were to be opened at 0.100 hours, and not a minute before. Normal human curiosity flexed under the strain, but would not take on the forces of discipline in open combat.

Tzann thrust the sealed orders to one side, on top of a small pile of unopened mail. There were other matters to attend to. Serious matters. The extremely disquieting matter of Lt. Vologsky, for instance.

Tzann flipped a switch on his intercom. "Put out a general call for Lt. Vologsky at once," he snapped. "He is to report here to my office immediately."

Vologsky lay back in the flightcouch, his body quiescent but just short of the point of relaxation. The cockpit hood was open; the sun played upon his swarthy face. The only sounds he registered were the faint rumblings of hangar doors and the occasional roar of powerful engines as his fellow-pilots tested their jets.

To a casual observer, he was at peace, yet the tension in his body remained only just dormant, simmering uneasily below explosion point.

"Vologsky! Wake up, Vologsky. Major Tzann wants to see you in his office, right away."

Vologsky was alert immediately, the tensions now on the surface, his nerve-endings tingling with anticipation and fear. This was it, the confrontation-point which he had been dread-

133

ing for the best part of a week. In an instant, all the deadness, the withdrawal was wiped away, leaving his mind clear to operate with the precision of a surgeon's scalpel. The inner robot switched off, leaving the conscious man to cope with real problems, the immediacy of living.

Pumping adrenalin lent a shrill, neurotic edge to his voice as he answered. "Tzann? Do you know what he wants with me?"

The messenger shook his head, grinning roguishly. "No, but I don't think he wants to give you a Hero of the Motherland medal. Sounds like you're in trouble, Vologsky." Still grinning, he turned and began to walk away.

The photograph. In his mind's eye, Vologsky could see Major Tzann seated at his desk, holding it between trembling fingers. He could imagine the man's eyes, filled with loathing and disgust, unable to register the full extent of the blazing fury which lurked beneath. When that fury finally broke through, the hand of retribution would come down with the strongest power in the world behind it.

Vologsky wanted to flee then, at that moment. Snap the cockpit hood into place, gun the mighty engines of the Foxbat into life, taxi toward the nearest runway and let her go. Streaking down the tarmac, against the wind. Reaching takeoff speed, rotating the aircraft into flight altitude and leaving the ground, his motherland, Major Tzann and his fury behind. Arrowing into the sky, blasting the thin air behind him into a long trail of ionized particles, cracking the air and land below with the plane's supersonic footprint, outflying anything or anybody they sent up in his wake. In less than two hours he could be free, safe and looking forward to a future.

It was impossible, of course. Vologsky made no move to close the hood, or warm up the aircraft's engines. An unscheduled take-off would be reported immediately; he would stand little chance of clearing the vicinity of the base itself. More important, perhaps, he was in normal uniform, which grounded him as surely as if he had been chained to the nearest hangar door. Without his pressurized flying suit, the supreme aerial technology of the MiG was useless, utterly wasted. Vologsky might as well try to take off and escape in a hot air balloon. Without the suit, supersonic flight was an impossibility, high-speed evasive action out of the question. Long before he could goad the aircraft to anywhere near its optimum ceiling, Vologsky would be frozen, evacuated or crushed to death.

The feeling of deadness returned to him, damping down the fear. Stiffly, like some crude automaton, Vologsky clambered from the plane's cockpit, dropped to the ground and began to march towards Major Tzann's quarters.

"You wanted to see me, sir?" Vologsky stood in front of Tzann's desk, stiffly to attention. Upon entering, he had braced himself and executed a formal salute. Major Tzann had given no sign, either physically or verbally, that he could relax.

Tzann fixed him with a stern, cold gaze. It was meant to be intimidating, and it served that purpose well. He was silent for a long time. Delay itself was another powerfully disorientating factor.

Finally, Major Tzann spoke, his lips hardly moving. "You know why you are here, of course?"

The years of formal drill and training came to Vologsky's assistance. His body remained stiff and taut, even though he wanted to tremble violently. He masked the fear in his eyes with the vacant, subservient glaze which became second nature to military personnel. "No sir," Vologsky lied, vaguely surprised that his voice came out strong and low-pitched instead of quavering and shrill.

Major Tzann frowned slightly. Without taking his eyes from the young pilot's, he slid his hand across his desk until his fingers encountered a brown, official-looking envelope. Grasping it, Major Tzann raised the envelope in the air, brandishing it like a talisman. Coldly, he said: "I received this today, Lieutenant Vologsky. I find the contents very disquieting, to say the least. It concerns your quite unforgiveable behavior, of course."

Still Vologsky remained rigid, his blank face giving nothing away. Cold was spreading up through his body from his feet, like a creeping gangrene. Surprisingly, it helped rather than threatened his self-control.

Faint annoyance began to show on Major Tzann's face. His heavy-handed tactics usually had their desired effect in reducing men to quivering wrecks. It seemed that Vologsky had more resistance than most. Major Tzann could not help regarding it as something of a personal affront, an act of mute insubordination. He tried the ploy of self-incrimination one more time. "You know what I am talking about, of course?"

Vologsky licked dry lips. "No, sir."

Major Tzann glared angrily, then forced himself to relax. He dropped the envelope back on to his desk, drawing in a deep breath. "Very well, Lieutenant. It would seem that your general behavior and sense of discipline has become so lax and sloppy that you do not even remember serious breaches of conduct. Allow me to remind you. Some weeks ago, during the course of a top-security reconnaissance mission, you committed a serious breach of discipline and security by voicing certain dangerous comments over an open radio transmission. You remember now, Vologsky?"

Vologsky wanted to relax, let out his breath and break into nervous laughter. So that was what it was all about! The stupid business with the radio controller at Alma-Ata. In contrast to what he had been fearing, it was a trivial matter. With a great effort, he remained still and silent.

"You do not attempt to deny these charges, I see," Major Tzann said icily.

Vologsky kept his face grave, but the surging relief inside him made it impossible to inject quite the right note of abject apology into his voice. "No, sir."

Major Tzann could not help but pick up on the missing contriteness. He glowered angrily. "Perhaps you do not fully realize the gravity of your actions. Lieutenant?"

Vologsky bowed his head slightly. "On the contrary, Major. I realize that my unconsidered remarks were dangerously indiscreet."

"Indiscreet?" Tzann bellowed. "At the very least, Lieutenant, you committed an act of crass stupidity. If any hostile power monitored that transmission, it could well be regarded as a major breach of national security. Treason, Vologsky . . . do I make my point clear?"

Vologsky lowered his voice to a whisper. "Yes, sir."

The assumed humility seemed to have a soothing effect upon Major Tzann. The faintest shadow of a smile flickered across his lips, quickly controlled. "The matter has not, as yet, been reported to the Soviet Supreme Command. It was passed on to me, as your commanding officer, to take whatever steps I felt necessary. The entire episode might have gone unnoticed had there not been a routine monitoring of the base communications tapes last week. I will not make a snap decision, Lieutenant. This matter is of the gravest concern to me, and to the good name of this unit. My eventual decision may very well depend upon your behavior over the next few weeks. Do I make myself absolutely clear?"

Vologsky nodded faintly. "Perfectly clear, sir." It was obvious that Major Tzann had blown the matter up purely for his benefit. He would not risk bringing himself and the Kharkov base into disrepute by pursuing the matter any further. The concealed threat was meaningless.

"Very well." Tzann was sure that he had made his point. He pressed home one more turn of the knife, just for effect. "I shall, of course, consider some form of punishment, Lieutenant. Normally, I would have withdrawn all future leave for some considerable time, but under the circumstances, such action is impossible. Therefore, I shall consider it and inform you of my decision when you return to this base."

"Return, sir?" Vologsky blurted out the question without thinking.

Major Tzann looked temporarily sheepish. He had made an unfortunate slip of the tongue himself. He covered up, hastily. "Of course, Lieutenant, you will already have realized that this morning's scramble is no exercise. The entire squadron is being transferred, temporarily. Your exact destination will be announced at the briefing."

"Of course, sir." Vologsky saluted again. "Will there be anything more, sir?"

Tzann shook his head. "Not for the moment, Lieutenant. "You are dismissed."

"Yes, sir." Vologsky clicked his heels together, executed a perfect swivel and marched toward the door.

After he had left, Major Tzann turned his attention back to the pile of papers and correspondence on his desk. He sifted, somewhat peeved, through the remaining unopened mail. There was rather a lot of it, and he had enough work already, dealing with a mass transfer of pilots and ground staff. Idly, Tzann picked up another brown envelope, addressed to him in crudely fashioned capitals. He toyed with the envelope for a couple of seconds, then thrust it back to the bottom of the pile. The letter was obviously unofficial, probably some cranky rubbish from a relative or a sweetheart

137

of one of the men in his squadron. He would not bother himself with it now. It could wait until later. Glancing at his watch, Major Tzann noted that it was almost time for the briefing.

CHAPTER TWENTY

The encounter with Major Tzann had merely rattled Vologsky. It took the briefing to break him. He came out of the briefing room trembling and dry-throated. Major Tzann's monotonous rendition of the flight orders still echoed in his mind.

"Timberwolf Squadron will scramble at 1300 hours and fly a direct course to Omsk at Mach 0.8. Individual pilots will conduct in-flight supersonic tests over the Virgin Lands, accelerating to Mach 2 before dropping to subsonic speed and contacting Omsk control for landing clearance. After refueling at Omsk, the squadron will again scramble at 1630 hours and proceed at Mach 0.8 to the final destination of Irkutsk. There will be a further briefing at Irkutsk at 0.800 hours tomorrow morning."

The words ringing and re-ringing in his ears. Vologsky stumbled away from the administration buildings, toward the hangars. Outside, on the parking aprons, the line of Foxbats lay in readiness, like a flock of silvery birds of prey.

Most of his fellow-pilots were heading either for the mess or their private quarters, bunched in small groups, talking excitedly about the sudden transfer and what it meant. Vologsky had no desire to be with or near them. He *knew* what it meant, and he needed to be alone.

He reached the nearest hangar and stopped, leaning up against its metal sides and sucking great gulps of air into his lungs in an attempt to quell the trembling. It had little or no effect. His body continued to quiver like a jelly; his legs felt like rubber beneath him.

The numbness, the sense of vague disorientation had gone completely now. Vologsky was fully alert and alive once again, and his entire being was tuned in to one single emotion. Fear was everything. He knew nothing else. It consumed him with the primal instincts of an animal—a trapped animal, facing the certain knowledge of its own destruction.

Vologsky was trapped as surely as if he were locked in a prison cell, chained to solid metal bars. Yet the prison was not small and confined. Vologsky's prison was the largest landmass on the face of the earth.

Irkutsk, on the shores of Lake Baikal. Less than 150 miles from the Mongolian border. Vologsky had no illusions about the purpose of the transfer. The Soviet High Command was preparing for war; the men of Timberwolf Squadron were the front-line troops.

Less than 150 miles from the border. From Chinese missiles and fighter planes and whatever new machines of death they had dreamed up in their inscrutable little minds and built in their unknown factories. Yet combat, warfare, honorable death were not the sources of Vologsky's fear. The 150 miles which would separate him from danger were nothing against the 3000 odd miles which would separate him from Turkey, life and freedom. Once he landed at Irkutsk air-base, Vologsky could only wait for the hammer to fall.

Desperately, Vologsky searched for a faint glimmer of optimism in the bleakness of his future. There was only one, slightly cheering thought, a bizarre kind of hope. Given luck, for want of a better word, he might get a chance to overfly Chinese territory before Kirov had a chance to betray him. With more of the same sort of luck, he might get shot down and killed. It seemed a minimally more desirable fate than to face a dishonorable execution, or a lifetime in the frozen hell of the labor camps.

Major Tzann returned to his office immediately after the briefing. Meticulously, he destroyed the orders and the covering missive from the Soviet Air Command before seating himself at his desk. The squadron was free from his command, temporarily. For an indefinite period, he would be in command of a virtually abandoned base. For reasons best known to themselves, the powers-that-be had chosen not to transfer him to Irkutsk with his pilots.

Moodily, Major Tzann found himself reflecting upon this apparent inconsistency. It was usual, in such cases, for the commanding officer to stay in the high seat. Why then, this change in normal routine?

There seemed to be only three possibilities. The unusual move meant absolutely nothing at all, or he was being singled out for either a positive or negative reason. If he had incurred disfavor somewhere in the higher echelons of power, the transfer of his squadron could be seen as a punishment, a prelude to even further demotion and disgrace. On the other hand, it was just as conceivable that his two-year command of the Kharkov air-base had earned him official approval, and that the transfer of the squadron was to leave him free to take up a new and perhaps more important posting.

Narrowing the possibilities down in this manner did nothing to ease Major Tzann's discomfort. As long as the possibility of disgrace presented itself, it engendered worry. Power was a fragile thing. He began to review his career over the past few years, looking for possible trouble-spots.

There was nothing in his personal career. As far as he knew, Major Tzann had never made any enemies in the ranks above him. He had always been a good, if somewhat unspectacular, officer.

The record of the Kharkov base, then? Over the past twelve months, he had lost nine planes and pilots. Not a particularly bad record, all things considered. The modified Foxbats had had certain teething troubles; the increased thrust of the enlarged Tumansky R31 engines had initially proved too much for the existing wing structure. That accounted for two crashes, which could in no way reflect upon the safety record of the base, or Major Tzann's command. Of the remaining seven losses, five aircraft had failed to return from missions over the Chinese border, which was well within the current thinking of Air Command, given the number of successful sorties. The only possible problems lay with the Foxbat which had crashed on landing, and the old Yak 18T trainer which had apparently broken up in mid-air. Subsequent inquiries had recorded pilot error in both cases, so any blame to be laid at Tzann's feet was purely secondary.

There were no other incidents of any sort. Kharkov ran as a trouble-free base, there were rarely problems.

Remembering this, Major Tzann began to smile. It was inconceivable that Supreme Air Command could find fault with his command of the base. That being so, an impending promotion was more than possible. It was a warming thought. In a splendid mood, Major Tzann set about dealing with the remainder of his morning mail.

With death accepted as an optimistic alternative, Vologsky's objective changed. He regained control of himself; the violent trembling died down. He was able to think again, with cold, clear logic.

Seen from this new viewpoint, one fact became immediately clear. Since he had accepted the idea of death in his aircraft, it made little or no difference when and where that death occurred. That being so, Vologsky reasoned with himself, he might as well perish in an attempt to find freedom as wait for the Chinese to shoot him down. Missiles were coldly impersonal agents of death; whether of Chinese or Russian construction, their effects were exactly the same. It mattered absolutely nothing to Vologsky what words were emblazoned on the outside of the thing which blasted him and his Foxbat into a thousand pieces.

An attempt, then. Die trying to escape, rather than give in now and curl up like a cringing dog. Vologsky glanced at his watch. Take-off was scheduled in just over forty minutes. The squadron would not be flying in a regular formation, so his first chance to make a break for it would occur within the hour.

But was it a chance worth taking? Methodically, Vologsky ran possibilities through his mind. He would, of course, be picked up on radar as soon as he changed course. It might take perhaps fifteen minutes at the most before someone, somewhere, took the decision to bring him down. They would attempt to contact him first, of course. Some stalling-time might be gained at that point. Vologsky could concoct some fictitious navigation trouble which might account for his wildly erratic course. There might be temporary doubt which could give him valuable extra minutes of life.

Twenty minutes, then, at most. Before all the stops were pulled out. On a course for Turkey, assuming a flight speed of Mach 2, he would be somewhere over the Caucasus

Mountains, above his beloved Georgian homeland, when they blasted him out of the sky. It was as good a place to die as any. A slight point in favor.

Points against. Vologsky sucked at his bottom lip as he enumerated them in his head. The twenty minutes of grace was a highly optimistic assessment. It might be a lot less. He might be far short of the Caucasus when the decision came. The shores of the Sea of Azov bristled with missile sites. If he was in the vicinity when the order was issued, he would have little chance of getting through. The single plane would make perfect target practice, and at supersonic speeds, he would be leaving a sonic footprint as clear as a smoke-trail across the sky. Miles ahead of him, other fighters and interceptors could be sent up to wait for him. He would be a fly buzzing straight toward a fly-paper.

On balance, immediate flight seemed to be a fifty-fifty affair. It presumed slow thinking, even stupidity, of ground personnel and radar units. There was one other, very important point. For the transfer flight to Irkutsk, via Omsk, the Foxbats would be stripped of armaments, not in combat condition. Instead of the usual complement of "Acrid" missiles, the planes would carry extra fuel tanks. If Vologsky chose to flee now, he would have absolutely no defense at all. He would be helpless, a sitting target. 23 mm cannon against SAM's would be like taking on an entire tank regiment with a pea shooter.

Vologsky turned his attention to the single remaining alternative; to fly as ordered to Irkutsk, and seek an alternative refuge from there. He dredged the depths of his memory, conjuring up a mental map. Assuming a maximum range of just over 2000 miles, he projected the aircraft's flight-path in various directions.

Firstly, he had to consider which countries might, conceivably, offer him at least temporary asylum. Finland came to mind, but had to be rejected almost at once. There was no way that the Foxbat could make it anywhere within a thousand miles of the Finnish coast. If Vologsky tried to fly in that direction, he would certainly perish in the icy waters of the Kara or Barents Seas.

To fly due North offered him nothing at all. There was only the vast ice-floes of the Arctic Ocean and a similarly frozen death. A slight course correction to NNE put Alaska in his direct flightpath, but although he would be welcome enough there, the distance was again utterly impossible. In this case Vologsky would come down over land rather than sea, and his death would come not from freezing water but from impact with the mountains of the Cherskogo Range. And even then only assuming he could fly the Foxbat that far. The whole area absolutely bristled with missile sites, guarding this potential attack route from the United States of America.

Nothing to the North or the West of Irkutsk held out any hopes at all, then. Flight toward the South meant certain death at Chinese hands. There was only one way left to go— due East. To Japan.

Left with a single target, Vologsky taxed his memory anew, trying to throw an exactly-to-scale map of the world up as a mental image. Somehow, the maximum range of 2000 miles did not seem quite enough. Vologsky knew instinctively that Hokkaido would be the safest bet of the two main islands in terms of flight distance. The 2000 miles would be safe with that as a destination, but there would be precious little spare fuel for evasive maneuvers, or high-speed flight. The major snag seemed to be that such a course would take him peri-lously close to Vladivostok, where Russian defense systems would be highly concentrated. Quite apart from land-based missile sites which protected the major Russian sea-port, the Sea of Japan was permanent home to many dozens of patrol-ing Soviet subs and surface vessels, each and every one of them well equipped with anti-aircraft guns and missiles.

In terms of potential attack, Vologsky would be far better off in evading Vladivostock and Russian territory altogether. A minor deviation in his course would enable him to overfly some 400 miles of sparsely-populated Chinese territory. In that delicate air-space, he might have a ghost of a chance. Chinese radar systems were not as sophisticated as those of Russia and the West. It was possible that he could fly low un-der the radar net, evading detection for long enough to enter North Korean airspace. Hundreds of MiGs had been supplied to the Koreans—it was possible that he would be mistaken for a local pilot, off-course. In any case, there would be room for doubt, and doubt bred time.

Once he was over the Sea of Japan, he would still have to face Russian naval defense systems, of course . . . but the is-land of Honshu was there waiting for him if he could make it. Kyoto, or possibly Kobé, would offer him safe landing sites.

Still the doubt persisted in Vologsky's mind. The 2000 mile limit left him absolutely nothing to play with. There was no room for evasion, no guarantee that his fuel would not run out shortly after clearing the North Korean coastline. Still, even that left him with a chance of survival. He would be ditching into warm rather than freezing, waters, and it would be a strictly three-way split as to whether a Russian, American or Japanese vessel got to him first.

This last thought seemed to clinch it all. It was his best chance. Vologsky made his decision on the spur of the moment, knowing that he really had no other choice at all.

Major Tzann held the offensive photograph between finger and thumb, his face pulled into a grim mask of disgust and fury. He forced himself to stare at the face of Mikhail Vologsky. "You depraved piece of filth," he muttered under his breath, as though addressing the man personally.

The curse helped to lighten his burden of loathing, if not his rage. Major Tzann's hand began to tremble. The obscene photograph dropped from his fingers to the floor. He made no attempt to pick it up.

Sitting rigidly upright in his chair, Tzann lit a cigarette and sucked in the smoke greedily, as if its flavor could drive away the taste in his mouth. Also, he felt that smoking might aid his concentration, enable him to think more clearly. And Major Tzann needed to think.

His initial reaction upon seeing the incriminating photograph had been immediate and predictable. He had reached for the phone and desk intercom simultaneously, to issue orders for Vologsky's immediate close arrest and contact Air Command. Something had made him stop, his reaching hands freezing in mid-air, then slowly dropping to rest on the desktop.

The something, whatever it was, niggled at the back of his mind for several moments, refusing to be isolated and understood. Then it dawned. Fear was the underlying emotion clouding his instinctive judgement and actions. Fear for himself, for the chance of promotion he had so recently promised himself.

To have had a practising pervert under his command for two years would be a direct reflection upon him. There was

145

no other way it could be, Tzann realized quickly. A commanding officer is supposed to know his men, know every little thing which went on within the base. A scandal could only result in doubts falling upon him, an enquiry which must, by necessity, prejudice his chances of gaining a higher command. Yet, confronted with the damning evidence of the photograph, what other choice did he have but to turn the matter over to a higher authority? He could not just let it drop. That would be like trying to sleep with a smoking bomb under the bed. If there was one obscene photograph in existence, there would be others. Copies might already have been sent to other people, higher than himself. The possibilities of blackmail and other crimes were endless. The photograph was only the thin edge of the wedge, the tip of the iceberg.

Only time would tell, Major Tzann reflected. A few days, a few weeks perhaps, should be enough to see if there would be any further developments. If there were not, it might be possible to get rid of Vologsky quickly and quietly, trump up some excuse to have him dismissed from the Air Force without revealing his sexual proclivities.

Time! With a sudden surge of hope, Major Tzann reminded himself that time was a commodity which he had just been handed on a plate. For an indefinite period, Vologsky was not his direct concern. He, and his attendant problem, had been dropped in someone else's lap. It was entirely up to Tzann to use that time, make plans to extricate himself from a potentially delicate and embarrassing situation.

Major Tzann examined the problem in minute detail, running it all over in his mind and looking at every possible angle. One thing was sure; he had got rid of Vologsky only temporarily. The real answer lay in getting rid of him for good. Remove the man himself, and no scandal could break. At least, not within the confines of the Kharkov base. The good name of the squadron would be preserved, and Major Tzann himself untainted.

An idea formed in his mind, and a faint smile began to creep over Major Tzann's grim face. He was a commanding officer; it was his prerogative and nature to delegate responsibility, get other people to do things for him. Why not make use of this facility to deal with the problem of Lt. Vologsky? The more he thought about it, the better it felt. Tzann's smile increased, becoming almost a beam of satisfaction.

Coming to a final decision, he picked up the telephone and

dialed the Irkutsk air-base. He knew Major Smelenkov, the commanding officer, very well. They were old comrades, understanding each other's ways.

"Felix? It is Nikrova Tzann, at Kharkov. How are you, old friend?" Tzann started, his voice jovial and benign.

The response was equally cordial. "Nikrova. You call to excuse yourself in advance, eh? To apologize for that motley crew of yours they have pushed on to me?"

Tzann laughed politely, accepting the jibe in good humor. "They are good lads, Felix. I want you to look after them while they are in your care."

Smelenkov laughed in return. "Like you, Nikrova, I shall be like a mother hen with her chicks."

"There is just one thing," Tzann said, letting a faint change in his tone announce the move on to more serious topics. "There is one young pilot . . . a Lieutenant Vologsky . . . I have had certain disciplinary problems lately. You understand?"

"Of course," Smelenkov assured him. "You want me to carry a heavy hand for you."

"Exactly. The heavier the better, if you get my meaning. It would please me greatly if Vologsky were volunteered for the most hazardous missions while he is under your command. I am sure you appreciate the sort of thing I have in mind."

There was a temporary pause. Finally Smelenkov answered, in a voice soft but firm. "I understand perfectly, Nikrova. You may rest assured that your young pilot will give his all for the Motherland."

"Good, good," Tzann muttered with great satisfaction. "Let me know if there is ever anything I can do for you, Felix Smelenkov." He dropped the receiver into its cradle and sat back in his chair, tapping the ends of his fingers together sat nodding to himself happily. He had done all that needed to be done. It was an even chance now that the Chinese would solve the problem for him.

Major Tzann bent to the floor and picked up the photograph again. Dropping it into his ashtray, he carefully lit one corner and blew on it gently to spread the flame. In a few seconds, it was just a black, charred rectangle. Major Tzann picked up his paper knife and crumpled it into ashes. He repeated the procedure with the envelope in which the photograph had arrived. Finally, he pushed his chair from his desk and lolled back in it, lighting another cigarette and smoking it with relaxed enjoyment.

Outside, the Kharkov air-base became alive as the pilots scrambled to begin their mass exodus. Major Tzann continued to enjoy his smoke as he heard the faint roar of the first Foxbat climbing into the sky.

CHAPTER TWENTY-ONE

Dwight Ennis, the top Presidential Advisor, was one of the small handful of Washington personnel who had nothing to fear from Franklin Hayman, and it showed in his attitude toward the man. He remained seated at his desk, apparently engrossed in paperwork, as Hayman was ushered into his prestigious office. Without speaking, or even bothering to glance up, Ennis gestured vaguely toward a chair and continued to study the papers in front of him. Hayman seated himself, tactfully keeping quiet.

When Ennis finally deigned to speak, it was with the tone of a college professor addressing a freshman student. "I'm sure you know why I sent for you, Hayman. The President is not happy . . . not happy at all." Ennis paused, sucking the inside of his cheek. A slightly sarcastic smile puckered the corners of his lips. "The thing is, what are we going to do about it to make him joyful once again?"

Hayman knew that he could not intimidate Ennis, but, equally, he knew himself to be on a more or less level par in terms of prestige and power. He hit straight back at the man's offensive superiority.

"You can cut the crap, Ennis," he said, almost wearily. "We both know that you get splattered just as much as me when the shit hits the fan. So let's level, shall we?"

149

Ennis regarded him coolly for a few seconds, as if trying to make up his mind whether or not to be annoyed and lose his temper. He appeared to decide, by a narrow margin, against it. "Eloquently put," he murmured quietly. "You really missed your vocation in the Diplomatic Service, Hayman." Despite the attempted sarcasm, it was obvious that Hayman's directness had got through to him, sobering his attitude. He lapsed into silence, waiting.

Hayman picked up the initiative. "All right, let's talk. Strictly off the record, of course."

Ennis nodded, his eyes making a careless sweep of the huge office. "Off the record," he agreed. "This office is clean."

Hayman took the assurance at face value. "You're worried about Operation Cuckoo?" It was a statement rather than a question.

"Very," Ennis said, with heavy emphasis. "I sent you a directive which asked for a cast-iron assurance that all overt acts of subversion against the USSR had been shelved indefinitely. You were unable to give me that assurance. Specifically, you cannot guarantee that a Russian pilot will not drop in on us with a stolen top-secret combat aircraft at any moment—when the President happens to be chatting happily away in the Kremlin and we are playing host to the Supreme Soviet Ambassador and half a dozen trade delegations. Yes, I find that very worrying indeed. Now, why the hell can't you stop this piece of insanity dead in its tracks?"

Hayman spread his hands in a gesture of frustration. "There's nothing we can do. We've lost contact with our Russian agent. There is no way of knowing whether he had initiated the defection or not."

"Lost contact?" Ennis demanded, penetratingly. "Was he arrested?"

Hayman shook his head. "Not as far as we know."

"Then how did you come to lose contact? Have the batteries on your radio run out?" Ennis asked, reverting to sarcasm. "More to the point, didn't you have some back-up plans, a contingency scheme to initiate if anything went wrong? Are you telling me that a major act of international espionage was launched without a fail-safe?"

Hayman bristled under the attack, which he found unfair and unwarranted. His voice rose to an angry shout. "This operation was conducted with every safeguard and meticulous

150

planning. The order to re-schedule at short notice came from your bloody department, Ennis. To make abrupt changes to a delicate operation at such a late stage was almost bound to create serious problems. This bloody cock-up doesn't sit on my shoulders—let's get that perfectly straight."

Ennis rode the attack, wearing a slightly pitying smile. When Hayman had finished, he said: "You know better than that, Hayman. This department knows absolutely nothing about Operation Cuckoo. It never did. No orders were ever issued to you or any other organization. It follows, then, that we could hardly have authorized you to change the schedule of something we did not know about."

Hayman's anger evaporated. It was useless. He lapsed into a mood of sullen resignation. "Yes, all right. I know the form," he mumbled. "We all have to cover up as best we can."

"You?" Ennis asked. For once, there was a trace of genuine sympathy in his voice.

Hayman shrugged. "I've done what I can. It wasn't much. It looks as though I carry the can." He broke off to give vent to a sudden new burst of anger. "Bloody Manville!"

"Paul Manville, huh? It was his foul-up?"

"Hayman shrugged again. "His, mine, anybody's. It doesn't really matter, does it? I can't crawl out from under, that's the crunch."

"Can't you offload on to Manville?" Ennis asked.

Hayman smiled, without humor. "Manville? Never heard of him. Your department isn't the only one where records and documents suddenly never existed. There is absolutely no record of a man named Paul Manville ever having been employed by the Central Intelligence Agency, or any other Governmental body. In non-official phraseology, his career has been totally terminated."

Ennis wrinkled his nose in a faint gesture of disgust. "God, you bastards are worse than cannibals."

Hayman made no comment. There was no need.

"So, what have we got?" Ennis muttered. "We have no Operation Cuckoo, no agent named Paul Manville to put it into operation, no Russian agent, no knowledge of any plans to steal a Russian fighter aircraft. What we *do* have is a Soviet pilot, somewhere, who may or may not be planning an unscheduled visit at a most inopportune time. Would you call that a fair assessment of the facts to date?"

Hayman nodded. "On the button."

"And you are absolutely sure that there is no way of getting through to the pilot, or stopping the defection in any other way?"

"Short of blowing the whole thing to the Soviets, no."

Ennis considered the suggestion seriously. "Could it be done at diplomatic level . . . discreetly?" he asked at length. "Have you any contacts with double-agents, or sympathetic Soviet personnel who might play along just to avoid embarrassment?"

Hayman scratched the side of his nose, distractedly. Interlocking his fingers, he flexed them, cracking the joints. Finally, he clicked his tongue against the roof of his mouth. "I don't know. It's impossible to be sure just what the Soviet reaction would be," he muttered guardedly. "It is perfectly possible that we could come to some agreement to cover the whole thing up. On the other hand, the Russians might decide to play it up for all it's worth. There's really no way of putting out feelers without giving the game away. On balance, I should say we're better off just sitting back on our asses. There's always the chance that our Russian agent didn't get through to the pilot, or he won't be able to make it. Again, if the Soviets shoot him down en route, there will be no way they can prove his destination, or the fact that we put him up to it."

Ennis listened intently to the conversation, his head cocked slightly to one side, like a bird. As Hayman finished talking, Ennis began nodding to himself, agreeing with his own inner thoughts. His eyes twinkled, momentarily. "Or if *we* bring him down, of course," he muttered thoughtfully. "If we, or our Allies, shot him out of the sky, we'd be proclaiming our baby-faced innocence to the whole world. We'd be in the clear."

New hope showed on Hayman's face. "It would have to be outside Soviet air-space, of course," he pointed out. "We'd find ourselves in another kind of mess if it weren't."

"Oh yes, of course," Ennis agreed. "He wouldn't have to be too far over the border. Just enough to create a violation of air-space, perhaps trigger off some over-conscientious controller who could be discreetly transferred immediately afterwards."

The idea took root in both men's minds. "There would be wreckage, as well," Hayman said happily. "We might learn

152

something from that. Not a lot, perhaps, but enough to make the exercise worth while. Save the project from being a total loss. Who knows, we might all come out with clean faces after all."

Ennis appeared to have accepted the idea without the need for any further discussion. "What was the pilot's destination?"

"Turkey. On or before July 4th."

Ennis considered for a few more seconds, then smiled with satisfaction. "I'll get straight on to the Turkish authorities. I'm sure we can come to some sort of an arrangement."

"Have you got that sort of weight?" Hayman asked.

"I can get it," Ennis replied, with supreme confidence. "This is top priority stuff."

Hayman could hardly believe his luck. A thin smile began to spread across his face. "It certainly seems to be the answer."

Ennis nodded. "The only answer there is. Manville should have thought of it himself. It could have saved him."

At the mention of the name, Hayman's smile turned into a full-blooded, wicked grin. "What were you saying about bloody cannibals?" he asked, pointedly.

Ennis made no attempt to answer.

CHAPTER TWENTY-TWO

SUPREME SECURITY: CLASS ONE PERSONNEL ONLY.

KGB MOSCOW. COPIES GRU HQ, MARSHAL GRIKO NYLESKY, SOVIET AIR FORCE COMMAND: FIRST SECRETARY, POLITBURO.

REPORT: FIELD HQ: ANKARA, TURKEY.

UNCONFIRMED COUNTER-ESPIONAGE REPORTS ORIGINATING IN ANKARA SUGGEST THAT UNITED STATES MILITARY ADVISORS HAVE BRIEFED TURKISH AIR TRAFFIC CONTROL CENTERS AND DEFENSE MINISTRY TO BE ON THE ALERT FOR AN UNSPECIFIED ROGUE AIRCRAFT ON OR BEFORE JULY 4. THIS AIRCRAFT SUGGESTED TO BE COMBAT ARMED AND HOSTILE. BELIEVED ADVICE TO BE DESTROY ON SIGHT. WE HAVE NO KNOWLEDGE OF UNSCHEDULED FLIGHT, ORIGIN OR PURPOSE. PLEASE ADVISE IF SOVIET MILITARY OR CENTRAL KGB CAN SHED LIGHT ON THIS MATTER. ALSO ADVISE IF HOME SECURITY FORCES KNOW OF ANY NATO PLANS WHICH MIGHT FIT THESE UNCONFIRMED REPORTS. WILL CONTINUE TO OBSERVE AND INVESTIGATE PENDING YOUR ADVISED ACTION.

UNION OF SOVIET SOCIALIST REPUBLICS EMBASSY, WASHINGTON.

EYES OF CULTURAL ATTACHE KOTIK ZHAGOV ONLY.

MEMO: KGB CENTRAL.

REPORTS ORIGINATING IN ANKARA, TURKEY SUGGEST UNITED STATES KNOWLEDGE OF, AND POSSIBLE INVOLVEMENT IN, ATTACK PLANS ON UNSPECIFIED HOSTILE AIRCRAFT DUE ON OR BEFORE JULY 4. INVESTIGATE AND REPORT IMMEDIATELY ON ALL KNOWN OR UNCONFIRMED UNITED STATES MILITARY AND CIA PROJECTS INVOLVING HOME OR FOREIGN AIRCRAFT. FURTHER SUGGEST FULL INVESTIGATION AND REPORT UPON CURRENT CIA ACTIVITY WITH SPECIAL REFERENCE TO AIR FORCE, NASA OR PENTAGON LIAISON. THIS MATTER SUPREME PRIORITY BUT DELICATE. USE ALL AVAILABLE PERSONNEL AND RESOURCES.

SUPREME SECURITY: CLASS ONE PERSONNEL ONLY.
KGB CENTRAL, MOSCOW.
REPORT: USSR EMBASSY, WASHINGTON.

INITIAL INVESTIGATION HERE REVEALS NO ACTIVITIES OUT OF ORDINARY. NO KNOWN UNITED STATES INVOLVEMENT WITH FOREIGN AIR FORCES EXCEPT USUAL NATO PLANS (SEE MONTHLY REPORT D.59907). IF PLAN IS IN OPERATION, IT MUST BE UNDER HIGHEST SECURITY. REGARDING SECONDARY INVESTIGATION, ONE UNUSUAL DEVELOPMENT. CIA OPERATIVE PAUL HENRY JAMES MANVILLE HAS DISAPPEARED, PRESUMED TO HAVE BEEN ELIMINATED. MANVILLE WAS LAST KNOWN TO BE ACTIVE IN PRAGUE, 1968. SINCE THEN BELIEVED TO HAVE ACTED AS PENTAGON LIAISON OFFICER, NON-ACTIVE IN FIELD. IS KNOWN TO HAVE BEEN IN CONTACT WITH NASA AND PENTAGON SHORTLY BEFORE DISAPPEARANCE, BUT PURPOSE UNKNOWN. ADVISE IF FURTHER INVESTIGATION JUSTIFIED.

UNION OF SOVIET SOCIALIST REPUBLICS EMBASSY, WASHINGTON.
EYES OF CULTURAL ATTACHE KOTIK ZHAGOV ONLY.
MEMO: KGB CENTRAL.

INSTITUTE IMMEDIATE HIGHEST LEVEL INVESTIGATION INTO CIRCUMSTANCES SURROUNDING MANVILLE DISAPPEARANCE. ABSOLUTE PRIORITY, IMMEDIATE ACTION.

SUPREME SECURITY: CLASS ONE PERSONNEL ONLY.
KGB CENTRAL, MOSCOW.
REPORT: USSR EMBASSY, WASHINGTON.

BELIEVE ON TO SOMETHING REGARDING MANVILLE. LAST KNOWN ASSIGNMENT LIAISON CIA/PENTAGON ON TOP SECRET PROJECT, NOW BELIEVED TO HAVE BEEN ABORTED. LITTLE KNOWN AT THIS STAGE AS SECURITY EXTREMELY TIGHT, BUT OPERATION APPARENTLY CODENAMED CUCKOO. AMERICAN TERMINOLOGY AND SENSE OF BOYISH HUMOUR WOULD SUGGEST INVOLVEMENT WITH FLIGHT, POSSIBLY FOREIGN AIRCRAFT. WILL PROCEED WITH DETAILED INVESTIGATION AT ALL SPEED. IF JULY 4 IS DEADLINE, SITUATION NOW CRITICAL. WILL INITIATE DIPLOMATIC EMBARRASSMENT HERE TO INCREASE PRESSURES.

Time was running out.

PART THREE: THE MIGRATION

CHAPTER TWENTY-THREE

Vologsky did not find it ominous, or even slightly odd, that he had been chosen for the first solo reconnaissance flight over the border. That was what Timberwolf Squadron were at Irkutsk for, and someone had to make the first flight. He was probably the best pilot in the squadron, hence the choice. It was logical. The only factor which told him that his mission was anything other than normal routine was the full combat readiness of the MiG 25. In addition to its full complement of four "Acrid" air-to-air missiles, the Foxbat had been fitted out with four more of the new lightweight AAMs and he had orders to test his guns immediately after take-off. The flight was not intended to be a milk-run, that was certain. Vologsky was headed for where there was potential trouble. And he would be expected to deal with it.

Walking awkwardly in his cumbersome padded flight-suit, Vologsky made his way along the corridor between the pilots' rest-room and the flight briefing room to receive his final, verbal orders.

Major Smelenkov regarded the young pilot before him with a detached curiosity, nothing the stiffness of his athletic young body and the stillness of his eyes. He appeared, to all intents and purposes, to be a perfectly trained young officer. Smelenkov had already familiarized himself with Vologsky's service record. On paper, there was nothing against him. He was a fine pilot, who should have been a credit to his squadron and his commanding officer.

With this committed to his memory and his first real look at the young man's bearing, Smelenkov felt a slight sense of surprise that his old friend Major Tzann should have had trouble with him. Smelenkov prided himself on being able to gauge a man's mettle from visual observation alone. What he saw now, coupled with what he had read, suggested a well-disciplined young officer with a secure future in the Red Air Force.

"Stand easy, Lieutenant," he muttered, his eyes still firmly fixed on the rigid figure in front of his desk. Once again, Smelenkov could not help but be impressed with the fluid ease with which Vologsky made the transition from a position of attention. There was no sign of sloppiness, of resistance to orders. However, he had Major Tzann's assurance that the man was troublesome. More than that; he was a source of extreme embarrassment to his old comrade. Perhaps it was something delicate, which Tzann could not spell out in great detail.

"Major Tzann tells me that you are the finest young pilot in your squadron," Smelenkov lied. "He suggested that I make the best possible use of you during your stay on this base."

Vologsky said nothing. His eyes betrayed no emotion at all. Clutching his flying helmet tightly to his side under his left arm, he continued to stare fixedly, focusing his eyes, as training had taught him, at a point about one and a half inches under Major Smelenkov's nose.

"Your mission today is an extremely important one," Smelenkov went on. "You may well feel honored to have been chosen for it."

It was time for a limited response. Vologsky allowed a fleeting smile to cross his lips, followed with a curt, almost imperceptible nod. "Yes, sir," he whispered quietly.

A slightly puzzled frown showed on Major Smelenkov's face. There was no faulting the young man. Asked for a snap judgement, he would have said that Vologsky was ideal material for promotion. Still, he had not been asked. Smelenkov shook the slightly irritating thought from his mind and returned to the issuing of orders.

"You will take off and pursue a course SSW, which will take you within fifty miles of Ulan-Bator. The purpose of your mission will be to study and photograph the air-defense systems there. Our latest intelligence suggests that you are unlikely to come up against any large-scale opposition. Certainly we have no knowledge that any missile launchers are in that immediate area . . ." Smelenkov broke off, to let his words sink in. The last statement was a deliberate falsehood; recent reconnaissance had shown that both missile launchers and mobile radar tracking units had been building up steadily for some days. However, those were facts which Vologsky did not need to know.

"You will realize, of course, that your aircraft is in full combat condition," Smelenkov went on. "Should you encounter any hostile aircraft, let me remind you that we are not at present in a state of war. Your first priority will be to take evasive action and attempt to return to home base. Under no circumstances will you initiate any form of attack, on air or ground-based targets. However, if you are yourself attacked, it will be your clear duty to defend yourself and your aircraft. Do I make myself clear?"

"Perfectly, sir." Vologsky allowed himself the faintest suggestion of a nod. Mentally, he registered the fact that he was to be a sitting duck.

"Good," Smelenkov said. "Carry on, lieutenant. You are cleared for take-off immediately. You will maintain complete radio silence, by the way . . . under any circumstances. For 24 hours, this entire base is on communications shutdown."

The words left one small doubt. Vologsky voiced it. "Mayday, sir?"

"Complete radio silence," Smelenkov repeated firmly. His meaning was clear enough. The sitting duck was not even allowed a quack of distress.

Vologsky walked slowly around his aircraft, ostensibly carrying out a pre-flight check. In reality, he was playing for time, pandering to his own personal doubts and insecurities. His brain screamed out to delay the moment when he climbed up into the Foxbat's cockpit, for, deep down inside, Vologsky knew it could well be the last time his feet touched the ground of his motherland. It would be a traumatic instant to his life. Oddly, his thoughts ran wild to reflect upon another footstep, another man. American astronaut Neil Armstrong;

163

July 20th, 1969. The position was reversed, the matter of purely personal rather than international and historical interest. Yet the significance was exactly the same. One small step, and a giant leap in his life, after which things could never be the same. A giant leap . . . but forward, backward, or into limbo?

There were other considerations, equally personal, and to do with the immediate future. Vologsky had not been taken in for one second by Major Smelenkov's assurance that his target area was free from missile launchers. Vologsky had no doubts that he would be flying into territory swarming with newly-established offensive bases. His orders to take only evasive or defensive action had been the clue. Mikhail Vologsky and the Mikoyan MiG 25 were both guinea pigs, expendable objects in the pursuit for new knowledge. He and the Foxbat were flying out to test just how good the Chinese anti-aircraft capability was. When, rather than if, Vologsky's plane blinked out of existence on the Irkutsk tracking radar, the computers could go to work, assessing the odds for future sorties, working out the degree of pilot loss to be expected. Vologsky could not feel bitter about this, or even surprised. If war was an illogical madness, then the conduct of it was a perfectly rational science. There was no room for emotional side-issues.

Vologsky reached up and patted the lower edge of the gaping rectangular air-intake on the aircraft's port side. It was a gesture almost of affection, certainly of trust. Vologsky knew that his very survival lay with that structure of steel, titanium and plexiglass. His control of it was a secondary thing; his performance only an inferior imitation of the Foxbat's true capability.

With that lay Vologsky's only thoughts of comfort. He would be flying the best aircraft of its type in the world. The only doubt was if the best were good enough.

Thinking of the plane as a life-support and preservation system was more encouraging. Vologsky ran the specifications of the aircraft over in his mind. Defensively, the twin Tumansky turbo-jets, uprated from the original R 31 series, gave the aircraft over 60,000 lbs of thrust, with afterburning. The Foxbat could climb out of trouble at nearly 45,000 feet a minute, flash away from an enemy at a maximum speed in excess of Mach 4. Over 34,000 pounds of fuel gave him a range of well over a thousand miles, even at full evasion speed. The AAM capability allowed him up to eight chances against other aircraft, or missiles. Four thermite discharge bombs in the rear section of the plane could take care of an equal number of heat-seeking missiles on his tail. Anti-tracking devices included radar jammers, ejectable decoys and SLAR, Side-Looking Airborne Radar. On top of all that, the flying machine held the fastest time-to-height record known, and had flown safely at a good 15,000 feet higher than any other conventional airplane. Its maximum ceiling remained unknown. No wonder official NATO sources had described the Foxbat as "probably the best aircraft of its type in the world."

If anything could get Mikhail Vologsky to Japan, then it had to be the Foxbat. It was the ideal vehicle to freedom, and his currency of negotiation when he got there. With new heart, Vologsky took his small step on to the boarding ladder.

He eased himself into the cockpit and swung the starboard-hinged canopy into place above his head. Adjusting his helmet, he coupled in his oxygen supply and set the anti-G device. The radio and communications systems were already plugged into place, requiring only the flick of a couple of switches to make them fully operative. A quick visual sweep of the main panel controls completed his pre-flight check. From the corner of one eye, Vologsky saw the ground mechanic scuttle across and remove the boarding ladder and front-wheel chock. The man retreated to a safe distance and signaled a thumbs-up. Vologsky was clear to go.

Carefully, without haste, Vologsky primed the ignition switches and set the fuel cock for take-off pressure. His thumb moved to the starter, hovering above it momentarily. He jabbed down with something of a grand gesture, tensing his body against the padded flightcouch as the twin starter cartridges fired simultaneously. The mighty Tumansky turbos throbbed into life, whining up to an ear-splitting crescendo. The Foxbat strained against the brakes like a chained animal, snarling with anger. As Vologsky released the brakes, the aircraft began to move, jerkily at first, then smoothly efficient as the mighty thrust came to terms with the weight of the aircraft.

Vologsky upped the throttles gently, his eyes on the straight runway ahead and the ground-speed indicator at the same time. The needle swung around the dial smoothly, coming swiftly up past the 100 knot mark and continuing to climb. At just over 150 knots, Vologsky rotated the Foxbat into flight elevation and the aircraft took to the air, streaking away from the ground at an angle of 38 degrees, its speed moving rapidly past 300 knots as it continued to climb.

CHAPTER TWENTY-FOUR

"So good of you to receive me at such short notice, Mr. Ennis. My Ambassador appreciates it deeply." Zhagov was on his diplomatic best behavior; warm, effusive, bubbling over with bonhomie. But his beaming smile revealed only the poor quality of Soviet cosmetic dentistry.

Dwight Ennis responded in like fashion. "It is an honor to make you welcome, Comrade Zhagov. As you know, we welcome every opportunity to expand the cultural bonds between our two countries."

Zhagov nodded. "Of course. Our wish also." He fell silent, continuing to mask any contrary feelings behind a fixed smile.

Ennis gestured towards a beautiful antique walnut and velvet Chesterfield. He had decided against using his office and settled for one of the more ornate State-rooms. The meeting had been hurriedly arranged at top level. It was obviously important.

As Zhagov seated himself, Ennis asked: "A drink, Comrade Zhagov? Vodka?"

Zhagov nodded deferentially. There was a slight twinkle in his eyes as he answered. "Bourbon. Old Grandad, if you have it."

"Of course." Ennis permitted himself a knowing smile, to

show Zhagov that the diplomatic gesture had been noted and appreciated. He crossed the room and rang the service bell.

Minutes later, the two men sat facing each other, sipping at their respective drinks. Silently, they appraised each other, neither wishing to begin the conversation which would lead them to the real business at hand. There were still the gestures to be made, the banter exchanged, and the moves of the diplomatic game to be played out on an invisible board.

"A toast, perhaps? To detente?" Zhagov said suddenly.

"Of course." Silently, Ennis cursed himself. That speech should have been his, as host. He lifted his glass. "To detente. To a new era of co-operation and understanding between our two great nations."

They both drained their glasses. Ennis stood, crossing to the cocktail trolley which had been brought into the room. "Another?"

"Why not?" Zhagov smiled, proffering his empty glass. Ennis filled it, adding ice. Zhagov took a drink, nodding thoughtfully. "Yes, I think that perhaps we really are entering a new era this time. All the old fears and mistrust must be swept under the carpet, forgotten. There are new frontiers, new priorities."

"Indeed. We must do everything we can," Ennis agreed.

"It will not be easy, of course," Zhagov went on. "Old habits die hard, old wounds take time to heal."

Ennis smiled, continuing the small-talk. "We must trust in our politicians, Comrade Zhagov. We do not elect them to perform easy tasks."

"We are all politicians, in our own various ways," Zhagov said pointedly. "Anyone and everyone close to the seat of power has an important role to play. Our mistakes can be just as damaging, perhaps just as costly, as those made by our immediate superiors."

"Mistakes, Comrade Zhagov? A Russian admits to mistakes?" It was a gentle, good-humored jibe, all part of the game.

Zhagov smiled broadly, to show that it had been accepted in the spirit in which it was delivered. "Indiscretions, then," he suggested. "The small failures that the human being is heir to. Even, perhaps, things which are not quite within our control. Accidents, things which go wrong."

"Quite," Ennis mused. He had the distinct feeling that Zhagov was hinting at something at last. Perhaps he was about to reveal the reason for his visit. Still, it did not seem to be the correct time to push the matter. It would all come out in its own good time. That was the Russian way. For the moment, then, the cosmetic chatter of diplomacy must continue. "Let us hope the current round of SALT talks are successful," Ennis said. "Both our countries have already wasted far too much money and resources on weapons of war. It is time for the insanity to stop."

The statement, although lightly made, was serious enough. Zhagov responded suitably. His smile faded for a moment. He nodded gravely. "You are right of course. The arms race did neither of us much good . . . except, perhaps, in pushing forward our frontiers of science and technology."

Zhagov paused for a second, then muttered what appeared to be an afterthought, a corollary to the initial statement. "In the field of aero-space design and technology, for instance . . . we have both made amazing progress. Our aircraft and missiles have new and frightening capabilities. We have built machines of terrible destructive power. If one of those mistakes I mentioned earlier should occur there, the results could be catastrophic, for both our countries. Or, indeed, for any other country, who happened, by a quirk of fate, to become involved."

Again, Ennis got the feeling that Zhagov was alluding to something, but he was being devilishly subtle about it. He began to feel a sense of irritation, a desire to get whatever it was out into the open, throw it out into the public arena like a challenge. But again the timing didn't seem right. Ennis let it drop again, choosing another topic of conversation. "I trust your trade delegation are enjoying our hospitality?"

"Greatly," Zhagov said simply, as if suddenly tiring of the pointless verbal smokescreen.

Both men were thoughtfully silent for several seconds. Their eyes met, probing gently beyond pinpricks of reflected light to explore each others' uncertainties, finally signaling an unspoken agreement.

Zhagov coughed gently, nervously, prefacing his words. "I think it is time, Mister Ennis, to, in your vernacular, take the gloves off."

"Quite." Ennis gave a brief nod. His face registered a fleeting look of relief, which hid his very real worry. The strain of diplomatic small-talk was a minor irritation compared to that involved in full-scale international discussions—and Ennis was now quite convinced that Zhagov's visit concerned nothing less. "I take it there is some sort of problem?"

Zhagov shrugged. "People make problems for themselves. With careful thought, and positive action, they can often be avoided. Or, at least, dismissed before they become embarrassing."

Ennis forced a thin smile. "I thought we had agreed the gloves were off, Comrade Zhagov?"

"Yes." Zhagov lowered his eyes, staring down at the floor pensively. When he looked up again, it was to stare directly into Ennis' eyes with a steely, purposeful glare. "We know about Project Cuckoo," he said in a quiet, but assured voice.

Only years of training saved Ennis from letting his shock register fully. It would have completely disorientated a lesser man. Gathering himself, Ennis returned Zhagov's cold stare. "Cuckoo? I'm afraid I do not understand you, comrade Zhagov."

"Ah." Zhagov sighed regretfully. "That is a pity, Mister Ennis. It is important for us to understand each other clearly. Perhaps if I explained myself a little more explicitly?"

Ennis nodded deferentially, maintaining his forced smile. "Please do," he muttered.

"Project Cuckoo . . . Turkey . . . July 4th . . . Paul Henry James Manville. Our security services are highly efficient, as you see."

Names, Ennis reflected, his mind working at speed. Just random names with no apparent facts to link them, fill in the gaps. Just how much did the Russians know, he wondered. Was Zhagov just teasing him, trying to make him squirm, by letting out their full knowledge in little bits and pieces? Or had the diplomat shot his bolt, thrown out his entire limited knowledge of Operation Cuckoo in one go, hoping to provoke a full-scale confession? There was no way of telling; Zhagov was giving nothing away. His face was impassive. He would make a superb poker player, Ennis found himself thinking.

But poker was an American game. Let the Russians have their world mastery of chess and gymnastics. Zhagov was playing an away game now, against a master. Maybe he held aces . . . maybe just one lonesome king. There *was* one way to find out—by carrying the game right through to its conclusion, bluff it out. Ennis knew he had no other choice, for the stakes were too high.

"Sorry, Comrade Zhagov, but you are confusing me even further. I really have no idea what you are talking about."

"No?" Zhagov's smile was mocking, supremely confident. He was not ready to throw in his hand yet. "Then perhaps your President has more knowledge. I have only to pick up a telephone to contact the Kremlin. It would be tragic if he were to leave Moscow under a cloud."

Silently, Ennis cursed himself for his stupid oversight. Not only did the Russians not practice the game, they did not follow the rules. Bluff was one thing; threats were another. Not a standard ploy in poker, by any means.

Throw in both hands, then. Shuffle the pack and re-deal. Play a completely different game; Happy Families. Ennis began to understand the exact nature of Zhagov's visit. How much the Russians knew, or suspected, about Operation Cuckoo was not really important in itself. What really mattered was the fact that they wanted to talk about it rather than take any positive action. That was what Zhagov had been hinting at all along . . . the Russians were desperately keen to maintain the current diplomatic status quo. It was more important to them than to the people of the United States . . . at least for the moment.

"We are dealing on a purely diplomatic level?" Ennis asked.

The Russian nodded curtly. "For the present, yes. Quite obviously, the matter will be passed on to the appropriate branch of the military in due course, but you have my assurance that it will be done with all possible discretion. Perhaps a formal notice of complaint, nothing more."

It was confirmed, then. Ennis knew that he had no reason to doubt the Russian's word. Operation Cuckoo had to be brought out into the open and dealt with. That way, a momentary political embarrassment would not be allowed to escalate into a major international incident. No more gunboats to Cuba, the world couldn't afford them any more. Both the Americans and the Russians possessed a stockpile of nuclear weapons powerful enough to annihilate the entire population of planet Earth several times over. Overkill was the word in current usage.

"You must realize, of course, that the United States Government was in no way connected with the events which led up to this embarrassing situation?" Ennis said. It was still time for saving face, even under the glaring light of truth.

Zhagov merely shrugged, signifying that he accepted the lie, knowing it for what it was.

"Very well, then. Basically, one of your pilots decided to defect to the West, flying one of your modified Foxbat-D aircraft from the Soviet airbase at Kharkov to Turkey. Naturally, when we learned of the plan, we were worried, just as you are now. The people of the United States have no wish to provoke hostility between our two countries. It was decided to shoot your pilot down as soon as he left Soviet air-space. The plan was codenamed Cuckoo."

Zhagov accepted the information, nodding thoughtfully. He raised one eyebrow a fraction of an inch. "So you know of our new toy? Your security services are to be complimented, Mister Ennis. They are almost as efficient as ours."

"What now?" Ennis asked.

Zhagov shrugged. "We pool our resources. You are quite right, of course. This pilot must be brought down, discreetly. Preferably over Russian territory."

"Of course. I will furnish all the information you require," Ennis promised. "It would, of course, be infinitely preferable if you were able to handle the matter yourselves."

Zhagov's eyes twinkled. He was unable to repress one further jibe. "Oh, I assure you that we can handle it, Mister Ennis. Our anti-aircraft systems are the finest in the world. We can shoot anything clean out of the sky—or space, for that matter."

Ennis could not fight against the smile which crept over his lips. In the relief from tension, he warmed to the Russian diplomat. "Let us hope you never have to back up that boast with proof, Comrade Zhagov. The running of the world would best be left to us diplomats . . . we only fight with words."

Zhagov smiled his agreement. Then his face became suddenly serious again. "There is not much time. We will need names, times, places."

"Of course. The pilot's name is Mikhail Vologsky, Lieutenant Vologsky. He is based at Kharkov, as I told you. There was no specific timing for his flight. It was just expected to happen on or before July 4th."

"Your agent?"

"Georgi Kirov. A tailor, working in Tbilisi. You want his full address?"

172

Zhagov shook his head. "It will not be necessary. We shall find him very quickly. I assume that his sudden disappearance will not raise any awkward questions?"

"None at all. You have my full assurance. The Lubyanka?"

Zhagov smiled roguishly. "That is an awkward question, Mister Ennis."

"Of course. My apologies." Ennis acknowledged his indiscretion graciously. "Do you think that you have all the information you will need?"

"Oh, I think so." Zhagov glanced down at his wrist, checking the date on his calendar watch. "We have three full days of grace. If this foolish lieutenant is sticking to his planned schedule, we should be able to stop him from even taking off on his insane mission. He will not get a chance to fly again, I can assure you." Zhagov rose to his feet briskly. "It is good that you and your fellow countrymen take detente so seriously, Mr. Ennis. Your co-operation has been much appreciated—and will, of course, be appropriately rewarded."

Ennis accepted the proffered hand, shaking it firmly. "You should know that you can always count on our whole-hearted co-operation, Comrade Zhagov."

The diplomatic screens had been re-erected. Things were almost back exactly as they had been—with one subtle difference. It was as if Operation Cuckoo had never existed. Still, there remained the need to add something, go over the top as it were. Ennis felt it his duty to show willing.

"The agent, Kirov . . ."

"Yes?" Zhagov appeared to be only vaguely interested.

"He will probably have made a run for comparative safe ground by now. I would imagine you might find him somewhere in Prague."

Zhagov accepted the additional information without emotion. "We shall find him wherever he is," he muttered firmly. He gave Ennis a knowing smile. "I assume that he is of no further use to your espionage network?"

Ennis briefly affected a look of shock. "Espionage network, Comrade Zhagov? You know that the United States government would never condone meddling in the internal affairs of a friendly power. The man is one of your own countrymen, a traitor. He acted for purely personal reasons, contacting us with his insane scheme."

"Yes, of course," Zhagov murmured. "As you say . . . a

traitor. Such a man can expect no sympathy from any nation. Or the pilot no sanctuary."

Ennis escorted the Russian diplomat to the door, nodding his head in agreement. The illusion, at least, was once again complete.

CHAPTER TWENTY-FIVE

Unaware that he had just become a figure of international importance, Mikhail Vologsky flew on at a steady 700 knots toward the Mongolian border, now less than fifty miles away. Since take-off, he had stuck rigidly to his orders, more from indecision than anything else. Making a definite course correction, striking out for the Great Khingan Shan and the Sea of Japan beyond it, was still a decision that his mind was loath to make.

Yet the decision had to be made, and made soon. His limited fuel reserves left no margin for dithering. Vologsky knew full well that his only real chance of passing over the Chinese mainland with any degree of safety would lie in boosting the Foxbat to its maximum tested airspeed, maybe even beyond. At Mach 4, he might just overpass the hostile territory before the Chinese radar systems could track and identify him, and be out of range of their land-based missile sites before they could be mobilized against him.

Inside his flying helmet, Vologsky could feel cool beads of perspiration breaking out on his forehead. The moment of decision was pressing upon him, transferring the strain from his mind to his body. Dimly, Vologsky realized that he needed to override his own brain, force his hands to make the vital movements which were necessary to place the aircraft on its new course. Ahead and to the left of him, he could already see the towering peaks of the Yablonovy Range, and to the right the high country had begun to concede to the desert wasteland of the Gobi.

Decide, screamed a silent voice in his brain, and in the fraction of a second it took his hands to follow through, it was already too late.

The shrill, warning bleep from the automatic missile detection system cut through all thought. Vologsky's eyes flashed, automatically, to the radar screen. From size alone, Vologsky identified the two small blips which had just shown up as aircraft rather than missiles. A split second later, the in-board computer verified this, positively identifying them as a pair of Chinese Shenyang F-9 fighter/interceptors.

Vologsky registered a moment of shock and surprise. His SLAR system was set to scan over a diameter of just over 200 miles, yet the two aircraft seemed to have come from nowhere, popping up on the radar screen at a range of less than fifty. It could only mean that they had come up from more or less directly beneath him, either scrambled hastily from the ground or from a low cruising position beneath the sweep of his radar scan. Either way, the aircraft were violating Soviet territory. They could only mean business.

In a purely reflex action, Vologsky's fingers snaked out toward the control panel, flipping on the Foxbat's radar-jamming devices. Even as he did so, Vologsky could not help reflecting that the action was a rather pointless one. The F-9's were the latest addition to the Chinese Air Force, and the cream of their fighting force. They undoubtedly possessed the most sophisticated electronic equipment, quite capable of unscrambling any defensive counter-measures and obtaining a positive fix on the Foxbat. As if to confirm this, the two blips on the radar screen changed course as Vologsky watched, diverging from each other and turning on to a path which would directly intercept that of the MiG. There was no doubt; they were coming straight at him.

The warning bleeper sounded again, briefly prefacing the appearance of a third blip on the screen, this time behind him. Vologsky took in his situation at once; he was roughly in the center of a triangle made up of hostile aircraft, closing upon him fast. In seconds, the first two fighters would be within missile range. Vologsky needed time to plan defensive measures.

Instinctively, he threw the Foxbat into a steep climb, catching his breath as the G-force tore at his body despite the cushioning effect of his padded flightsuit. A quick glance at the control panel told him two things, each of them a warning. The G-meter registered over plus 6, and the entire panel swam in a reddish mist, a circular pool of light surrounded by inky blackness. The vision tunneling effect was a sort of early warning system, preparing the brain for a complete blackout if greater acceleration and higher G-force placed any further strain upon the body. Vologsky ignored both warnings, knowing that he had to use the superior climbing power of the Foxbat to gain the time he needed. At 100,000 feet, he leveled out, banked the Foxbat around into a tight turn and streaked northward, accelerating toward Mach 2.

The ploy served its purpose well. Caught off-guard, the three Chinese pilots continued on their fixed height and course for several moments too long. Before they could correct themselves, and begin to climb in pursuit, Vologsky had used the fantastic acceleration of the Foxbat to open up his safety gap to well over a hundred miles. Safe, for the present, from anything they could launch at him. Vologsky cut his airspeed to Mach 1.5 and took time off to consider his position.

Before he attempted to make any plans, there was one thing that he needed to know. How determined were the Chinese pilots to get him? The next few seconds would show. Vologsky was now heading directly into the supposed safety of Soviet airspace. If the Chinese continued to pursue him, penetrating even deeper into Russia, it could only mean that they were committed to the kill. If they were content merely to chase him off, he could expect all three planes to turn and make for home almost immediately.

Ten seconds passed in complete silence. It was more than long enough to tell Vologsky what he wanted to know. On the radar scope, the three blips kept their position, having reached the same height as the MiG, and gradually began to close up again.

It didn't make sense. Vologsky racked his brains, trying to find a valid reason why the Chinese should be willing to risk three of their best aircraft violating enemy territory in pursuit of one surveillance aircraft. Vologsky had seen nothing; his missile detection systems had picked up no trace of offensive weaponry. The three F-9's had swung directly into the attack with no other provocation than a course obviously set for the Mongolian border. Vologsky wondered, momentarily, whether full-scale war had been declared, and the authorities had somehow neglected to inform him of the fact. Or had war been declared in the few minutes since he had taken off? If was a ridiculous thought. Vologsky pushed it from his mind with a sense of irritation. Deprived of a solid fact, he could only partially satisfy himself with a fairly logical speculation. Even though he had not seen anything, it was highly likely that there *had* been something important to see and the Chinese were taking no chances. It was the only explanation for the ruthless dedication with which the pilots were pursuing him.

However, such issues were really quite irrelevant to the situation. What mattered to Vologsky was the pure, and now undisputable, fact that the three F-9's were out to bring him down. It affected him in two ways. Firstly, he was in immediate danger, and secondly he was being forced back into Soviet territory, burning up precious fuel at a phenomenal rate.

As coolly as he could, Vologsky considered each problem in turn. The danger from the three Chinese fighter planes was not a very real one, all things considered. Vologsky had several factors in his favor, all of which made the Foxbat reasonably safe. Strictly in terms of fuel, the pursuing Chinese could not hope to chase him for very much longer. It seemed logical to assume that they had been cruising at a low altitude before the attack, therefore they could not be carrying a full fuel load. Also, the Chinese planes were heading into hostile territory, from which they had to make a retreat, whilst the Foxbat was streaking straight for home and safe ground. One mile to Vologsky was two to each of the Chinese pilots.

The main safety factor, however, lay in the superiority of the MiG's performance. Vologsky was in little doubt that he could outrun and outmanoeuver the Chinese aircraft. Unless they too had been modified from the original specifications, the F-9's were incapable of a maximum airspeed much above Mach 2.4. The Foxbat could outfly them at all times, staying safely beyond the range of their 30mm NR-30 guns and Sidewinder missiles. Oddly, the Chinese themselves did not apparently know this. Soviet security must be tighter than a limpet to have protected the secret of the improved Foxbat aircraft.

The second problem, however, could not be dismissed quite as lightly. Vologsky was still headed in the very last direction he wanted to go—toward home. He was, at present, hopelessly trapped between two fates, equally frightening. In evading death from the three Chinese fighter planes, he was merely speeding back toward death at the hands of his countrymen.

Vologsky glanced at his fuel gauge. It was already registering slightly below the three-quarters full level. With a sinking heart, Vologsky realized that it was already too late to contemplate the third alternative of making a run for Japan. With the remaining fuel in his tanks, he would be lucky to make it as far as the coast, with absolutely no reserves to evade the anti-aircraft systems around Vladivostock.

His situation seemed hopeless. He suddenly found himself settling back into the numb, uncaring state of torpor which had preceded his flight, and had to make a conscious effort to fight it off. There had to be some sort of hope, at least. Even the slim chance of ditching in the Sea of Japan and being picked up by a foreign ship was surely better than accepting certain death without argument.

With this thought, primal instincts were aroused, pumping adrenalin into his system. Only a weak, frightened little animal accepted death with equanimity. The smallest creature with any hold on life would at least put up a fight. It suddenly occurred to Vologsky that he could die in combat, with at least his own personal pride intact. The entire episode with Kirov had soiled him, made him mentally and physically unclean and ashamed of himself. Now there was at least a chance to redress the situation partially in a glorious death. Three fighter planes against one; a last challenge, a test of himself and the technology of his country. In death, he might be remembered as a hero rather than as a traitor. It was something to gain, when he had absolutely nothing to lose.

The decision made, Vologsky primed his cannons and activated the missile launching systems. Briefly firing a test burst from the guns into the empty sky, he began to bank the Foxbat into a gentle starboard turn, back toward the three pursuing F-9's. The gentle tug of G-force on his body had a soothing effect, enabling Vologsky to think coldly and clearly once again. Now he would be the hunter rather than the prey, and the superior performance of his aircraft would partially negate the odds of three to one against him. The coming dogfight would be more of an open contest, a reasonably fair challenge. Vologsky sensed a rising excitement, even pleasure, at the prospect.

Completing the turn, he tore his eyes away from the three blips on the radar scanner and stared out through the perspex canopy into the cloudless sky ahead, seeking visual contact with the three F-9's. Suddenly, he caught the first faint glint of sun on shiny metal, and he knew that the fight was on.

CHAPTER TWENTY-SIX

Vologsky had the advantages of surprise and height on his side as he streaked toward the oncoming Chinese fighters. His abrupt turn had caught them all hopping; it was not common for the hare to turn on the hounds.

Even now, the three pilots were only just beginning to climb upward to meet Foxbat on level terms. From a distance of three or four miles, Vologsky could see them clearly, brightly illuminated by the sun. Ahead and below him, the three F-9's were strung out in a slightly ragged V-shape, a tempting target for a couple of "Acrid" missiles. Vologsky's finger hovered above the firing button.

Major Smelenkov's words at the briefing came to him, causing a vital second of delay. "Under no circumstances will you initiate any attack". With a sense of annoyance, Vologsky realized that the conditioned reflex to orders had cost him the initiative. The three F-9's had flashed below him, and were beginning to break away as individual fighting units. Two of them were up to his height now, and probably already beginning to turn around on to his tail. In seconds, they would be in a position to loose off heat-seeking missiles to home in on the exhaust gases from his engines.

Cursing his stupidity, Vologsky barrelled the Foxbat over to port and started a diving turn which would bring him down behind the third F-9, which appeared to be laboring somewhat. He fixed his mind to operate purely for himself, his survival. It was kill or be killed, and to hell with anything else. How could a man preparing to betray his country possibly worry about following orders?

The straggling Chinese aircraft came into view, and Vologsky suddenly realized why its pilot was having difficulty in keeping pace with his companions. The aircraft was not an F-9 at all, but one of the older F-6 *Farmer-C* types, originally built as a copy of the Mikoyan MiG 19. Its performance was far inferior to that of the later fighters in the series. For a fraction of a second, the tail section of the aircraft flashed across his gun-sightings. Vologsky's finger flew to the firing button, loosing off a short burst of tracer. He was just too late. The flaring path of the 30mm shells passed above the aircraft's starboard tailplane, missing by yards. Startled, the Chinese pilot reacted by winging over to port and attempting to gain speed by entering a power dive.

Vologsky dismissed the plane from his thoughts for the time being. His main worry was the other two on his own tail. A cannon burst could be chewing into his rear section at any second—or a brace of deadly Sidewinder missiles come streaking to find him.

Closely following on the thought came the urgent shrieking from the missile detection system, accompanied by a flashing red light just to the left of the radar scope. Vologsky did not have the need or the time to study the small new blip which was steaking away from one of the F-9's at Mach 5, homing on the Foxbat's exhaust heat. The digital readout gave time to impact at 12 seconds—all the time that remained of Mikhail Vologsky's life, unless he acted swiftly. Terror, and years of training came to the fore, snapping his mind into overdrive. Twelve seconds were not long enough to arm and use the thermite decoys. Even if he managed to release them before the missile closed upon him, the aircraft would still be too near the actual explosion to survive. There was only one way, and Vologsky took it without a moment's hesitation.

Seconds before, he had been closing in on the limping F-6 for a cannon attack. Now, Vologsky needed that aircraft for a different reason. He had been ready to track it as the Sidewinder missile was launched; he was still moving on his course of interception. Vologsky needed only a slight change of plan.

Throwing the control yoke over savagely, Vologsky sent the Foxbat shrieking down in the wake of the F-6's evasive power dive. The glinting body of the aircraft flashed into view through the canopy as though suddenly projected there by some cleverly hidden hologram device. Straightening up, Vologsky gunned the twin Tumansky engines into a roaring crescendo of power, heading the Foxbat straight for the rear end of the Chinese aircraft.

His skill as a pilot was about to be tested to the full. Vologsky was gambling for his life, and the odds were short. Life or death depended on almost inhuman accuracy—a matter of a few feet, at a speed rapidly approaching Mach 1.

The missile detection system's digital display showed that there were less five seconds to detonation of the missile as the Foxbat shot like an arrow under the belly of the F-6, the MiG's tailplane clearing the Chinese fighter by a matter of inches. Immediately, Vologsky hauled back on the control yoke, coaxing the Foxbat into a desperate climb for survival. There was going to be a massive aerial explosion, and Vologsky needed to be as far above it as he could get in just five seconds.

The Foxbat shuddered violently under the sudden strain of abrupt climb, then jolted forward with renewed power as the mighty turbojets chewed on the thin air and found something to push against. Just as the acceleration of the Foxbat was settling to a smoother mode, the aircraft shuddered again, this time more violently. Even with the source of the explosion behind and beneath him, and the blinding glare of the sun ahead to his port side, Vologsky was aware of the searing orange flash of the explosion all around him.

Vologsky slowed his rate of climb, banking slightly to level the aircraft out before starting a proper turn. As he came around, Vologsky saw what was left of the F-6 as a huge red and orange fireball, spewing shattered, blackened and smoking metal toward earth in a deadly rain. Then it was gone, only a few streamers of oily black smoke marking the fact that anything had ever existed in that particular part of the sky.

Vologsky breathed again, streaking away toward the sun and breaking through Mach 1 and the sound-gate as he did so. The strategem had worked well. By leading the Sidewinder missile under the F-6, Vologsky had given the homing device a choice of targets. Unable to differentiate between the

183

exhaust heat of one aircraft from another, the missile had chosen the nearest. As Vologsky had pushed the Foxbat into the sky, away from the F-6, the Sidewinder had made contact with the wrong target, swiping the Chinese aircraft from the air like a giant fly-swatter. There was no way the pilot would have had a chance. So it was one down, two to go.

He continued to fly directly into the sun, accelerating rapidly upward toward Mach 1.8. The radar scope showed that the two F-9's were still too close on his tail, still well within effective missile range. Vologsky could not help wondering why they had not launched a pair of missiles at him while they had the chance, or, indeed, why others were not already on his tail. The most reasonable explanation was that the Chinese fighters had been stripped to a weight minimum for a lengthened cruising time, and were restricted to a pair of Sidewinders each. Neither pilot would thus want to shoot off his entire payload in one go, and the Chinese were probably aware that the Foxbats carried thermite anti-missile devices. So, they would bide their time, keep the missiles in reserve.

Even so, Vologsky corrected his earlier oversight and armed the anti-missile systems in readiness. If there was a next time, he could not be so lucky again—to have a perfect decoy target in such a perfect position.

Still accelerating, Vologsky kept the Foxbat running for the sun, constantly checking the distance of the F-9's behind him. He opened up a gap of nearly fifteen miles before considering his next move.

He studied the radar scope carefully. The two Chinese pilots had obviously taken a hard-learned lesson from the fate of their colleague, and were flying well apart, though at the same height. Checking the computer, Vologsky figured that both aircraft were pushing themselves toward maximum performance, while he still had quite a bit of reserve speed in hand.

What had almost worked once would work again, Vologsky decided. Acting immediately, he pushed the Foxbat through Mach 2 and continued on his course until the gap between him and his pursuers had increased to nearly twenty-five miles. Then, rotating the aircraft in a shallow climb, Vologsky started to turn back on his hunters, just as he had done before.

He chose his target at random from the radar scope. The

184

F-9 on his starboard side. Completing his turn back on himself, Vologsky returned to the attack.

It was classical fighter-plane tactics, made a part of aerial history by the Royal Air Force pilots of World War II. Attack out of the sun, sudden and deadly. The oncoming Chinese pilot saw only a blinding glare of diffused ultraviolet playing optical tricks on his canopy. By the time he picked out the streaking arrow of death hurtling toward him, it was too late.

As he came into effective cannon range, Vologsky attacked again. The line of tracer pulsed out as if in slow motion, probing like licking tongues of flame around the body of the F-9.

The Chinese pilot, realizing his danger, had to take evasive action, fast. He chose to bank off to starboard. It was a fatal mistake. He would have been better off plunging the Shenyang into a sudden dive. Suddenly, as the F-9 banked up and away, it no longer presented just a small, head-on target to Vologsky's guns. The whole underside surface of the aircraft's port wing was exposed. Tracer streaked below it, almost on a parallel with the line of the fuselage. Vologsky inched back on the stick, inclining the Foxbat's nose up a couple of degrees. The line of tracer crept upward, finding its target. Nearly half the F-9's wing suddenly shattered into shards of torn metal, exposing the girder construction underneath. Then, flapping a couple of times like a wounded bird, the end-section of the wing drooped momentarily and was then torn away by the screaming air.

The aircraft went into a slow-motion spin, rapidly building into a full-scale spiral. Finished, the F-9 dropped out of the sky toward the lower hills of the Sinkiang-Uighur.

With a somewhat detached professional interest, Vologsky watched the stricken plane plummet. The Chinese pilot made no attempt to bale out, and Vologsky was sure that none of his cannon shells had found their way into the cockpit. It more or less confirmed the prevalent rumor that the Chinese removed the ejector seat facility from their combat aircraft. They did not care for the idea of dropping live pilots behind enemy borders to be picked up and interrogated.

Vologsky checked his radar scope quickly, looking for the position of the last Chinese aircraft. With a sudden relief flooding through him, he saw that the F-9 was streaking for home, rapidly drawing out of range. Either the pilot had reached the end of his fuel reserves or the deaths of his two companions had made him lose all taste for the fight. Whichever was the case, this battle was over. Vologsky returned his attention to the spiraling F-9 somewhere below him, picking it up again a split second before it plunged to the ground and blossomed into a multi-petaled flower of fire. Seconds later, as the holocaust slipped out of Vologsky's field of vision, he heard the dull roar of the explosion, followed by half a dozen booming echoes bouncing off the sides of the surrounding mountains.

Vologsky flopped back in his flightcouch, his energy suddenly sapped, as though a switch had been thrown into the off position. His eyes found their way to the fuel gauge almost subconsciously. It read slightly under half-full.

Quickly following upon the sense of physical exhaustion, Vologsky's emotional reserves drained away. All the excitement and intoxication of winning the dogfight left him, leaving only a mental vacuum. He felt drained and empty in the knowledge that he was back exactly where he had started. Vologsky was once again a man with no hope, a pilot and an aircraft with absolutely no place to go.

The Foxbat was cruising at little over 500 knots, with Vologsky's fingertip control merely a nominal, halfhearted one. His dull eyes scanned the control panel with complete detachment, the aircraft's flightpath of little interest or importance. Only a basic instinct told him to keep the machine flying, level, and at a constant height. Somehow, Vologsky sensed that he owed the Foxbat at least that. It would have been an act of the most callous ingratitude not to repay the aircraft for its recent efforts.

Minutes fled away, miles slipped away beneath the silver belly of the Foxbat. Neither time nor distance meant anything at all to its pilot. On the ground, however, it was an entirely different matter. Chinese radar scanners had already picked up the image of the unknown Soviet plane, apparently set on a direct course toward Peking. The dogs of war strained at the leash.

On the other side of the border, there was equal activity and concern. As the Foxbat flew high across the Gobi desert, a Yakolev Yak-40 short-range transport aircraft, bearing no less than four top-graded KGB personnel, was radioing the control tower at Kharkov base for landing clearance. The reasons for their presence were contained in a single, terse intelligence report, received shortly before.

SUPREME SECURITY: CLASS ONE PERSONNEL ONLY.
KGB CENTRAL, MOSCOW.
REPORT: USSR EMBASSY, WASHINGTON.
FULL EMERGENCY PRIORITY. AMERICAN OPERATION CUCKOO
NOW KNOWN TO INVOLVE DEFECTION OF SOVIET AIR FORCE
PILOT WITH TOP-SECRET MILITARY AIRCRAFT. IMPERATIVE
THAT THIS PLAN IS RENDERED INOPERATIVE AT ONCE. FULL
DIPLOMATIC COVER WILL APPLY TO ALL INVOLVED
PERSONNEL. RUSSIAN PILOT NAMED AS MIKHAIL VOLOGSKY,
ATTACHED TO MILITARY AIR BASE AT KHARKOV. DATE OF
DEFECTION ON OR BEFORE JULY 4. DESTINATION TURKEY.
PREFERABLE THAT PILOT VOLOGSKY BE PLACED UNDER
CLOSE ARREST BEFORE FLIGHT. IF NOT POSSIBLE,
IMPERATIVE AIRCRAFT BROUGHT DOWN OVER SOVIET
TERRITORY. AMERICAN SOURCES HAVE ALSO EXPOSED
TRAITOR GEORGI KIROV, TAILOR, OF TBILISI GEORGIA.
CURRENTLY BELIEVED TO BE IN OR ON ROUTE FOR PRAGUE
SUGGEST IMMEDIATE ARREST AND DETENTION. CENTRAL
FILES ADVISED THAT CIA OPERATIVE PAUL HENRY JAMES
MANVILLE NOW TERMINATED,

CHAPTER TWENTY-SEVEN

The rubber stamp stopped, suddenly, in its descent toward the documents spread out on the desk. The hand holding it paused in mid-air, knuckles whitening slightly. The stamping of transit papers was usually a routine affair. This particular instance was different.

The Czech official glanced up from the name printed on the documents to the man in question. His eyes narrowed slightly. "Kirov? Georgi Kirov?"

"Yes," Kirov answered, his voice perfectly level. He saw no reason to be alarmed. Regulations decreed that alien transit papers be presented for renewal every two days while Soviet citizens remained in foreign territory. This was Kirov's first renewal, and an inbred cynicism had led him to expect some minor tribulations. The authorities invariably made some kind of trouble, turning what should essentially be a simple act into a major and complicated procedure. It was the nature of the system, and people had to accept it.

The Czech official's eyes showed a trace of sympathy. "I am sorry, Comrade Kirov, but these papers do not appear to be quite in order."

Still Kirov felt no real anxiety. All officials seemed to take a certain pleasure in causing delay and frustration. Such tactics served to remind the Soviet traveller that he was enjoying a rare and special privilege, and that such generosity had to be paid for in terms of other limitations upon personal freedom. Since the quelling of the uprising, Czechoslovakia bureaucracy was little different to that of his homeland. In this case, the only subtle difference was that the Czech had prefaced his statement with an apology. In Russia, there would have been no such courtesy.

With a faint shrug, Kirov demurred gently: "I cannot see why there should be any problem. Those papers are new, issued quite properly in Tbilisi only a few days ago. I assure you that they are quite in order. What appears to be wrong with them?"

The Czech official thumbed a button on the underside of his desk. "I am sorry, but I cannot stamp these papers as they are," he muttered firmly.

Kirov studied the man's face carefully, as old instincts took hold of him, warning him of danger. There was a certain shiftiness, even fear, in the official's eyes. Underlying that was another emotion, even harder to define. Pity, was it? Suddenly, Kirov knew that he was in trouble.

Even as he started to react, it was too late. Behind him, the door opened and two men, summoned by the hidden buzzer, entered the room. They moved quickly, coming up either side of Kirov and each placing a restraining hand upon his elbows.

Kirov looked them both over quickly, coming to an inescapable conclusion. They were not Czechs, that was for sure. Both men were in civilian clothes, suits of different patterns but which had a certain sameness about them. They were two of a kind, a pair of terrible twins. The bulges showing beneath their jackets did nothing to change that impression. With a sudden sinking feeling, Kirov knew that they were KGB, and that they were there for one reason only. Vainly, he tried to bluff it out.

"I do not understand. What is wrong with my travel documents, please?"

The grip on his arms increased in pressure. "Come with us, Comrade Kirov," one of the men said, gruffly.

It was useless to resist. Without further protest, Kirov allowed himself to be manhandled toward the door. Outside in the corridor, the two men pressed themselves close against his side, and their grips upon his elbows changed to half-nelsons.

Kirov was frogmarched down the corridor toward the elevator.

As the doors of the elevator sighed shut, one of the KGB men let out a sneering laugh. "Too bad, Kirov. Your game is up. Your imperialist puppet-masters betrayed you. A traitor has good friends, yes?"

"I don't know what you are talking about," Kirov replied quietly, but there was little conviction in his voice.

The elevator came to a gentle stop. Roughly, Kirov was pushed out into another plain corridor and marched toward an unmarked door. One of the men opened it and his companion thrust Kirov inside with a vicious punch in the kidneys.

The room was starkly functional. In the way of furniture, it boasted only a desk, behind which were two comfortable chairs. In front of the desk was a third chair, this one of solid plain wood construction with stout leather straps dangling from each arm-rest. Facing the chair from the desk was a powerful swivel lamp. Lying close by were two short lengths of rubber hose and a gas lighter. Kirov was under no illusions as to the function of the objects. Neither did he imagine that they were the only "persuaders" in the interrogation room. No doubt the innards of the desk boasted a whole armory of more sophisticated devices of torture. And all this for what was surely only a preliminary grilling. Once his bruised body arrived home, there would be further interrogations, unresticted use of more up-to-date equipment to aid the old question-and-answer game. Drugs, sensory deprivation, electrical torture. Anything and everything which could open up Korov's mind would be used to dredge the last piece of information from it. When the KGB arrested a leading agent, they liked to get full value for their money. With over thirty years of action behind him, Kirov had a lot of information stored up. It was highly unlikely that his body would be able to hold out for the amount of time it would take to extract it all.

Quickly, Kirov paraded this battery of unwholesome facts before his consciousness, assimilating them and pursuing a conclusion. There was only one; Kirov was a dead man.

The KGB men had begun to propel him toward the wooden chair. In a matter of seconds he would be strapped down and the torture would begin. Once started, it would not stop. A long and painful road to death would be irrevocably set out upon. Escape, or a shorter route, were both preferable. It was a time for desperate measures.

Kirov had already considered two possibilities. He tried the most optimistic one first. Bribery among the KGB was not completely unknown. Kirov had heard of many stories. He tensed his body, resisting the pull toward the interrogation chair. "I have money . . . thousands of roubles. I could make you both rich."

Neither was impressed. The man who had sneered at him in the elevator laughed outright. "It is very difficult for a dead man to spend roubles, Kirov," he observed. "You are far too big a fish for us to let you slip out of the net."

Kirov let his body sag, as if with final resignation. He had not really expected to buy his way to freedom. That left only one alternative. As the two men thrust him into the chair, he looked up, smiling. "What floor is this room on?"

Thrown by the apparent insignificance of the question, one of the men frowned in puzzlement, answering him automatically. "The sixth . . . why?"

"My lucky number," Kirov said, putting on a brave grin. Uncoiling from the chair with an agility which belied his age, he was up and moving before either of the men could restrain him. He was across the small room in a fraction of a second, finishing his sprint with a leap and a headfirst dive at the window. His weight and momentum took him straight through the glass with a crash.

Shocked and dumbfounded, his would-be interrogators could only gape at the smashed window as Kirov's body plummeted toward the concrete pavement below. He had found his short route to death.

CHAPTER TWENTY-EIGHT

"You bungling, incompetent fools. You had him in your hands and you let him trick you like children. You have not heard the last of this, I promise you. Return home immediately and make out a full report. I will deal with you both later."

As an outward expression of his fury, Nikolai Chersky slammed the telephone receiver back into its cradle with a crash. He turned on Major Tzann, his anger not yet spent. "And you, Major . . . I find myself completely surrounded by fools, blind idiots. You had a dissident pilot under your direct command and yet you suspected nothing. The traitor Kirov was known personally to you, he made several journeys here and still you did not see fit to question his motives." Chersky broke off to gesture towards the telephone. "You are no better than those two mindless morons. They had Kirov in their hands and they allowed him to jump out of a sixth-floor window before they could even ask him a few questions."

Major Tzann shifted uneasily in his chair, seeking some words of defense against the unfair attack. "There was no sign that anything was wrong," he pleaded. "Vologsky seemed a disciplined young officer—a good pilot. He was never in any kind of trouble, I had no reason to doubt his allegiance.

And the tailor, Kirov. He appeared to be only that. How could I know he was a foreign agent?"

"Fool," Chersky repeated. "Did you expect him to wear a badge, proclaiming the fact? Did you not reflect upon the fact that the pilot Vologsky had made several applications to be transferred to the Space Program and was thus obviously unhappy, and a possible dissident? You are supposed to be in command of your men and your situation at all times, Major Tzann. It is your job and your duty to look beyond the obvious, pick out potential trouble before it arises."

Tzann shivered uncomfortably under the scathing attack. Unwarranted or not, Chersky could bring the heavy guns to bear upon him. He had the power. His position, high in the KGB ranks, made him one of the most feared and powerful men in the country, and his total arrogance reflected this. If Chersky decided to make him a major scapegoat, then he would do so. The minor fact that Vologsky had been a member of his squadron would become total, damning evidence against him. Right now, in the absence of anyone else to vent his wrath upon, Chersky was making out a formidable case against him. Personal survival decreed the need to justify himself, despite his fear of the man. "I must point out, Comrade Chersky, that no one in your own organization was aware that either man was potentially subversive. I received no direct orders to conduct any form a surveillance, or even to treat Kirov or Vologsky with any suspicion. I trust you will make a note of that, comrade."

Chersky glared at him intimidatingly. "I am making a note of many things, Major," he said, in a slightly quieter voice. "Not the least of which is the fact that you do not appear to regard this matter with the seriousness it merits. Quite apart from personalities, Major Tzann, it boils down to one basic fact. You were in charge of, and directly responsible for, several of this country's top-secret military aircraft. One of those aircraft might now be on its way to a hostile power. Is that not an accurate assessment of the facts?"

Tzann's eyes were lowered as he answered, in little more than a hoarse whisper. "Yes."

There was a loud rap on the office door. Chersky barked: "Enter." The trio of KGB men who had accompanied Chersky from Moscow walked into the room. "We have searched the pilot's quarters, thoroughly," one of them announced. "We found nothing of interest."

"You checked with the radar room?" Chersky demanded. "You obtained a current fix on this pilot and his aircraft?"

The spokesman shook his head silently. Major Tzann hastened to explain. "We have not the facilities on this base, Comrade Chersky. Our radar equipment is only short-range, for our immediate needs. Only a base like Alma-Ata would have the long-range radar scanner necessary to track the single aircraft."

Chersky cursed. "Damned inefficiency," he muttered. "Fools and inefficiency, that is all I seem to come up against."

Major Tzann could not help making another small point. "With respect, Comrade Chersky, it is the nature of our military security rather than the fault of individuals. You yourself could have been spared this pointless journey had the authorities seen fit to check in advance and inform you that my squadron had been transferred to Irkutsk."

"You do not need to remind me, Major," Chersky retorted coldly. "There will be repercussions, I assure you." He turned back to his men. "Talking of Irkutsk, have you managed to make contact with the commanding officer there yet?"

"No sir, all forms of communication appear to be shut down. It must be a security operation, sir."

"Get on to the Marshal of the Soviet Air Force," Chersky snapped. "Absolute top priority. There must be a way of getting through to that airbase. Some form of emergency contact. Find out what it is and get me on it." He whirled on Tzann once again. "I take it that your radio officers *are* competent? There is no chance that the communications problems are at this end?"

"None at all," Major Tzann replied confidently. However, it could only help to show willing. "I shall check personally, however," he announced, rising from his chair. "With your permission, Comrade Chersky?"

Chersky nodded. "Yes, go ahead Major. One of my men will go with you. Please instruct your radio operator to clear a telephone channel to Soviet Air Command for him."

"Of course." Gathering as much dignity as he could muster, Major Tzann marched from his office, the KGB escort firmly on his heels.

After he had left, Chersky glowered at his two remaining underlings. Frustration and a sense of impotence were boiling up in him once again, and they were the only people to take it out on. Besides, a little bit of bullying kept people on their toes, he reasoned. "And what are you two idiots doing, standing around and twiddling your thumbs?" he roared at them. "Make yourselves useful, can't you? Find out whether that transport aircraft is refuelled and ready to fly again. And interrogate some of the service mechanics, the ground staff. Find out anything there is to know about that traitor pilot."

"Yes, sir." Both men bowed obsequiously and backed toward the door.

Left alone, Chersky vented his pent-up anger on Major Tzann's desk, smashing his clenched fist down upon it so hard that a penholder jumped a good four inches to tumble over the side on to the floor. "Damned incompetence," he grunted, yet again.

Chersky's anger was exacerbated by the fact that he felt physically uncomfortable. He was hot and sticky, perspiring heavily in Major Tzann's overheated office. Chersky felt another wave of antagonism against the man. He was soft, spineless, having his heating turned up to such a level. Tzann was a man who obviously liked his comforts to the point of self-indulgence. The Major liked to be warm, and comfortable, and secure. It was something to remember for the future.

CHAPTER TWENTY-NINE

The Foxbat shuddered, briefly, as it encountered a small patch of turbulence. The jolt snapped Vologsky out of his reveries at once, returning his mind with concern for the aircraft. With an automatic reaction, his hands tightened on the control yoke, establishing firmer control to steady the Foxbat. It settled quickly, the level flight indicator on the control panel sinking back into place gently. With a pilot's natural instinct, Vologsky knew exactly what had happened. A swiftly spiraling thermal rising up from the desert floor had caught the Foxbat under its starboard wing, giving it a gentle nudge. But even a nudge, encountered at 500 knots, packed enough power to make a pilot sit up and take notice.

Aware of the aircraft as a vulnerable entity once again, Vologsky made a quick visual check of his instrumentation. The sudden realization that his present course was taking him straight towards the Chinese capital came as something of a mental jolt. It was like a fly deliberately homing in on a swatter. Already, Vologsky knew that he was too close to densely populated Chinese territory to have been overlooked. The entire country's radar tracking stations must be going mad with activity, every missile silo within three hundred miles preparing to launch all they had available at him. It was surprising that a whole salvo of surface-to-air missiles were not already showing up on his detection gear. Perhaps the Foxbat's incredible course had confused the Chinese military. A lone fighter plane, homing in on the Chinese capital, was so unthinkable that it might just be totally mind-blowing. Stunned by disbelief, they might just be sitting back to wait and see what was going on, confident in the knowledge that they had more than enough firepower to blast him out of the sky a hundred times over, whenever the need arose.

It was a chilling thought. Vologsky veered off to the northeast, putting the Foxbat into a steep power dive which took the aircraft through Mach 1. The boom carpet he would leave behind him was almost as good as a flare advertising his position, but Vologsky didn't care. He was getting out, fast.

He began to level out at 12,000 feet, continuing to accelerate. If necessary, whilst the flat wastelands of the Gobi remained below him, he could dive even lower, hopefully slipping under the Chinese radar net. For the present, a speedy departure from Chinese territory seemed the most sensible course of action. Winding up his radar detection system to its maximum extent, Vologsky pursued that course, running out the turbo-jets to deliver maximum thrust, shoving the Foxbat forwards like a blow from a huge hand. The Mach-meter crept steadily up to 2.8 and settled, as Vologsky cut back the power. He was content to stay just on the lower side of Mach 3. It was an optimum figure, more than fast enough to evade pursuit from any known Chinese aircraft, with something in reserve to let loose if any SAMS came up at him. Also, it left him precious extra minutes of flight time. Over Mach 3, the Tumansky engine gulped down fuel like a hydro-electric turbine takes water.

Fuel. The clock by which Vologsky could measure the minutes of his life remaining to him. He had forgotten. Now, he suddenly remembered again. Like a hypnotist's medallion, the gauge drew his eyes toward itself.

Five hundred miles, maybe? With two hundred miles more in the reserve tanks. Give or take a twelve to fifteen per cent error and a speed reduction once he was clear of hostile territory and Vologsky's rang was something around six hundred miles—an hour's flying time at subsonic speeds, and twenty minutes or so if he continued to fly at his present rate.

Time suddenly mattered a lot more than distance. It made no difference to Vologsky *where* his life ended, but the chance to multiply his life expectancy threefold most certainly did. He cut power savagely, the sudden jolt of the change slamming him in the back of the head despite his helmet and pressurized flying suit. The Foxbat shuddered briefly as the returning shockwave engulfed it, then slipped into its new mode smoothly. Vologsky's ears popped as the crash of sound pounced out of the silence. He thought of gunfire, remembered the two dead Chinese pilots, and realized there was something he had forgotten to do.

With the Foxbat skimming smoothly across the desert at 600 knots, Vologsky engaged the autopilot, clasped his hands together, closed his eyes and began to pray.

He prayed to a God whom he had largely forgotten over the past few weeks of his life. In his final minutes, Vologsky wished to atone for that, and more. He had deaths on his conscience, and the betrayal of things he had once held dear in his heart. Although short, Vologsky's plea to the God he believed in was a very deep and personal one. He did not expect forgiveness, nor did he demand it as his right. He merely asked, with humility, the pure strength of his faith—all the hope he had, or really needed.

Opening his eyes again and glancing up, Vologsky saw the towering peaks of the Great Khingan Shan on his starboard side. Ahead, in the distance, the flat plain at its foothills was broken by a thin, winding strip of silver. Vologsky recognized it almost at once. He was less than twenty miles from the border. The silver line he could see was the Amur river, its slow-running waters reflecting the sunlight back to him. The Amur ran due north for about another two hundred miles before describing a huge and ragged half-circle, almost turning back on itself. The Soviet border had been marked by its course. It was a natural boundary.

He must have been picked up by Russian radar scanners by now, Vologsky realized. He found himself wondering what they could be thinking, observing one of their own aircraft flying in from deep Chinese territory. He was more than a thousand miles off his original course, and it was highly unlikely that any bases this far to the East had been briefed to expect returning surveillance aircraft. Unless, however, they had sent over sorties of their own. But then they would have their own strictly defined flightpaths, and identification arrangements. No doubt they were frantically trying to contact him at that very moment, unaware that his communication system was completely shut down. Any minute now, they would start to get worried. What would happen then was anybody's guess. If they were worried enough, they might just blast him out of the sky to be on the safe side.

Vologsky's reflections remained largely academic. The Foxbat was doomed anyway—he had already accepted that. Any second, Vologsky intended to change course due East, mentally committed to the idea of running for the coast. In its dying minutes, the Foxbat might just give its pilot a chance to ditch into the sea, with some minimal chance of survival.

He was about to make that course change when the detection system bleeped out in warning once again. Vologsky's hand froze on the control yoke, holding the Foxbat steady while he checked the radar scope and computer identification. There were four blips on the screen, closing on his position rapidly. Obviously, the Soviet ground staff had succumbed to curiosity. They wanted to know more about the lone aircraft, and had scrambled four interceptors from the ground to take a close look at it.

The computer identified the four aircraft as Sukhoi Su-15s, an all-weather interceptor which had been largely superseded by the Foxbat series. There were still several hundred of the aircraft in service, however, and they could maintain a steady flight speed in excess of Mach 2, which made them quite formidable machines. However, they were rapidly being phased out of elite Soviet Air Force service, and this led Vologsky to conclude that they had been launched from the combined operations base just outside Blagoveshchensk. The military base, although not a large one, fulfilled several important defense functions. Largely in the hands of the Army, it maintained surveillance over the border toward Harbin, Changchun and Shenyang, operated regular inspection flights over the Sea of Japan and served as an early-warning radar base covering seaborne assaults on the coastal city of Vladivostok. With all these things in mind, it was unlikely that the Su-15s were the best thing they had. They would no doubt have at least half a dozen Foxbats, probably also modified to the improved performance of Vologsky's own aircraft. For this routine interception and inspection, however, it had obviously been considered advisable to use the Sukhois.

Two thoughts struck Vologsky simultaneously. While the airbase at Irkutsk remained in a state of communications shutdown, there was no way that anyone could check out any story he chose to tell. For the next twenty hours, at least, he could be perfectly safe within the confines of the Blagoveshchensk base. It was possible, of course, that he would be placed under close arrest as a security precaution, yet Vologsky could not help feeling that there must be a plausible story which he could construct which would prove acceptable to the authorities. He might even modify the story of his encounter with the three Chinese warplanes to show himself up as a hero, flying on a secret mission which only his commanding officer at Irkutsk could reveal. That being so, he might well be given VIP treatment until his story could be checked out the following day. Twenty hours with the chance to be free on a military base was not a thing to be sniffed at. It was a pretty good life expectancy to a man with less than forty minutes of flying time in his fuel tanks.

Better still, his aircraft would probably be completely checked and refueled soon after landing. Keeping Soviet aircraft in a constant state of readiness was standard procedure on Air Force bases, and there was no reason that a combined operations unit would not operate the same system. Failing that, Vologsky's assumption that the base would boast at least some Foxbat-D aircraft was a promising alternative. The Americans only wanted a specimen of the aircraft's type, not one specific plane. Assuming he kept his freedom, Vologsky might well gain access to those Foxbats and be in a position to steal one, or bluff his way into a return flight to Irkutsk. Once airborne, nothing need stop him making an all-out dash for Japan, and freedom. At best, only aircraft of equal performance could pursue him, and with luck he could gain valuable minutes of surprise before anyone realized that anything was amiss. Fuel would no longer be a problem, since the base was nearly a thousand miles nearer the coast, and Japan beyond. Vologsky could streak straight there at Mach 3 without once having to glance at the fuel gauge with any concern.

With a surge of renewed optimism, Vologsky gazed ahead through his aircraft's perspex canopy. He had visual sighting of the four Su-15s now, approaching him in a line about five hundred feet above him.

201

Making a sudden decision, Vologsky snapped on his radio communications system and flipped a switch onto standard channel A. There was a brief hiss of static and then he heard the sound of a Russian voice, making air-to-air contact.

CHAPTER THIRTY

The insistent jangling of the bedside telephone woke Dwight Ennis from the terminal stages of an alcohol-induced sleep. Through a blurry haze, his eyes finally focused upon the faint red glow of the digital clock and bedside lamp just to the left of the priority telephone. With fumbling fingers, Ennis snapped on the light and lifted the receiver, holding it to his ear.

"What the hell?" he grunted, irritably. As his eyes accustomed themselves to the sudden light, he managed to read off the time on the clock. "Christ, it's five in the goddamn morning."

The voice at the other end of the telephone was suitably apologetic. "Yes, sir, I know that, sir. Sorry sir, but this call just came through on your emergency line here at the White House. It's the Soviet Embassy, sir. The caller insisted upon talking to you personally."

Ennis had managed to shake himself fully awake now. The message sobered him immediately. It had to be important. "OK, put it through—but keep it on monitor," he snapped.

"Wilco, sir." There were two faint clicks on the line before a new voice came on.

"Mister Ennis. Please forgive me for disturbing you," said Zhagov politely.

Ennis grunted. Protocol was one thing, but there were

limits. He could not help but leave an edge of annoyance in his voice as he replied. "Please forgive Western decadence, Comrade Zhagov, but we do tend to sleep through the hours of night."

"Russians also," Zhagov said flatly. "I too have been disturbed from my bed. However, most unfortunately it is only noon in Moscow, where everyone is most certainly awake, and somewhat agitated."

"Trouble?" Ennis forgot his irritation at once.

"Perhaps," Zhagov replied. "Your Operation Cuckoo—it has, how do you Americans say it?—laid an egg."

"Oh Christ." Ennis groaned. "You'd better give me the details."

Zhagov coughed. "Excuse me for asking, Mr. Ennis, but is this telephone conversation being recorded?"

"Yes," Ennis said. There seemed no point in lying.

"I would prefer if it were not," Zhagov murmured. "It might be better for all concerned."

Ennis thought for a few seconds. "Yes, perhaps you're right," he muttered finally. He flipped the recall button on the telephone a couple of times. "Please take a note of that, monitor. You will erase this recording and establish a direct security line. That is an order."

There was no reply, but Ennis heard the final click which told him the order had been followed. He returned his attention to the Russian. "Now, what's the problem, Zhagov?"

"The problem is exactly the same, Mr. Ennis. It's just that now we can be sure we have it."

"Explain," Ennis said, not fully understanding.

"The agent, Kirov, was tracked down earlier today," Zhagov volunteered. "In Prague, as you suggested. Unfortunately, he committed suicide before we could ask him any questions."

"Then how can you be sure that Operation Cuckoo is live?" Ennis interrupted. "Surely we are no better informed than we were before?"

"On the contrary. Now that Kirov's defection to supposedly safe ground is confirmed, we must assume that he had completed the final stages of the plan. The pilot Vologsky must have been ready to go."

"Yes, but surely it is not too late to stop him," Ennis protested. "There are still two days left. Surely your security forces can prevent him from taking off?"

"Ah." Zhagov muttered unhappily. "Unfortunately, that is not the case, Mr. Ennis. Certain unforeseen complications have arisen. This pilot's entire squadron was transferred two days ago to Irkutsk, which, by yet another unfortunate quirk of fate, happens to be shut down tight on a security practice. For all we know, Vologsky may at this moment be on his way."

"Irkutsk . . . Irkutsk," Ennis murmured to himself, struggling to recall his sketchy knowledge of Russian geography. "Isn't that several thousand miles to the east?"

"Just over three, to be precise," Zhagov confirmed.

"Well there you are then," Ennis concluded triumphantly. "Defection is out of the question. Turkey will be completely out of range to him. Your pilot can't go anywhere."

"We can't be sure of that," Zhagov said. "Certainly Turkey is out of the question—but there are other places. Can you be sure that your man Manville did not lay in any contingency plans, an alternative landing site?"

"Such as?" Ennis asked.

"I haven't the faintest idea," Zhagov admitted. "But several possibilities remain open. We know, for instance, that Vologsky landed and refueled at Omsk as ordered. He took off again with a full tank at 10.00 hours, Moscow time. He was ordered to fly directly to Irkutsk. He may not have done so. There are several other destinations within his aircraft's range. Finland, perhaps even Sweden, the Barents Sea, the Arctic Ocean. I am not a specialized military man, Mister Ennis, but I assume one of our aircraft could, in an emergency, make a landing on one of your aircraft carriers, if advance plans were made to modify the arrester gear in some way?"

Ennis digested Zhagov's speech thoughtfully. Finally, he asked: "Are you making an accusation, Zhagov? Are you trying to accuse the United States Government of duplicity in this matter?"

"Not at all," Zhagov demurred. "I am merely pointing out the possibility of a secondary destination. Can you be absolutely sure that your man did not make some emergency arrangement with the Navy?"

"No, not at this precise moment in time," Ennis had to admit. "But I can damn well check it out in double-quick time."

"Then I suggest you do," Zhagov murmured gently. "We have already discussed the possible ramifications of this ill-timed scheme coming anywhere near fruition. They remain just as unpleasant, potentially dangerous."

"I'm well aware of that," Ennis snapped, a little irritably. He didn't need the reminder. "I'll get on to the U.S. Naval Command at once. I should be able to give you a firm answer within the hour."

"An hour is a long time," Zhagov pointed out. "A jet fighter plane can travel a long distance in an hour."

"I'll get back to you as quickly as I can," Ennis said. He prepared to hang up the receiver, but Zhagov wasn't quite finished.

"There is just one last matter to consider, Mr. Ennis. I mentioned Finland and Sweden as possible destinations. There is one more, of course."

"One more?" Ennis couldn't think offhand.

"We know the pilot landed at Omsk as ordered," Zhagov went on. "He may, therefore, also have continued on to Irkutsk. If he managed to take off again from there, he is marginally in range of Japan. The one thing which bothers me in all this is the pilot himself. We do not have fools in the Soviet Air Force, although, in this case, one man is obviously seriously misguided. However, he is also obviously an intelligent and rational young man. He may well have chosen a secondary destination for himself. This would be extremely awkward for both of us, would it not? If a neutral country becomes involved, our efforts to deal with this matter on a diplomatic level might well be ruined, the entire thing taken out of our hands entirely. That would be embarrassing to say the least, Mr. Ennis. Do you not agree? At this present moment, the eyes of the world are upon us. We should be very concerned that they only see good things."

"Your point is well taken," Ennis muttered thickly. "I shall make it my immediate business to check out every possibility you have brought up. Can I assume you will do likewise?"

"You can, most certainly," Zhagov assured him. "It might be in the best interests of diplomacy if you left the Finnish question to us. We have, perhaps, a slightly greater proximity in attitudes as well as purely geographical terms. You, by the same token, are in a much better position to deal with the Japanese. Do I make myself clear, Mr. Ennis?"

"Perfectly," Ennis said. He knew exactly what Zhagov meant. The gentle hand of diplomacy had a lot more power when it could also be clenched into a fist of threat. Zhagov's discreet hint carried a whole wealth of meaning beneath it.

"I will leave you to make your investigations, then," Zhagov said. "I hope to have some assurances from you in the very near future."

"Right." Ennis dropped the telephone into its cradle for a few moments, then lifted it again. He began dialing the number of Supreme Naval Command.

CHAPTER THIRTY-ONE

Two of the Su-15s peeled off on either side of Vologsky's aircraft and rolled into diving turns which brought them up behind him. They buzzed him closely, obviously looking for the Foxbat's visual identification. The remaining pair of Sukhois fell into an escort pattern, remaining slightly above him.

Vologsky's radio crackled into life. "Please identify yourself, Timberwolf Seven. Set your radio to standard communications channel A and respond. Over."

Vologsky took a deep breath, preparing his story. Then he flipped the radio switch and began to talk.

"This is Lieutenant Mikhail Vologsky, of Timberwolf Squadron, Soviet Air Force base Kharkov, currently on transfer to Soviet Air Force base Irkutsk. I am in trouble, repeat, trouble. Request emergency permission to make landing at Blagoveshchensk. Please respond."

The radio went dead, emitting only a faint crackle of static. Vologsky assumed that the pilot of the Sukhoi was changing channels to make contact with his ground control, both to relay Vologsky's message and ask for further orders. After a few moments delay, the pilot came back on the air.

"Please give the exact nature of your trouble, Timberwolf Seven. You appear to be undamaged. Over."

"I am undamaged, but I have a critical fuel situation," Vo-

209

logsky responded. "Am unable to return to base. Situation near critical, repeat critical. Request immediate clearance for emergency landing."

Again the radio went dead, but this time the delay was a lot shorter. "What is your mission, Timberwolf Seven? You were tracked coming in from hostile air-space. Please confirm your orders and the commanding officer who issued them. Over."

It was time to pile on the bluff, Vologsky realized. He flipped the radio switch, forcing himself to take on a more authoritative tone. "Negative," he said firmly. "My mission is classified. Irkutsk base is on security shutdown. I am not at liberty to reveal my orders at this moment. Now please clear me a direct channel to ground control for landing instructions. I repeat, fuel situation critical."

Once again, the crackle of static and a short pause. Finally, the Sukhoi pilot's voice came across again, sounding far more sympathetic. "Please reset your radio to standard channel D, Timberwolf Seven. Blagoveshchensk ground control will take you in from here. Good luck. Over and out."

All four Sukhois streaked away at once, clearing the immediate area. Vologsky changed channels and snapped into the intercom. "Ground control, this is Timberwolf Seven. Please instruct for immediate landing."

The reply was immediate. "Confirmed, Timberwolf Seven. Do you require full emergency landing procedures?"

Vologsky thought quickly. It might not be a good idea to overplay his hand. He was going to have quite a job explaining why he had complained of a critical fuel situation when he had fuel reserves anyway.

"Negative to that, control. I am still able to make conventional approach and landing. Instruct, please."

"You are clear to make immediate approach and landing on runway five," came the reply. "You are advised that windspeed is 24 knots, gusting to 30, steady SSW. Do you copy, Timberwolf Seven?"

"Wind 24 to 30, SSW. Confirmed," Vologsky acknowledged. "I am about to make my initial approach for a landing on runway 5."

Vologsky checked his instrumentation. The base was still a good eight miles away, and the four Sukhois had pulled well away from him, loitering on the fringes of his radar screen, now set for a sweep of twenty miles. Vologsky ran through his brief story, checking it over in his mind before making his landing preparations.

The lie about the fuel niggled at him. Perhaps he had been a little too hasty in concocting it. Even a cursory examination of the Foxbat would reveal that he had exaggerated his situation wildly. It would doubtless raise awkward questions, arouse suspicion. On impulse, Vologsky decided to tidy things up a bit. He busied himself jettisoning the remainder of his primary fuel, and switched to reserve. It was a calculated risk. Now, at least, his story would be corroborated by his instruments. The deliberate jettisoning of the fuel would show up on his flight recorder, of course, but Vologsky was gambling that no one would have the audacity to subject his aircraft to such close scrutiny, at least until his story could be checked out with the Irkutsk base.

There was no way the fuel-dumping could be observed by the Blagoveshchensk ground control, Vologsky felt confidently. In a matter of moments, it would be dispersed into the atmosphere in tiny droplets, which would evaporate long before they reached the ground. The twin turbojets coughed on vapor for a split second, resuming their normal whine of power as the re-igniters chattered briefly and smoothed over the transition from the blown main tanks to the reserve supplies. Satisfied, Vologsky cut back and the Foxbat slowed to a minimum cruising speed of 250 knots. He began to lose height slowly, dropping at just under 200 feet a minute. His course was spot on. With luck, his landing should be a straight run-in, with no need for a primary approach and fly-past.

Less than two miles from the runway, Vologsky dropped his undercarriage, checking the red panel light which told him that the wheels were down and fully locked. He throttled back to 180 knots as the altimeter dropped below 1000 feet and the end of the runway sprang into clear visual. Flaps three-quarters down, the Foxbat began to sink toward the tarmac.

The aircraft dropped smoothly toward its target, a perfect landing just as Vologsky had anticipated. As the gray runway loomed up beneath the Foxbat's rear wheels, Vologsky completed his flare-out and virtually killed the twin engines. With a faint jolt, the Foxbat was down, tires squealing momentarily in protest. As the nose-wheel made contact with the

211

ground, Vologsky threw both engines into full reverse thrust and the Foxbat rolled to a standstill.

Coming to a halt, Vologsky peered sideways out of his canopy. From the direction of the main administration buildings, four jeeps were speeding toward him. As they drew nearer, Vologsky saw that each one was full of military personnel, every one fully armed to combat status. Whether they had swallowed his story or not, they were taking no chances, that was obvious.

Vologsky cut his engines and began to unstrap himself from the flightcouch, and disconnect his oxygen supply. Slowly, he operated the canopy release and the perspex cockpit hood swung to starboard.

The jeeps had surrounded the still aircraft now. Facing the muzzles of at least a dozen sub-machine guns, safety catches released, Vologsky began to clamber out of his aircraft, a tight lump rising in his throat. Now came the awkward part.

CHAPTER THIRTY-TWO

The unexpected conversation with Zhagov had stimulated a completely fresh channel of thought in Dwight Ennis' mind. Up to that moment, he had not even considered the possibility of granting the Russian pilot any element of free thought. He had simply assumed, in strictly military terms, that Vologsky would be an obedient slave to orders, rigidly controlled by the terms of the original plan. Zhagov's point that the man might now be acting as a free-thinking human being, choosing a new escape route for himself, opened up whole new areas of speculation. Acutely aware that they were well worth investigating before taking any definite action, Ennis dropped the telephone receiver hastily back into its cradle before Naval Command could answer.

He shook off the last vestiges of sleep, clambered out of his bed and pulled on his bathrobe. Pausing only to splash cold water on his face, he made his way to his study, turned up the central heating and sat down at his desk. Concentrating hard, he ran the conversation with Zhagov over and over in his head, probing beneath apparently simple statements for hidden messages.

Point one: Zhagov's reticence to have the conversation recorded. Ennis considered it objectively, on different levels. Purely and simply, it could be that the Russian was protecting himself, personally. On a slightly deeper level, Zhagov was also protecting the Soviet diplomatic machine. That suggested a very real, deep-felt need to avoid an international incident. The fact that the Russians had initiated the contact lent strength to his view.

Point two was Zhagov's apparent frankness. If the man was telling the truth, and Ennis saw no real reason to doubt that he was, then the Soviets had some doubts about their ability to stop the pilot. This consideration, in turn, pointed toward the fact that the Foxbat was indeed a very superior aircraft, possibly capable of out-running conventional Soviet anti-aircraft systems. This underscored the original need for U.S. technicians to get a look at it.

Point three raised a whole series of interesting speculations. Because of the communications shutdown at Irkutsk, the Soviet security system was actually operating against itself, giving the pilot a unique advantage. Ennis had no idea how long it could last, but for the moment, at least, the Russians had no idea where their man was, or where he might be headed. One thing they *did* know, obviously, was Vologsky was an intelligent and resourceful young officer, able to make an independent decision. Zhagov had let that slip quite easily. All in all, the Soviets appeared to be at a serious disadvantage, albeit temporarily. It followed, therefore, that if the Russians were at a disadvantage, then the United States held the upper hand.

But was it a hand they still wanted, and if so, how should they play it? Those were ticklish questions, the answers to which would obviously depend on other factors.

The most important of these, obviously, was the Russian pilot's most likely destination. Knowing that made all the difference. If the Soviets could be sure of it, then the balance was redressed in their favor. If Ennis had the information, then his hand was strengthened even more. Leaving, possibly, a large enough area of free play to put one over on the Soviets. That was a delicious thought, to be investigated in detail.

Ennis opened his desk drawer and drew out a sheaf of large-scale world maps. Choosing the one he wanted, of the Central and Eastern sectors of the USSR, he spread it out in front of him and began to study it carefully.

As Zhagov had pointed out, the Russian pilot had a choice of destinations outside the Soviet Union, given his last reliably reported position. But which would he choose? That was the million dollar question.

Ennis had severe doubts that Paul Manville would have had the time or opportunity to develop any contingency plan for Operation Cuckoo. The scheme had been hastily conceived, and even more hastily changed, and then dropped. Unfortunately, the man was no longer available to confirm or deny the fact, but Ennis felt that he was on a 99% safe bet in making the negative assumption. That was one more small point in his favor; the Soviets would be more inclined to the view that a back-up plan was probable.

On that basis, a flight toward the Arctic or the Barents Sea was unlikely. Deprived of a sure landing site, the Russian pilot would only be flying to an icy death in those deserted waters.

Ennis tried to put himself in Vologsky's place, think in his terms. Given a full tank of fuel at Omsk, where would he be most tempted to go? Omsk was the crucial point, that was obvious. The Russian pilot would have had to make a decision within seconds of taking off and clearing the immediate vicinity of the airfield. His choices were simple; flee for Finland or continue to follow orders and head for the base at Irkutsk.

Thinking in Russian terms, Ennis could not help suspecting that he would plump for Finland, given a split-second choice. There was a certain geographical proximity which somehow made it seem less alien than Japan. Added to this feeling would be the psychological jump of actually committing himself to the run, a mental pacifier to a man whose nerves must obviously be in a state of some turmoil. To complete his ordered mission, and thus be nearer Japan, the young pilot must have been aware that he was flying into his own territory, thus using up valuable time. It would tell against any decision.

Yet there must equally be arguments against such a decision, Ennis reasoned. He studied the map in front of him in greater detail, concentrating his attention upon Omsk.

For nearly a thousand miles, towards Finland or the Barents Sea, there was nothing but the utter bleakness of the Siberian Plain. Vast uninhabited areas of ice-covered tundra, with virtually no mountains anywhere along the route. Plus factor, or minus? A definite plus, Ennis concluded. If the pilot was thinking rationally, he would realize that his own radar trackers would be on to him as soon as he set an uncharted course toward the North-West. Flying low over the Siberian Plain, he might have a chance to slip under the net, gain many hundreds of miles before he was picked up again.

This positive reflection triggered off its negative cousin almost at once. True, Vologsky could make a run for it across the tundra, but in doing so, he must alert the authorities immediately. This would count against him in the long run, since he must sooner or later gain height to pass over inhabited areas, coming into radar view once more.

And they would know exactly where to be looking for him, Ennis realized. His original flight would point like an arrow to his destination. The Soviet military could telephone ahead, setting up an almost impervious barrier long before he came up from the plains. Also, a North-Western course toward Finland would put the Foxbat dangerously near the heavy concentration of defense systems around Moscow and Leningrad. No pilot with any sense would want to run that gauntlet, given any choice at all.

The arguments for and against more or less canceled each other out. Ennis turned his attention towards Irkutsk, to apply the same sort of reasoning.

Irkutsk was a different kettle of fish. It left only the one possible destination—Japan. Once again, making the assumption that there was no emergency back-up plan, Vologsky would have to make it to one of the islands, or perish in the sea. But a warm sea rather than an ice-cold one. A sea which was crawling with shipping, both military and civilian, a high proportion of which would belong to the Western Powers.

Given a take-off from Irkutsk with a full fuel load then, what were Vologsky's immediate flight possibilities? A glance at the map showed Ennis that the desert regions of the Gobi were just as deserted as the Siberian Plain. Once again, he might have up to 500 miles of low-level flight before he reached any really mountainous terrain. Even the mountain ranges themselves might serve as radar cover, if the pilot had the skill and guts to fly through valleys, below the mean land level. A direct course might mean crossing the Mongolian border, even overflying Chinese territory, but that might just be a risk worth taking. It was unlikely that the Chinese anti-aircraft capability was anywhere near as sophisticated as that of the USSR. If border skirmishes were hotting up as latest Pentagon intelligence suggested, then the Chinese might well be busy with other things, have too much on their minds to pay undue attention to a solitary fighter aircraft which was incapable of carrying much in the way of heavy offensive weaponry.

Also, there were no massive Soviet defense concentrations to worry about. Certainly nothing to match the saturation coverage of Moscow and its suburbs. Vladivostok would be well protected, of course, but intelligence had always suggested that the emphasis there was on naval rather than inland surveillance. With luck, Vologsky could be out over the Sea of Japan before the authorities there knew what was going on.

So there was nothing in it, really. Finland, or Japan. They both came out about even, from the Russian pilot's point of view. From Ennis' point of view, however, there was a third factor which tipped the balance. If Vologsky had chosen Finland, then it was already finished. The Foxbat was at this minute either spiraling down in flames or about to make an emergency landing where the Russians could easily get to it first. Working on the premise of a flight to Japan however, gave Ennis time, and a chance to double-cross the Soviets even yet. Zhagov had been slightly wrong in assuming that the involvement of a third power would cause international publicity and embarrassment. The Japanese military would like to get a good look at the Foxbat too, Ennis figured. If Vologsky *did* manage to land the aircraft safely, it was an odds-on bet that the United States and Japan could come to a speedy arrangement to throw up a smokescreen. The Foxbat could be at least examined for a few precious hours before the Russians were any the wiser. At a pinch, the success of the flight could be covered up by the deliberate shooting-down of another, dummy aircraft over the Sea of Japan, in waters far too deep for any form of inspection or recovery of wreckage. That way, the United States military got to have the MiG 25, and the diplomatic cool remained intact. The Russians would suspect, maybe, but they could prove nothing. Nor were they likely to try, Ennis thought. The Soviet determination to preserve the renewed state of detente showed that they were really rattled this time. They needed close relationships with the United States as never before. Somehow, the Chinese had really managed to put the frighteners in.

Suddenly, Dwight Ennis saw it all clearly, and realized that he had absolutely nothing to lose, personally. If anything went seriously wrong, he still had Hayman as his own private scapegoat, to absorb most of the blame. Putting one over on the Soviets and gaining the Foxbat would be a large feather in his cap.

Having considered his personal position, Ennis considered the matter on a national and international level. Again, there were certain safeguards which could be invoked at any time, to prevent the matter getting out of hand. Right up until the very last minute, Ennis would be able to warn the Japanese Air Command of the aircraft's approach. What they did then was entirely their affair. By *not* warning the Japanese for the time being, the United States Government was safely out of it. They could hardly be blamed, internationally, for the defection of a Soviet pilot to another country. Such was the fabric of diplomacy.

Whether Vologsky intended to fly the Foxbat to Japan or not no longer really mattered, Ennis concluded. Merely accepting the possibility gave Ennis time to make plans and the opportunity to bring off the political double-cross of the decade.

With a new sense of purpose, Dwight Ennis picked up his security telephone, and put in a call to the Pentagon. He needed to know exactly what naval strength the U.S. War Department had within immediate striking distance of the Japanese coast. Already, he had started to formulate the germ of a plan to confuse the Russians even further, if the need arose. Having once committed himself to the game of intrigue, it was important to stay a few jumps ahead. That was the name of the game, if you wanted to be a winner.

CHAPTER THIRTY-THREE

The armed guards clustered around Vologsky as he stepped down on to the tarmac. There was nothing overtly threatening about their presence, but it was obvious that they meant business, and were not there to form a guard of honor for the conquering hero. Vologsky allowed himself to be escorted to the nearest jeep and driven toward the administration buildings. He said nothing. It seemed prudent.

Immediately outside the de-briefing room, a young Major stood ready to greet him formally, standing stiffly to attention. Vologsky's guard stopped dead, two paces to either side. Vologsky clicked his heels, executing a perfect salute.

The Major dropped his arm, letting it dangle at his side. "Identify yourself," he snapped curtly.

Vologsky rattled off his name, rank and serial number automatically, still remaining at attention.

It was not enough. The Major extended his arm, the palm of his hand upturned. "Your papers."

Vologsky unzipped his flying suit and extracted his service documents. Wordlessly, he handed them across to the Major, who made no attempt to inspect them. Instead, he tucked the papers into his own uniform pocket. "Colonel Lenkaya would like to see you in his office as soon as you have refreshed yourself. My men will escort you to the mess." The Major saluted once again, spun on his heel, and walked away briskly. The armed guards fell into close formation at Vologsky's side once again, pressing him into a slow march toward the recreation area.

"Stand at ease, Lieutenant." Colonel Lenkaya regarded Vologsky from underneath a pair of dark, shaggy eyebrows. He seemed almost friendly, in a patriarchal sort of way, and there was even a faint smile on his face. Nevertheless, the look jealously guarded the suspicion, even mistrust, which the Colonel really felt.

Colonel Lenkaya folded his arms upon his desk, glanced down at Vologsky's service documents spread out on his desk, then up again at the pilot himself. "Well, Lieutenant Vologsky. You are a man of mystery, it would appear. A pity. I do not care for mysteries. Perhaps it might clear matters up if you were to tell me more about this "secret" mission of yours?"

"With respect, Colonel, I do not consider myself free to discuss the matter," Vologsky said politely. "Unless you wish to issue a direct order, sir. I feel duty-bound to report to my commanding officer before saying anything."

Vologsky was playing a gamble. He knew full well that Colonel Lenkaya could order him to give a full account of himself and his orders, but it could only be done by pulling rank, breaking military protocol. Vologsky doubted that the Colonel would take the risk. He was right.

Colonel Lenkaya skirted round the direct approach. "You took off from Irkutsk airbase . . . is that correct?"

"Yes sir."

"And who issued your orders, Lieutenant?"

"Major Smelenkov, sir."

"A pity he can not confirm your story," Lenkaya mused. "You say that the Irkutsk base is completely shut down on a security exercise?"

Vologsky was being led, and not very subtly. He refused to fall into the trap. "I believe so, sir."

"Ah." Colonel Lenkaya's eyes narrowed. The smile faded from his face. His fatherly approach was not yielding the results he had expected. "Tell me one thing, Lieutenant Vologsky. How do you come to be this far from your home base, without sufficient fuel to return there? You *were* ordered to return to home base, I take it? Or did you disobey your orders? Is that the answer to our little mystery?"

Vologsky thought quickly. His immediate answer might well determine the sort of treatment he could expect for the next few hours. If he chose to remain silent, he might well anger the Colonel, and end up in a state of close arrest until Irkutsk base could be contacted. It seemed best to say something, show willing, yet keep the "secret" mission as an ace card. He spoke haltingly, as if unsure of how much he ought to tell the Colonel.

"I was attacked by three Chinese aircraft, violating Soviet airspace, sir. In the ensuing chase, I was forced to take evasive action which took me well off course and used up my fuel reserves. In order to protect my aircraft, I sought the nearest safe landing site, which happened to be this base."

"You said 'chase,' Lieutenant. In the ensuing chase. Do you not mean fight? Did you not engage these aircraft in open combat?"

Vologsky stiffened. "I am sorry, sir. Again, with respect, I feel that this discussion borders on a direct violation of my orders, sir."

"I have had your aircraft thoroughly checked over," Lenkaya said in a soft voice. "As you say, your fuel was almost exhausted. So, I might add, were the magazines of your guns. You are revealing no secrets by admitting combat."

"Very well, sir. I engaged the Chinese fighters in combat after they had first attacked me. My orders were specific on that point."

Lenkaya switched on the fatherly smile again. "And did you destroy the Chinese aircraft?"

"I shot down two of the three aircraft," Vologsky murmured, in a flat, emotionless voice. "The third aircraft flew off, presumably heading for home."

"Excellent," Lenkaya said, beaming now. "They will think twice before violating our airspace again, eh?"

"One would assume so," Vologsky said modestly. There was a momentary silence, in which Vologsky studied the Colonel very carefully. He was still smiling, apparently quite genuinely. He obviously liked the idea of blasting Chinese aircraft out of the sky. The information had put him in good humor. It might well be the time to try his luck out, Vologsky thought.

"Permission to make a request, sir?"

Lenkaya nodded. "Granted."

Vologsky executed a stiff salute. "With your permission, sir, I request permission to refuel my aircraft and return to my base. I feel that my commanding officer would be interested to hear my report at the earliest opportunity."

Lenkaya looked dubious. "I shall have to consider the matter," he said. "However, Lieutenant, you may rest assured that your aircraft will be completely refueled, flight-tested and restored to full combat condition, if, indeed, those operations have not already been carried out. However, as you can imagine, I would be failing in my duty if I were not a little concerned about unusual happenings on an important military base. And the sudden appearance of an unknown pilot, with a story which cannot be checked with a superior officer, is rather unusual, I think you will agree."

Vologsky hid his disappointment. "I understand, sir. Do I take it that I am under arrest until you contact Major Smelenkov?"

"Arrest, Lieutenant? What gives you that idea?" Lenkaya was guarded.

"I have been escorted everywhere by an armed guard," Vologsky pointed out. "Do I have your permission to personally supervise the refueling of my aircraft?"

"That will not be necessary," Colonel Lenkaya said flatly. "Our ground mechanics are quite competent, even though we do not have any of the Mikoyan series on this base. You may rest assured that your aircraft will be serviced properly, lieutenant."

It was a useful piece of information. So the base did not boast any aircraft better than the Sukhois. If he ever got off the ground again, it was something well worth knowing. The optimistic thought was buried almost immediately by the harsher realities of his situation. Thinking of getting off the ground again raised the question of the armed escorts once more. Colonel Lenkaya had very cleverly skirted around the problem; it was obviously time to force a confrontation, get things spelled out in capital letters. Vologsky realized that he had very little to lose. With unusual boldness, he spoke again. "With great respect, sir, I feel I must make a formal complaint about my treatment. As a loyal serving officer of the Soviet Air Force, I must take objection to being ushered around at gunpoint."

Colonel Lenkaya's face froze. For a moment, anger

222

threatened to erupt, but with an effort, he controlled it. He spoke in an icy voice: "Your formal complaint is noted, Lieutenant Vologsky. I shall make mention of it in my report." Lenkaya uncoiled from his chair, holding himself stiffly erect. "And now, Lieutenant, I am sure that you are tired and could do with some rest. I have made a room in the officer's rest quarters available to you. My men will show you the way."

Vologsky saluted briskly enough, but he felt weak and shaky inside. There was no mistaking the Colonel's real meaning. He was, to all intents and purposes, under close arrest. The vain attempt to bluff his way out of it had sealed his fate. He was trapped on the Blagoveshchensk base until such time as Colonel Lenkaya could make contact with Major Smelenkov at Irkutsk. When he did so, it would all be over. Still, he managed to keep his voice firm. "Will that be all, Colonel, sir?"

"You are dismissed, Lieutenant," Lenkaya muttered.

Vologsky turned smartly on his heel and marched toward the door. Outside in the corridor, the guards were waiting for him.

Colonel Lenkava frowned to himself as the footsteps faded away into the distance. He had learned nothing of importance from the young pilot, and as he had quite honestly stated, he hated mysteries. A sense of frustration gripped him, bringing anger in its wake. He picked up the telephone on his desk and dialed the radio room. "Have you made contact with the base at Irkutsk yet?" he demanded gruffly.

"Sorry sir, all systems still appear to be shut down," came the apologetic reply.

Colonel Lenkaya ground his teeth in annoyance. "Then get on to the Soviet Air Command," he barked. "Tell them that it is a priority matter."

"At once, Colonel." The line went dead.

Lenkaya sat back in his chair, slightly pacified by his decision and action. There was something not quite right about the pilot Vologsky, and he fully intended to find out what it was. Going straight to the top seemed the best way of setting about it.

CHAPTER THIRTY-FOUR

Colonel Lenkaya was not the only man anxious to get through to Soviet Air Command. On board the Yakolev transport aircraft, now more than mid-way on its flight from Kharkov to a refueling stop at Omsk, Nikolai Chersky continued to fume inwardly at the conspiracy of events which had rendered even the awesome powers of the KGB impotent.

He glanced up expectantly as one of his staff emerged from the flight-deck, hurrying down the empty belly of the aircraft toward him. He looked pleased with himself.

"You have news?" Chersky barked.

The man nodded. "I have a direct line to Soviet Air Command for you, sir. If you would like to come to the flightdeck."

"The Marshal himself?" Chersky queried. "I will not speak to underlings."

"The Marshal himself," came the confirmation. "He is holding on a priority line. I have briefly explained the position, sir."

"Good." Chersky rose, pushing rudely past his companion and making his way to the flight-deck. The co-pilot held out an extension intercom, plugged into the control panel. Chersky snatched it from his grasp without a word, gesturing for both pilot and co-pilot to disconnect their own headphones whilst keeping them in position over their ears. Satisfied that neither man could overhear his conversation, Chersky began to speak.

"Marshal, this is Nikolai Chersky, Second-in-Command to the Chairman of the KGB. I must advise you that I am operating under the direct orders of the Chairman and the First Secretary himself. This is a matter of extreme national emergency." Chersky spoke with complete authority, with little or no regard for the rank and position of the man he addressed. Such was his own exalted position. He feared no one, and respected only a few members of the Politburo and his own superior.

The Air Marshal appeared to accept a subservient position without question. "Let me just clarify the situation, Comrade Chersky. We are facing the possible defection of a Soviet Air Force pilot with one of the modified Foxbat-D aircraft . . . is that correct?"

"Exactly," Chersky said brusquely. "And at the moment, our efforts—my efforts—to track him down are being severely hampered by a security operation at the Irkutsk airbase. I want that operation suspended at once, and a direct line established between myself and the commanding officer on that base."

"It will be done at once. Is there anything else?"

"Yes. I want an immediate general alert put out to every Air Force base within 2000 miles of Omsk. This pilot, Mikhail Vologsky, must be tracked, contacted, and persuaded to bring that aircraft down."

"And if those efforts fail?"

"I do not need to remind you, Marshal, that this aircraft represents the finest piece of aerial hardware in the world. With it lie the bulk of our air supremacy hopes in the next decade. That aircraft must not be allowed to fall into enemy hands. If it cannot be brought back, it must be destroyed, completely. Do you understand?"

"Completely," the Air Marshal confirmed. "Do you have any other recommendations, Comrade?"

Chersky thought for a second before responding. He needed an outlet for the frustrated anger which had been building inside him. For the moment, he could not vent his wrath upon the pilot, but there was another scapegoat who would do, for temporary relief. "You have a Major Tzann, in command of the base at Kharkov," Chersky continued in a deceptively calm voice. "I find that he has been guilty of gross negligence and stupidity. It is my strongest recommendation that he be severely reprimanded, and transferred immediately."

"Transferred, Comrade? You have some specific place in mind?"

Chersky smiled wickedly to himself, pleased to have released some of his anger. "I will leave the actual posting to you, Marshal . . . but somewhere cold, I would think. There is nothing quite like a few degrees of permafrost to make a man think of better, warmer, times."

"I will see to it. And now, Comrade Chersky. I will clear an emergency channel through to the Irkutsk base for you. Please remain on this frequency. I will get back to you as soon as possible."

Chersky prodded the co-pilot in the back, proffering the intercom as the man turned toward him. He was about to let go when the Air Marshal's voice came over again, urgent and excited. "Comrade Chersky . . . are you still there?"

Chersky snatched back the intercom, holding it to his lips. "Yes, I am still here. What is it?"

"Something has just come in, Comrade . . . a bit of luck, I think."

"Out with it," Chersky snapped.

"A message has just been placed on my desk, another urgent request to make contact with Irkutsk. It seems that the military base at Blagoveshchensk have a rogue pilot, claiming to be from Irkutsk. There is something of a mystery about him, it seems."

It was too much of a coincidence. In a sudden flare of excitement, Chersky knew that he had tracked down Vologsky and the Foxbat. The same capricious fates which had protected him thus far had finally betrayed him. He shouted into the intercom. "We have him! We have the traitorous dog. Order his close arrest immediately, Air Marshal. He must not be allowed to leave Blagoveshchensk until I arrive there to take him into custody."

"At once, Comrade Chersky," the Air Marshal said. The intercom went dead almost immediately.

CHAPTER THIRTY-FIVE

From the small window of the rest-room, Vologsky could just see his aircraft, if he stood on tiptoe and craned his neck so that the side of his face was pressed against the glass. It stood, deserted, on a small apron at the side of an auxiliary runway, gleaming in the pale sunlight. The ground mechanics had long since finished servicing it, and had gone back to their routine chores. Vologsky felt a sickness in the pit of his stomach, a feeling of parting and loss. It was as if he were still connected to the Foxbat by some umbilical cord, about to be severed. In the womb-like cockpit of the aircraft lay protection, comfort, life itself. Without the Foxbat he was nothing, a totally insignificant fledgling, who had not yet learned to fly.

To be able to see freedom and yet not be able to get to it was a particularly sadistic form of torture. Vologsky found himself wondering whether Colonel Lenkaya had ordered that the aircraft be left within his field of vision on purpose. He decided against it, forcing himself to step back from the window. The torture was self-inflicted; he did not have to contort his body so that he could graze out on the aircraft.

Vologsky's eyes moved toward the door. It was not locked, he knew, but the room was a prison cell nevertheless. Twice he had opened that door, on some pretext or another, and each time the faintest click of the door-handle had been instantly followed by the metallic sound of gun safety-catches being slipped off in readiness. His armed guards had been cut from six to two, but that was the only concession granted him. He was still a prisoner; still under suspicion. And time was running out.

The window? Vologsky returned his attention to it, looking at it rather than through it. The metal frame was about 18″ wide, 14″ deep, the inner frame mounted on a central pivot. With the window fully opened, he would have to squeeze through a space just under 9″ wide, a virtually impossible feat for a man of Vologsky's build. Stripped naked, he might just have been able to manage it, but clad in his bulky flying suit he had no chance at all. And without the flying suit, the Foxbat was of little use to him. Vologsky considered stripping off, pushing the flying suit through ahead of him and then dressing again on the outside, but the idea was totally unfeasible. The only other answer lay in taking the central pivot out and removing the entire inner frame. A cursory examination revealed that this, too, was out of the question. The metal frame was sturdy; without tools it would take superhuman strength. Any attempt to smash the glass out of the frame would be sure to alert the guards outside. The window, then, led nowhere. Vologsky's sole avenue of escape lay through the door, despite the armed guards.

There were only two possibilities there. Brute force or trickery. Any plan must necessarily, involve one or the other, or both. The first option was not at all promising. One man against two, both armed with sub-machine guns.

A rising sense of desperation sent Vologsky's mind into overdrive. His thoughts over the last few minutes had all concerned options, one form of action balanced against another. Suddenly he realized that it was extremely limiting, a kind of binary thinking pattern which set up psychological blocks, by its very nature. Escape. That was the sole target to be aimed for. So it did not have to be a question of the door or the window, brute force or trickery, with or without his flying suit. All possible factors could be combined, with escape as the primary objective.

Working calmly and rationally, Vologsky began to turn everything over in his head, gradually progressing toward a total, cohesive plan of action.

It took him less than three minutes, once he applied himself in this fashion. Having formulated what seemed to be a workable plan, Vologsky checked it over a couple of times for flaws. Finally, having accepted all the necessary risks involved, he began to put it into action.

He crossed to the window again, looking carefully out from side to side. There were certainly no exterior guards, and no other buildings looked directly out on the block in which he was being held. A few odd personnel could be observed walking about in the distance, but there seemed no reason why any of them should choose to concentrate their attention on this particular window.

Stepping back, Vologsky began to peel off the bulky flying suit. Stripped of the garment, he connected the helmet back into position and zipped the suit up again, carrying it to the window. Opening it to its fullest extent, Vologsky carefully began to arrange the suit so that it was half in and half out of the window, the flying helmet carefully deflected downward toward the floor.

With a few minor adjustments, the job was finished. Vologsky walked backwards to the door, regarding his handiwork. It was not a perfect job, by any means. Through Vologsky's eyes, the flying suit in the window looked exactly what it was—an empty garment draped through a windowframe. Yet the suit was bulky enough to suggest the fullness of a body still inside it; the scene suggested a figure struggling to climb through a narrow gap. Vologsky tried to see it through the eyes of a stranger, coming suddenly into the room and seeing the empty suit for the first time. As the guards would see it, if they ran into the room quickly, under circumstances of emergency or panic. A thin smile crossed Vologsky's lips. Yes, under those circumstances, the brain might overide the eye, just for a few precious seconds. The guards would not see what *was*, they would see what they *expected* to see: their prisoner in the process of escaping through the window. Vologsky could only guess at their reaction, but he hoped that they would fulfil their part of the plan.

There was only one way to find out. Vologsky tiptoed back to the window, clenching his fist. He poised himself and took a deep breath.

Vologsky let out a loud cry, as if in considerable pain. At the same moment, he smashed his clenched fist against the metal frame of the window, making a loud crash. In a smooth, co-ordinated movement, he bounded away from the window and threw himself against the opposite wall, tucked in beside the hinges of the door.

Everything happened in a few seconds. Just as expected, the door flew open almost immediately, hiding Vologsky behind it. He heard, rather than saw, the two guards rush into the room with loud exclamations of surprise. Vologsky himself was already moving. He slid along the wall, clear of the door, bracing himself for a forward run. As the two guards headed straight for the window, he threw himself at their backs, his arms extended.

In the split second that the first guard's fingers closed around the shoulder of the flying suit and found it empty, Vologsky closed the gap between him and the two men. The nearest whirled in surprise, a cry of alarm springing to his lips. It got no further. Mustering all the strength in his right arm, Vologsky slammed his knuckles into the man's throat, just below the chin. With a sickening, choking sound, the guard buckled at the knees and slid to the floor, clutching at his throat and fighting for his life's breath. Eyes rolling wildly, he threshed on the floor in his death throes, his neck broken, but Vologsky could spare no time to pity him.

He was already busy with the second guard, a huge, bear-like figure of a man. Vologsky had tackled him close, knowing that the immediate danger was the machine-pistol which he carried. Chest against chest, Vologsky and the guard clutched each other's throat, the gun crushed tightly between them, pointing harmlessly into the air over their shoulders.

Vologsky's eyes began to water and mist over as the ham-like hands around his throat increased their grip. He felt his head begin to spin, like going into a high-G aerobatic maneuver, and knew that unconsciousness was only moments away. There was no time for the finer points of the martial arts. Vologsky kicked out wildly with his left foot, forcing his opponent to step back a pace, his legs slightly apart. Following through quickly, Vologsky brought his right knee up under the guard's groin as hard as he could.

The man let out a squeal of agony, and the tight grip around Vologsky's throat slackened off. Tearing himself free, Vologsky slammed a hard right-hand punch into the man's solar plexus, following it with a vicious rabbit-punch on the back of his neck as he doubled over. Vologsky jumped back as the heavy man toppled forward, knocked senseless. He fell

232

to the floor heavily, his head cracking against the hard, bare surface.

The first guard would be silent forever. Vologsky dropped to his knees beside his second victim, lifting his head slightly from the floor. A thin trickle of blood showed from just behind his right ear, dribbling down his neck on to the collar of his uniform. Laying his head back gently on to the floor, Vologsky lifted one of the man's eyelids. There was a flicker of movement. The man was not dead, but severely concussed. He would be in a state of unconsciousness for several minutes.

Hastily, Vologsky retrieved the empty flying suit from the window and began to pull it on. He had only just pulled one leg of the suit into position when he froze, a sudden thought striking him. It was a mistake, he was thinking too simply again. Blagoveshchensk was a combined operations base, rather than an Air Force one. It followed, therefore, that there would be many more Army personnel than Air Force, a fact which would be instantly reflected in the ratio of uniformed figures walking about. Quite obviously, a pilot in a flying suit would attract more attention than a soldier.

Peeling off the flying suit once again, Vologsky turned his attention to the dead guard. He was slightly larger than Vologsky around the chest, but more or less the same height. Vologsky bent over the body and began to hurriedly strip it of its uniform.

A minute later, he was fully dressed in a corporal's uniform. Checking on the unconscious guard one last time, Vologsky rose quickly, hoisting a sub-machine gun into position over his shoulder. Bundling the flying suit under his other arm, he headed toward the door.

Outside, Vologsky paused, flattening himself against the wall of the building and looking carefully in every direction. He could see the Foxbat clearly now, less than five hundred yards to his right. It stood waiting for him, ready to whisk him away from danger to a new life. All he had to do was to walk to it. Just five hundred yards, across open ground with no cover.

Vologsky slipped the sub-machine gun off his shoulder and snapped off the safety catch before hoisting it back into position. He was totally committed now; he could not afford to be squeamish. Nothing must prevent him from getting to the aircraft. If he had to kill again, then he would. Vologsky was operating under the most savage rules of survival, where only instinct and the preservation urge held sway. Crushing the flying suit into the smallest possible bundle under his arm, he pushed himself away from the wall and began to walk toward the Foxbat. That five hundred yards suddenly seemed more like five miles.

The sound of marching footsteps caused Vologsky to glance sideways, nervously. He froze in his tracks, his heart pounding. From around the side of the officers' rest block in which he had been kept, a small troop of soldiers came out into the open, marching in formation. Vologsky heard a barked order, and the troop left-wheeled at once, turning directly toward him.

Every instinct told Vologsky to drop the flying suit and run. His whole body trembled violently as the body of soldiers marched quickly toward him. His knees threatened to give way at any moment.

He could only go back. Vologsky's panicking brain forced his body to respond, turning on his heels and walking briskly back toward the room he had just left. He ducked into the corridor and closed the door behind him. Weakly, he flopped back against the wall to wait. The sound of the soldiers marching past him was almost drowned by the sound of his own blood throbbing in his temples. Only when the outside was completely quiet again could Vologsky force himself to make a move. He stepped outside once again, braced himself, and began to march at a brisk pace along the side of the building. He no longer headed directly for the Foxbat, realizing instinctively that a diagonal course, across the drill ground, would only draw unwanted attention to himself.

Also, there was one more factor he had overlooked. He still had to don his flying suit again. The aircraft would not give him sufficient cover to do that safely. Before he made the final run for the plane, Vologsky knew that he had to get inside somewhere.

He peered ahead, trying to identify the next block of buildings. They were the uniform gray concrete structures which could be anything, from sleeping quarters to administrative offices. Either way, they would contain people, and Vologsky needed somewhere completely deserted. An empty hangar, or a latrine.

There was neither, as far as he could see. The main group of hangars was well beyond the runway apron on which the

Foxbat was parked, at least as far again as he had already walked. It would take him too long to get there and return, even assuming he could make it safely without being challenged. Any minute now, the unconscious guard would be coming round, and once he raised the alarm, the game would be up. Given no other choice, Vologsky continued walking. He was abreast of the Foxbat now, some 50 yards away from it. The next block of buildings was less than thirty paces ahead of him.

Vologsky stared at the nearest window, trying to see what was inside. He picked out what appeared to be vertical lines inside the room, and frowned when he could not immediately identify them. A few steps more, and everything fell into better focus. The lines were ropes, hanging from the ceiling to the floor. The window looked into a large open space, rather than a small room. Suddenly, Vologsky realized what the block was. It was neither a barracks nor a suite of offices. It was a gymnasium. A new sense of optimism rose in him. In a gymnasium, there would be showers, toilets, changing rooms.

He reached the window and peered into the gym. His luck was holding better than he could possibly have expected. The gymnasium was not in use. The only people inside were a couple of instructors, checking over the equipment. Ducking back from the window, Vologsky walked around the back of the building, looking for a rear entrance to the changing area.

He tried the handle of the first door he came to. It was locked. Undeterred, he walked on to a second door, paused, and closed his fist around the handle. His hand slid around, but the handle did not move. Vologsky stared down at the smooth metal knob almost accusingly, a sob of frustration threatening to rise in his throat, choking him. Dimly, he realized that his palm was sweating profusely, the perspiration acting like a thin film of lubricant between flesh and metal. Increasing his grip, Vologsky turned the handle again, and the door sighed open.

Vologsky threw himself inside, closing the door quietly behind him. He was in a store-room, cluttered with pieces of broken gymnastic equipment and old packing cases. The only light came in from a small ventilator set high above the door. It was barely enough to see where he was going. Although he moved slowly and cautiously, the bad light, and the cluttered conditions of the room were against him. His shoulder brushed against an untidily-stacked pile of broken wall bars, sending them crashing down to the floor in domino-fashion. In the confined space of the small room, it sounded like a burst of machine-gun fire. Vologsky stifled a curse and held his breath, acutely aware that his whole body was trembling violently. He waited for what seemed an eternity before he heard the soft pad of feet outside the door on the opposite side of the store-room. There was the rattle of a key being inserted in the lock, and the door began to open.

Vologsky threw the flying suit to the ground, bringing his sub-machine gun up into a businesslike position. As the door opened fully, he pressed himself back against the wall, his heart hammering. A hand reached around the door, groping for the light-switch on the wall. The light snapped on suddenly, and one of the instructors stepped into the storeroom.

The gasp of surprise died on the man's lips as Vologsky jerked the barrel of the sub-machine gun under his throat. "One sound and you're a dead man," Vologsky hissed icily. Skirting around the frozen instructor, he gently pushed the door closed with his foot. The two men eyed each other wordlessly, both their minds racing, trying to identify and cope with the situation. Vologsky thought of the second instructor.

"Tell your companion that you are going to tidy up some equipment which has fallen down," Vologsky whispered. To emphasize his instructions, he shook the gun again, in what he hoped was a menacing gesture. It appeared to work. Trembling slightly, the instructor pulled the door a few inches ajar and called out to his colleague. "There is a bit of a mess in here, Felix. I had better clear things up."

Vologsky nodded with satisfaction. "Now, close the door," he hissed.

The instructor did as he was told, slowly extending his hands outward in a state of surrender.

"Turn around," Vologsky commanded. The instructor obeyed at once, shuffling around until he presented his back to the barrel of the gun. Swinging it around in his hands, Vologsky smashed the heavy butt of the sub-machine gun into the back of the man's head.

Even as the instructor crumpled to the floor, Vologsky knew that he had used far more force than was necessary. Fear had lent him extra power, power which he had been unable to control. With a dull, detached sense of pity, Vologsky looked down at the body of the instructor, knowing from the twisted position of the man's head that he had gone the way of the guard, the top of his spine shattered. Guilt crowded in on him, dredging up all the feelings of disgust and hopelessness he had suffered before. Like a man in a trance, Vologsky began to pick up the discarded flight suit.

Colonel Lenkaya dropped the telephone as though it had suddenly become red-hot. His shock was strangely mixed with a surging feeling of elation. He had been right. The feeling in his bones had been almost uncannily accurate. Something had told him that the pilot Vologsky was not what he purported to be. He had known that there was something wrong, a situation potentially explosive and dangerous. Now it was confirmed, from the Marshal of the Soviet Air Force himself. Above all other feelings, relief flooded over Colonel Lenkaya. He thanked the nameless fates that he had seen fit to place the pilot under close guard. His arrest would be a feather in Lenkaya's cap. What would have happened to him if he had let Vologsky go, he dreaded to think.

His fingers snaked to the intercom on his desk, flipping it on and punching out the button which would connect him with the guardroom. "Take a detachment of men and bring the pilot Vologsky to my office at once," he snapped. "He is a traitor, potentially dangerous. Take every possible precaution."

Vologsky zipped up his flying suit and crossed to the outside door of the storeroom. Opening it, he peered out cautiously from side to side. There was no-one about. Carrying the sub-machine gun loosely in his hand, he made his way to the end of the gymnasium block, from where he had a clear view of the Foxbat. There was no time to lose. With a purposeful stride, Vologsky stepped out from the side of the building and began making his way toward the aircraft.

He had covered no more than ten or fifteen yards when a shrill wailing blast echoed out over the runway area. The warning was immediately followed by Colonel Lenkaya's excited voice, amplified throughout the base by the series of loudspeakers attached to every building.

"Attention all personnel. This is an emergency. The pilot of the MiG 25 is loose somewhere on this base. He is subversive, armed and dangerous. He must be captured at all costs. Shoot on sight, repeat, shoot on sight."

Vologsky's heart seemed to drop through his stomach into

237

his feet. He tripped, almost falling over before he recovered himself and began to react. His mind and body surged with a massive injection of adrenalin into its system. Staring ahead, past the deserted Foxbat, he could see a dozen figures hurrying out of the hangars, fanning out into a search pattern. A glance either side of him confirmed that all the buildings were also discharging vast numbers of armed soldiers, as the entire base was scrambled to track him down.

The Foxbat was less than twenty-five yards away now. Vologsky broke into a clumsy trot, cursing the unwieldy flying suit which made running impossible. The gap between him and the Foxbat narrowed with almost painful slowness. Beyond it, the nearest of the soldiers from the hangar area was pointing excitedly towards him. The others changed direction, clustering together like a swarm of bees, homing in on the solitary aircraft.

Vologsky reached the port wingtip of the Foxbat, reaching out to touch it, briefly, like some sort of good luck charm. He half-fell against the side of the aircraft's fuselage, his hands scrabbling against its smooth metal side. The boarding ladder had been taken away. With every muscle straining, Vologsky found a hand purchase on the leading edge of the huge rectangular air intake and hauled himself up.

The cockpit hood was open. Vologsky scrambled into it, letting his body find its own position in the flightcouch. Feverishly, he operated the canopy closing control and reached for the ignition gear. There was no time for any attempt at a pre-flight check, nor could he spare any precious seconds to connect in his air supply. He could do that later, once the plane was moving.

His fingers moving in a practiced blur, Vologsky tripped the ignition switches and armed the starter motors. Turning on the fuel, he counted off three seconds and stabbed the ignition button.

The twin starter cartridges fired simultaneously, with a loud crack. The mighty turbines began to whine painfully, as if in protest at their rude awakening. Vologsky knew that there was no time for a proper warm-up. He pulled back on the throttles gently, his eyes on the rpm indicator. It quivered slowly up to the twenty per cent mark, jerking violently as Vologsky forgot all about normal safety routine and opened the throttles right up. He slammed off the brakes as the rpm indicator steadied and began to climb upwards toward the half-power mark. The Foxbat quivered momentarily, then began to roll slowly forward.

Vologsky made no attempt to steer the aircraft on to the runway proper. As it rolled off the parking apron, he let it pursue its own straight course, bumping up over a low concrete curb to continue across rough grassland bordering the tarmac runway. All that mattered was to build up speed, create distance between himself and the closing soldiers. Above the roar of the Foxbat's engines, Vologsky heard the sound of bullets whining off the fuselage and the nosewheel assembly. They were probably firing at the tires.

The aircraft was picking up speed now. Vologsky opened up the throttles a shade more, then busied himself coupling in his oxygen supply and performing the more basic preflight checks.

The aircraft was rocking dangerously as its speed built up to around 85 knots. Vologsky knew that he had to get the aircraft on to a proper runway quickly, for it could not cope with rough ground at its present speed. Staring ahead through the canopy, he saw the black strip of a main runway cutting across the grassland on his port side. It would have to do, Vologsky decided. No matter what the wind direction, he would have to try for an immediate take-off. Any second now it would not just be rifle bullets coming at him. They would be trotting out the heavy armament in readiness. Rather than see the Foxbat leave the base, Colonel Lenkaya would order it to be blown to pieces on the ground.

The Foxbat was traveling too fast over uneven ground to use the conventional steering gear. Vologsky dropped all the flaps on the port wing, and the drag gradually drew the aircraft round. The plane would intersect the runway about three-quarters of the way along. If the wind was against him, there would be more than sufficient runway for a clean take-off. If it happened to be with him, things might get a little sticky.

There was a sudden, blinding flash ahead of him followed by a shattering explosion. Someone had opened up with a mortar, or maybe a tank was shelling him. Vologsky pulled out all the stops, twisting the throttles back savagely. The Foxbat leapt forwards, narrowly missing the crater which had appeared in the soft ground. Two more explosions behind him told Vologsky that he had done the right thing, missing death by a matter of a few yards. At over 100 knots, the aircraft left the grass and cut onto the runway at an acute angle. Vologsky guided it into a more or less straight course with the flaps, trimmed the aircraft back to normal and opened up. Out of the corner of his eyes he caught a brief glimpse of the wind indicator, showing him that the wind was blowing almost directly across the Foxbat's direction. It would be a nasty take-off—if he could take off at all.

His hands were clenched tightly around the control yoke as the ground-speed indicator nudged upwards to the 150 knot mark. Vologsky kept up a steady pull on the throttles, watching the indicator continue to rise. 175 . . . 180 . . . 185 . . .

Under normal circumstances, Vologsky would have already begun to rotate the aircraft into flight elevation. Now he fought against his natural inclination and the plane's controls to keep it rooted to the ground.

200 knots . . . 210 . . . 220 . . . The aircraft was shaking violently, its wheels taking a terrific hammering. The end of the runway was rushing toward him with frightening speed. There was perhaps just over 300 yards of tarmac ahead of him now. In seconds, if the Foxbat did not lift off clean, it would all be over. Vologsky would be dead, the sleek Foxbat a cartwheeling, blazing hunk of scrap metal.

As the groundspeed indicator hit 240 knots, Vologsky yanked back on the control yoke, hugging it to his chest. The nose lifted, one rear wheel came off the ground, and with a sickening lurch, the Foxbat took to the air.

CHAPTER THIRTY-SIX

On board the U.S. Aircraft Carrier *Retribution,* Commander James Brant read the coded orders which had just come over the wire for the third time, trying hard to place a different interpretation upon them. It was no use. The orders were chillingly specific.

Brant suddenly felt all of his fifty-two years, and then some. The terrible responsibility of command had been thrust upon him again for the first time since Korea. It had been a long time, Brant reflected miserably. Too long, perhaps? At any rate, he had forgotten the tightness in the gut, the dull headache and the terrible sense of guilt which was like an itch, inside his skull where he couldn't scratch it. They all came back now, a hundred times worse because it was peacetime, and he had allowed himself to mellow with the years.

Brant looked at the Prime Clearance orders yet again, summing up his feelings in one expletive. "Damn," he swore loudly, shaking the offensive piece of paper in the air.

He wanted to screw the orders into a ball, and consign them to the nearest waste-paper basket. Forget about them, pretend that he had never received them, never had to make that lonely, terrible decision. He couldn't do it, of course. That was the trouble. You never could ignore orders, even when they went against the grain of everything you have

241

come to believe in. Especially orders issued directly by Dwight Ennis, top military advisor to the President himself, and fully sanctioned by the Pentagon together with a "Q" Prime Security Clearance.

So, he would obey. On the simplest level, he would follow his orders and issue directives of his own. A pilot, a plane— and a mission. That was all he had to authorize. Simple? Brant felt a bitter laugh rise in his throat. Yes, the act itself was simple. The hard part came in making the choice and then living with it afterwards. How did a man make a choice like that?

With eighty-five pilots at his command, Brant had to pick just one, give him his orders and see him safely launched on his mission. From then on, according to all the rules, he was absolved of all further responsibility, and, one would assume, any sense of guilt.

Maybe, in wartime, it worked like that. Brant vaguely remembered similar circumstances, in the heat of battle. You became hardened, and although you never actually forgot about things, and people, you put them out of your mind and in time, they just ceased to exist any more.

But this was different. Terribly different. This was peace-time, he was on a routine patrol off the Japanese coast, Vietnam was rapidly becoming a bad memory and even the Russians were making friendly noises. All that, and the vessel he commanded flew under the flag of a nation which purported to stand for liberty, equality and the pursuit of happiness.

Yet Brant had to choose a Marine, put him into a plane, and send him to commit suicide.

And the most terrible thing of all was, he had not even been told why. He probably never would be.

CHAPTER THIRTY-SEVEN

At six thousand feet, Vologsky drew the Foxbat clear of a
heavy cloud layer and emerged into brilliant blue sky. Leveling off, he brought the aircraft around in a tight turn, heading back toward the base. The heavy, low cloud had given
him an idea which he wanted to try out, and it was worth
risking a high-speed fly-past of the base to see exactly what
was being scrambled against him.

Vologsky eased the yoke forward, putting the Foxbat into
a gentle dive. He re-entered the cloud layer, homing in on the
base by radar. At just over three thousand feet, he came out
through the bottom layer of the cloud again, in visual range
of the base. Trimming his airspeed to just over 500 knots, he
dropped another fifteen hundred feet and closed on the base,
his senses on full alert. He had to be ready for anything now;
there had been more than enough time for the entire base to
get into a state of full alert. Anti-aircraft guns, missile
launchers and all tracking systems would be fully operational.

Having these fears to worry about, to concentrate his mind
upon, Vologsky felt better. The lethargy was gone again now,
replaced by a new surge of power. Flying the aircraft once
more, Vologsky had something positive to relate to. He no
longer felt quite so alone and vulnerable. He recalled the

feeling of elation following the dogfight with the Chinese aircraft, and warmed to the new challenge.

The main runway was in clear view now, and nothing had so far been sent up at him. Vologsky smiled inwardly. They had not expected him to come back. The only action apparently taken had been the mobilization of six of the Sukhois. Vologsky could see them taxiing into position at the far end of the main runway. They were strung out in pairs, some thirty yards apart. The fighters posed no serious threat to him, other than as tracking devices over the first three or four hundred miles of his flight. The Foxbat could easily outrun the inferior aircraft, and now that he had no fuel worries, Vologsky had no need to dawdle. Still, there was nothing to lose by cutting down the odds. Vologsky armed his missile launch systems and plunged the Foxbat into a screaming dive toward the first pair of Sukhois.

At 1500 feet, he launched one of the "Acrid" missiles under his port wing. It streaked straight down to its target as the Foxbat leveled and banked sharply off to the starboard. Vologsky heard the dull rumble of the explosion half-way through his turn. By the time he came round and had visual contact with the runway again, there was only a billowing cloud of oily black smoke to be seen. It obscured all six Sukhois. Vologsky had no way of knowing how many of the aircraft he had put out of action.

Looping round the outer perimeter of the base, he climbed gently back above the cloud layer, not yet ready to make a run for it. Vologsky was waiting for at least one of the Sukhois to get up after him. It was all part of his plan. One eye on the detector system, he continued to fly the Foxbat round in a lazy circle.

The cockpit chronometer ticked off nearly three minutes before a pair of blips appeared on the Foxbat's detection screen, climbing up toward the aircraft from 2000 feet. Obviously, his missile attack had done more damage than he could have hoped for.

It was time to act. Vologsky pulled away from the base and set a direct course toward the coast. He flew at a steady 600 knots, well aware that at that speed, the two Sukhois could close on him. That was exactly what Vologsky wanted. The cloud layer was about five hundred feet below him, stretching ahead, unbroken, for at least another twenty-five miles. It looked good, and the timing was just about right.

Something had to happen soon, for both Sukhois were well within missile range, and now that they were clear of the base, there was nothing to stop them letting loose.

Sure enough, the missile detection shrilled out its warning almost immediately. Vologsky responded at once, his mind finely tuned in to the streaking projectile of death homing in on him, and his body an integral working part of his aircraft. The strategy he had planned was a dangerous one, requiring nerves of steel and split-second timing. He was setting himself up as a target, relying only upon his fairly crude anti-missile system to save him.

The detector gave a time to impact of five seconds. Vologsky waited for it to drop to three before acting. He plunged the Foxbat down into the cloud layer, activating his anti-missile system as he entered it. From the rear of the Foxbat, a thermite bomb ejected and ignited at once, burning with a blinding intensity. As the decoy left the Foxbat, Vologsky gunned the throttles, increasing his angle of dive. His vision blurred, reddened and tunneled. Plunging down through the thick cloud, he was completely blind.

Behind him, obscured by the clouds, the missile's infra-red system located the flaring thermite bomb and detonated. In the Foxbat, Vologsky felt only a brief lurch, followed by the noise of the explosion and the spattering of a few odd pieces of shrapnel against the fuselage. He increased his dive even further, plunging almost vertically through the bottom of the cloud layer and toward the ground.

The two Sukhois were still up where he had left them, flying a good 1000 feet above the top of the cloud layer. The pilot who had fired the missile could not possibly have seen the decoy launched, and Vologsky had shaved it close enough not to register on radar or infra-red scanners. Hearing the explosion deep inside the cloud, the Sukhoi pilot would be bound to come to the conclusion that he had scored a direct hit on the Foxbat. All Vologsky had to do now was to reinforce that belief.

As the ground rushed up toward him, Vologsky launched another of his own missiles, homing it straight into the deck under radar control. As it blossomed into a fiery mushroom below him, he pulled back on the control yoke and pushed the Foxbat back up into the cloud at 3000 feet. Pulling into a tight starboard turn, he flew on through the cloud for thirty seconds, then pulled into a steep dive once more, finally leveling out well below the cloud at little over 120 feet.

A glance at his radar screen confirmed that the two Sukhoi pilots had fallen for the trick. They were still on their original course, and rapidly losing height as they dived to start sweeping the area for visual sighting of the wreckage. They could think nothing else. They had heard the explosion of the detonating missile, tracked the plunging Foxbat on their radar, and heard the secondary explosion as it hit the ground. By using the cloud again, for just that brief time, Vologsky had cut them well off from visual sighting, and was now safely below the radar tracking net. For the two Sukhois, and probably the Blagoveshchensk base, it was all over. The rogue Foxbat and its pilot had ceased to exist.

Chuckling to himself, Vologsky flew on, skimming low along the valley of the Amur river in the general direction of Vladivostock. He would worry about the defense systems there later. For the moment, for a few minutes, he could afford to relax, allow his pounding heart to return to normal.

CHAPTER THIRTY-EIGHT

Commander Brant had done an unprecedented thing; he had queried the Prime Security orders. Technically, he was at liberty to do so, under circumstances in which there was room for misinterpretation, or the orders involved an act of aggression against a foreign power. Brant had gambled his career on the latter, whilst knowing full well that his personal interest involved the first eventuality. Brant did not find the orders as they stood in the least ambiguous. He realized full well *what* he had been ordered to do. He only needed to know *why*.

Surprisingly, they told him. There was no obvious note of censure on the coded message which came back to him from the Pentagon. Someone, possibly Dwight Ennis himself, was treading on thin ice, Brant reckoned. The whole business stank of a half-baked, hastily concocted cover-up job, yet another compromise erected over yet another cock-up. The Pentagon and the USAF had dropped shit down the fan-shaft. Now they wanted the US Navy and the Marines to clear up the mess for them. Brant smiled bitterly. So what else was new? he asked himself. Peace or wartime, it happened too damned often. Historians of Pearl Harbor, please take note.

Knowing most, if not all the story hadn't really made a lot of difference, not to Brant personally. He still had to make

247

the agonizing decision, and he still had to live with it on a purely personal level. There was a measure of compromise, even for him, of course. Instead of choosing a pilot, he had asked for a volunteer for a dangerous mission. It didn't ease the guilt, but at least it removed him one small step from direct involvement.

Now, all other preparations completed, Brant awaited that volunteer in his cabin for briefing. He concentrated only upon the name written on the piece of paper on his desk, pushing aside all personal knowledge of the actual man. Major Harry (Hank) Meakin, United States Marine Corps. There was a light tap on the bulkhead outside. Brant called out, in an artificially casual voice: "Come in."

Hank Meakin strolled rather than marched into Brant's cabin. His salute was casual, only a shade short of being sloppy. He had been told that he was volunteering for a dangerous mission, but his features showed no real sign that he took it really seriously. Although his face was set in an outwardly serious mask, Meakin's blue eyes twinkled, like an excited schoolboy up before the principal on a minor charge of insubordination.

"You wanted me for briefing, sir?"

Brant nodded. "Sit down, Major."

Meakin lowered his six-foot two, athletic frame into a chair, facing Brant across his chart-desk. His movements were cool and casual, the only signs of tension being an over-eagerness, an excitement to know more.

Brant regarded him gravely, acutely aware that to Meakin, the entire business was a game, a welcome chance for excitement and a chance to escape from the dull routine of patrol duty. Brant wondered how much he was at liberty to tell the man; how much he ought to tell him.

Brant chose his words carefully. "You realize that this is a secret and dangerous mission, Major Meakin? You are still at liberty to withdraw your voluntary application. However, once I outline your briefing to you, that option is no longer open. You will be absolutely and totally committed. Is that clearly understood?"

Meakin nodded, his eyes still twinkling. "Perfectly understood, sir. Count me in, whatever it is."

"All right." Brant could not help a sigh escaping from his lips. "Briefly, Major, the position is this. Our intelligence sources have reason to believe that a Russian pilot is at this minute in the process of defecting with a top-secret Soviet military aircraft. His probable destination is Japan. This vessel is presently set on a course which will bring us into Japanese waters within the hour. Your mission is not yet confirmed, but immediately it is, you will take off. An aircraft has been made ready for you and put on stand-by."

"My aircraft, sir?" Meakin interrupted. "Last time I saw it, she was still down in the loading bay. No more than fifteen minutes ago, sir."

Brant coughed. He was coming to the first tricky part. "You will not be flying your normal aircraft, Major. One of the stand-by Skyhawks has been specially modified and equipped for this particular mission. I will explain these modifications to you in a moment."

"Sorry, sir." Meakin apologized for his interruption, relaxing in his chair to listen to the remainder of his briefing.

"Unfortunately, the Soviets also are aware of this defecting pilot," Brant went on. "They also suspect that the US government are connected with it in some way. Therefore, to avoid international embarrassment, we must tread very warily. We cannot be seen to give an open help to this defecting pilot. However, we want and need that aircraft, so we must do whatever we can to ease this Russian pilot's defection, covertly. That is where you come in. As soon as the flight of the Russian plane toward Japan is confirmed, you will take off and fly directly into Soviet airspace over Vladivostok. The Skyhawk you will be flying has been deliberately sabotaged, so that flying it will be difficult, although not impossible nor really dangerous. However, its flying characteristics will be altered enough to show Russian radar scanners and any pilots they send up to buzz you that the aircraft is in trouble. As soon as you are within Russian airspace you will send out an international Mayday and request emergency landing permission. Hopefully, they will swallow your story. The idea is that you will give them something else to think about while the Russian pilot is attempting to fly out through the coastal defense. It may be of some help to him." Brant broke off, staring into Meakin's eyes. They were still twinkling, although not quite as brightly as before. "Do you understand so far?"

Meakin nodded emphatically. "Then what, sir?"

"You will delay the Vladivostok air control for as long as possible. Under no circumstances will you actually attempt a landing. Your plane has also been fitted with a self-destruct device. At the last possible moment, you will activate that device and bale out over Soviet territory. You will realize, of course, that you are bound to be interrogated, and it is possible that you may be removed to the Lubyanka prison—with all that might involve. However, you may rest assured that diplomatic moves to rescue you will be initiated at once, and with luck, we should be able to get you repatriated within a few weeks." Brant shrugged. "Well, that's about it, Major. Any questions?"

Meakin forced a brave smile. "Only one, sir. Can I take a camera along? I'd love to get a few snaps of the Kremlin to show the boys when I get back."

Commander Brant also forced a thin smile. "I will of course make a special note of your willingness to volunteer for this mission in my log, Major. You have the gratitude of myself and your country. Good luck, Major Meakin."

Meakin stood stiffly, executing a formal salute. He had serious misgivings about volunteering now, but he was damned if he was going to let it show. Hell, they'd get him out safely somehow. He had implicit trust in Uncle Sam and his own immortality. At 32, tall and good-looking, there was no other way for a man to feel.

"Guess I'll be seeing you, sir," he said to Brant.

Brant did not attempt a reply.

CHAPTER THIRTY-NINE

Ahead, in the distance, Vologsky could see the shining V which marked the confluence of the Amur and Sungari rivers. Another hundred miles beyond that, Vologsky knew, came the foothills of the Sikhote Alin Range, which rose, in parts, to nearly 6000 feet above sea level. He would have to climb to at least 8000 feet to cross the range safely, and as soon as he did so, he would be picked up by every coastal radar station within five hundred miles.

It was an unpleasant thought. For the past twenty minutes, Vologsky had felt safe, even relaxed. Cruising down the Amur valley at less than 1500 feet and an airspeed of Mach 0.8 had been like taking a joyride, secure in the knowledge that he was leaving no radar trace or supersonic footprint behind him. To rise, and thus advertise his presence once again was like a positive act of false bravado, a deliberate tempting of the fates which had thus far smiled upon him.

Alternatives? Vologsky could not rely upon his own geographical knowledge, not this far to the East. He needed help. His fingers snaked out to the in-board computer, punching out instructions. In seconds, the required information came up on the moving map display.

It was there in front of his eyes, as sure as a glowing neon sign pointing the way to safety. He had only to continue following the course of the Amur river as it curved away to the North. The broad, deep valley continued up through the mountains, running parallel with the Gulf of Tartary. The only trouble spot was Khabarovsk, also set deep in the low-lands beneath the Sikhote Alin Range. Even keeping to his present height, the Foxbat would have to pass within visual as well as radar range of the defense systems there. Even so, Vologsky reasoned, it was infinitely preferable to risking his chances with the coastal defenses around Vladivostok. Comparably, it was like going against a pistol rather than a cannon.

Vologsky took the decision automatically, setting a new course toward the North-East. He would be in radar range of Khabarovsk in little over five minutes, and missile range fifteen minutes after that. Vologsky activated his radar-jamming systems as a precaution, winding them up to full power. At best, it might give him a few extra seconds and cause at least a minor degree of confusion.

This time, there were no interceptor planes, no attempt at a warning contact. The first pair of a fleet of SA-6 surface-to-air missiles blipped on to Vologsky's screen when he was still a good sixty miles from the outer perimeter of the Khabarovsk defense system. Vologsky glanced at the two harmless dots with contemptuous disregard. The missiles had been launched early, on an interception path. At that altitude, Vologsky knew, the SA-6 had a maximum range of little over 30 kilometers. Unless Vologsky obliged by flying straight toward them, the missiles would merely exhaust their limited fuel supplies and plunge harmlessly toward the ground.

He did not oblige. Banking the Foxbat into a lazy turn, Vologsky veered away to starboard, toward the mountains. There were perhaps five miles of flatland remaining before he would have to gain height. It was more than enough. Vologsky watched the two blips disappear from his tracking screen and then resumed his former course. He still had a fairly wide safety margin, at his present altitude. There was no point in climbing yet awhile, for it only lessened his chances of survival. The higher he took the Foxbat, the greater the range of the SAMs and the easier it was for the radar trackers to get an accurate fix. At anything over 20,000 feet, the missiles could be tracked in on the Foxbat on triangulated coordinates. At 50,000 feet and over, the maximum range of the SA-6 missile was more than doubled up to 70 kilometers. Vologsky saw no point in giving his hunters those twin advantages, for the present.

Another pair of missiles came up in the wake of the first, ranging ones. Vologsky let them close, not bothering to take any evasive action. They were still over ten miles short when they dropped out of sight.

Vologsky banked hard over to port and began a sweeping circle which took him back on himself. It was time to take a few minutes off to consider his position. The missile-launch control at Khabarovsk would have learned by their mistakes by now. They would be unlikely to waste any more missiles whilst the Foxbat remained out of range. Flying a good twenty miles back along the valley, Vologsky turned again and cut back the throttles to minimum power. Cruising toward Khabarovsk again at less than 400 knots, he weighed up his chances.

It was obvious, from the way in which Khabarovsk had greeted his first radar sighting, that the word was out. Every airbase, mobile missile-launch system within hundreds of miles would be on full alert, waiting for him to fly anywhere near range. The determination to shoot him down was equally obvious from the extravagant wastage of missiles. Vologsky found it vaguely flattering that an open-ended budget of many millions of roubles had so obviously been opened on his account. He found himself wondering what the tally was so far. Four Sukhoi fighters, four SA-6 missiles, plus all the fuel and energy which had been wasted on his behalf. It had to add up to a tidy little sum already.

He pushed the idle speculation from his mind. It was an irrelevance, a childish indulgence. There were far more important things to think about.

The immediate danger was still Khabarovsk. Seeing matters through the eyes of the ground control there, Vologsky realized that they would have already started launching interceptors, now that their ill-timed missile attack had proved such a miserable failure. Air-to-air missiles were a much different proposition to the SAMs which the ground-control could throw up against him. Therefore, continuing toward Khabarovsk was definitely unwise.

It was obviously time to turn for the mountains and make his final spurt toward freedom. Vologsky eased back on the control yoke, increasing thrust as he did so. The Foxbat began to climb at a shallow angle, still headed in the general direction of Khabarovsk. Vologsky waited until his altimeter read 8,000 feet before commencing his turn.

As he came on to his new heading, due east, he wondered, briefly, just what the Soviet military had waiting for him. If Khabarovsk had been alerted, then so would have been Sovetskaya to his north and Vladivostok to his south.Both bases would have launched interceptors to close in along the coastline, to form a flying carpet, a barrier which he would have to penetrate. Beyond the mountains of the Sikhote Alin Range lay the Gulf of Tartary. There was no way of knowing how many submarines and surface ships had already been ordered into the area, each one armed to the gills with missiles. It was a formidable prospect. Even with all the faith in the world, Vologsky had serious misgivings about the Foxbat's ability to break through.

Still, the plane's superb performance was about all he had on his side now, Vologsky reminded himself. All he could do was to use it to its full advantage. As the aircraft passed over the first low foothills of the Sikhote Alin, he angled the Foxbat upwards and pulled out all the stops.

Five minutes later, at 90,000 feet, and a speed of Mach 3, the Foxbat arrowed across the very roof of the world toward the Japanese island of Hokkaido.

CHAPTER FORTY

The McDonnell Douglas Skyhawk catapulted off the flightdeck of the *Retribution* and clawed its way into the sky above the Sea of Japan. Alone at last, Hank Meakin spoke to himself, relaying the reprimand which had been on his lips ever since he had learned the nature of his mission.

Hank Meakin, you are a bloody fool. One of these days you're gonna learn to keep your goddamn mouth shut.

The one-way conversation helped to keep his spirits up. Certainly, he needed something. Meakin had never faced the possibility of flying directly to Lubyanka prison before. He didn't care to face it now. Following on from the lighthearted self-reprimand came the more serious, inner anger which refused to lie buried. Why in the name of hell couldn't he have stuck with the old rule of the Services, never volunteer for anything. Goddamnit, it might take months before the Russians could be persuaded to release him, if at all. Worse, he could end up spiraling to death in the burning wreck of his plane.

Jesus! Maybe that was the bright side of things, after all. Meakin had only a sketchy knowledge of brainwashing techniques, but he remembered seeing "The Manchurian Candidate" on the TV less than two months ago, and it had frightened the living shit out of him. He liked his brain the way it was; obsessed with sex, hard drinking and raising hell every time he got a furlough. That was the way a man's brain ought to be—nice and dirty, not laundered clean by whatever fiendish techniques the commies had up their nasty red sleeves.

Meakin's rising paranoia peaked out at the ridiculous level, and he was able to laugh at himself again. It was a natural defense mechanism, he rationalized. A guy had a right to get frightened once in a while. Especially a guy who volunteers for an unspecified mission, just for the hell of it.

He relaxed slightly, checking his course for the Soviet coast. He was spot on for Vladivostok. He could expect initial radio contact within the next quarter of an hour.

That left him some dead time. The slight damage done to the Skyhawk's starboard tailplane assembly created a slight turbulence, but took little extra control to cope with. He needed only a fraction of his concentration to keep the aircraft flying on a straight and level course. The rest of his mind was free to wander.

Anxious to direct his thoughts away from his own predicament, Meakin considered the Russian pilot. He knew only that the aircraft had been picked up on long-range radar, streaking toward the Gulf of Tartary about 250 miles north of Vladivostok. Meakin had no way of knowing if the pilot was still flying, or whether his home team had managed to bring him down on first base. There was no radio contact with the *Retribution*—that was part of his orders. Meakin voiced his thoughts aloud, as if they would carry over hundreds of miles of airspace. "Hope you make it, you poor bastard."

He laughed, a shade bitterly. The Russian pilot, whoever he was, could expect a damned sight better treatment than he would be getting, that was for sure. He was taking Uncle Sam a present; Meakin was only delivering a headache to the Russian Bear.

Meakin chuckled, involuntarily. The reflection had cheered him, rather than increased his depression. Yeah . . . that was the good thing about Uncle Sam . . . he was a pretty good boss to work for. He'd see you all right, everytime. No sweat! They'd get him out, all right. A couple of days, maybe . . . a week at the most. Uncle Sam's boys would pull the right strings, make the right noises in the right places . . . and Hank Meakin would be flying home in air-conditioned

256

comfort to a hero's welcome. A medal, maybe? At least an honorable mention, a couple of weeks R & R. That'd be nice; there was the blonde in Pittsburgh . . . what was her name? Marjorie? Marlene? Marjean . . . he remembered now. Marjean Davisson . . . a real swinger. A couple of nights in the sack with her would wash away even the memory of a week in the Lubyanka.

Oh Jesus! Meakin groaned aloud, thinking of the girl. He shifted uneasily in his flightcouch, to ease the discomfort of the mounting erection inside his flying suit. It was time to think of other things.

Meakin transferred his attention to his instruments, noting with a cold resignation that he had just crossed the buffer zone between Japanese and Soviet airspace and was about to cross into hostile territory.

It was quite a reception committee. Rapidly counting off the blips on his screen, Vologsky totted up no less than fourteen aircraft lined up ahead of him. They were laid out in a typical search and destroy formation, obviously meaning business.

There were basically four groups of aircraft, spaced out across the sky, about 5 miles apart. The top group of four were flying at 60,000 feet, with another four immediately beneath at the lower altitude of 40,0000. Lower still, at 20,000 feet were two more aircraft, spaced ten miles apart. On either side of these main groups, individual planes flew in line, but a further five miles away. Two of them were at 30,000 and the last two were at 50,000 feet. The formation gave the pack a saturation coverage over an area 30 miles wide, at five different altitudes. Not even a fly could hope to buzz through such a pattern without being noticed.

At Mach 3, evasive measures were extremely limited, to say the least. Vologsky knew that he was already above his normal operational ceiling, which should have been no more than 70,000 feet. However, he had the singular advantage of piloting the aircraft which held the world altitude record. The Foxbat-D had flown at over 119,000 feet, unarmed. It was time Vologsky set his own record, and found out what the aircraft would do with an almost complete armament capacity. He coaxed the last erg of power from the twin Tumanskys, and eased the control yoke back. Even a shallow increase in the rate of climb, at that speed, was enough to test Vologsky's pressure-suit to its limits. The G-force tore at his body, threatening to crush his ribs in against his lungs. A sudden wave of nausea hit him, and passed, leaving his head strangely light.

The Foxbat strained upwards, its rate of climb falling back rapidly as the gulping turbo-jets tried to chew on ever-thinning air. The altimeter quivered just before the 110,000 foot mark, then dropped back a fraction to settle. Vologsky hastily trimmed the aircraft to maintain 108,000 feet and flew on toward the reception committee below him. Only the top line of fighters stood a chance of getting up anywhere near him before he was past them. Vologsky took some comfort from that fact. Even they could not hope to get close enough to him to engage him in gunfire. Their only chance was a missile strike, and four aircraft bearing six missiles apiece could put out a pretty lethal umbrella of death. Vologsky knew that he could not hope to outrun or evade such a salvo of missiles. At his present speed, given the distance still between him and the four hostile aircraft, each "Acrid" would only have to streak up toward him at a shallow angle of climb. That way, at almost maximum possible strike speed, they would home in on him in excess of Mach 4.

Twenty-four missiles, then—and only three anti-missile decoys left in the tail unit of the Foxbat. Bad odds, by anyone's standards.

It *was* possible to take evasive action against a missile, of course. Vologsky had only dealt with it in theory, but he had heard other pilots who boasted of putting that theory into practice and surviving. The idea was simplicity itself. The pilot let the missile close in on his tail and then threw his aircraft into an almost-vertical climb. If he survived the initial shock of the tremendous G-forces such a maneuver engendered, he had a slim chance. Heat rises; given the right timing and sufficient acceleration, the aircraft pulled out of the missile's flight path, leaving only an ionized trail behind it. The missile, lacking the maneuverability because of its high inertial speed, supposedly lost its heat source and flew straight on into thin air.

All this was of course purely academic, in Vologsky's case. He was flying toward the missiles, not away from them. He was at his ceiling, with nowhere left to climb and no power to do it anyway. And, of course, the theory was designed to cope with a single missile. Twenty-four coming at once was something completely different.

What chance did he have, then? On paper, the answer had to be zero. Based upon probabilities, the odds against him must run into millions to one. Vologsky resigned himself to accepting the end of his run, the conclusion of the whole unpleasant business. He had no chance of survival . . . all he did have was a vague hope and another theory . . . this one completely untested, and for all Vologsky knew, possibly unfounded as well.

His radar screen erupted into a flicker of moving dots as the four interceptors launched the battery of missiles against him. Instinctively, Vologsky realized that each aircraft had fired four of its six "Acrids," keeping a second strike in reserve. Or, more likely, saving unnecessary wastage.

Vologsky put his theory to the acid test. Reaching forward, he cut the engines and killed both ignition switches.

At normal operating altitudes, a Foxbat was designed to make nearly two miles of forward glide for every 1000 feet of height. That much Vologsky could count on. In the rarified atmosphere of 108,000 feet, however, the Foxbat dropped like a lead balloon, only its forward inertia keeping it level. Vologsky's stomach sloshed sickeningly about inside his abdomen, rising almost into his chest cavity. The trajectory of the missile salvo had been worked out and set by the computers of the attack aircraft. They had worked out the height and speed of the target with inhuman accuracy, operating to such a fine and critical level that no mere human could hope to pit his puny brain against them. Human logic was a very inferior substitute for the certainty of a sophisticated thinking machine.

But logic is based on the normal, the expected. A moving target, keeping a constant speed, does not radically change that speed in an instant. A trajectory, defined by the most basic laws of physics, cannot be altered in a matter of seconds. Yet the falling Foxbat did both those things, because the puny human brain had seen fit to do the unexpected, the illogical.

Deprived of their initial interception, perhaps the missiles could have changed course enough to still home in on their uncooperative target. But the delicate infra-red tracking systems were designed to seek out the heat from flaming turbo-jets, and now there was no heat. Only a patch of warmed air, desperately thin and tenuous.

The twelve missiles streaked upwards into the stratosphere, well clear of the Foxbat. Seconds later, Vologsky saw stripes of smoke flashing past either side of his cockpit canopy, as the Foxbat plunged through the smoky trails the missiles had left behind them.

Vologsky's fingers moved quickly to the ignition switches, tripping them in sequence. For a fraction of a second he tensed, waiting with a pounding heart for another kind of death in place of the missile strike. If the engines flamed out, it would all be over just as quickly and effectively as any missile detonation.

The re-igniters chattered briefly before a rolling shockwave caught the Foxbat under its belly, shaking it like a toy kite in a gale. Then the aircraft was flying again, shrugging off the noise of re-ignition behind it.

Vologky leveled at sixty thousand feet and boosted the throttles to full thrust again. Behind him now, the four interceptors continued on their course, their pilots utterly taken aback by the miracle they had just winessed. By the time they recovered themselves, made a turn and came after him again, Vologsky knew that he would be safely out of range of their remaining missiles. Ahead, he could see the glittering surface of the Sea of Japan. The sight brought an immediate rush of blood to his mind and body, warming him. He felt a surge of affection for his aircraft. The Foxbat had done it, brought him safely out of Russia. Even though he was still in Soviet airspace, Vologsky had the odd feeling of absolute certainty. He was clear, he was safe. There was nothing left to stop him now except the Japanese air defense systems. Somehow, Vologsky knew that they would not be mobilized against him. The USSR was a massive and menacing neighbor; the Japanese were an ancient and wise people. They would not risk a possible confrontation, not over one little aircraft.

Still, there was no point in tempting the fates. Safe as he felt, Vologsky had to face the facts. There would be Soviet vessels in the area, possibly more patroling interceptor aircraft. It was stupid advertising his presence by continuing to fly at his present height. Vologsky angled the Foxbat down toward the surface of the sea, losing height rapidly. At under 500 feet, safely under the radar net once again, the aircraft skimmed above the waves, homing in toward Hokkaido. The Japanese would not even see him coming. The first sign that they had an unexpected visitor would be when the Foxbat's supersonic boom shook the flimsy huts of the coastal fishermen around Wakkanai.

Hank Meakin flew on at a steady 500 knots, listening to the guttural Russian voice coming over his communications system. The Soviets had wasted little time in making contact, and they were making no bones about their position. "American pilot . . . you are in violation of Soviet airspace. Change course immediately or you will be intercepted and destroyed without further warning."

Meakin ignored the message for a few moments. Finally, after it had been repeated three times, he replied. He flipped his radio on to a wide frequency range and spoke in what he fondly hoped was a suitably worried voice. "This is an international Mayday, repeat, Mayday. I have severe steering damage, am unable to change present course. Request emergency crash-landing clearance at nearest possible landbase. Mayday, Mayday. This is a formal request for emergency landing procedure under international law. Repeat, am unable to change from present course. Urgently request emergency landing procedure . . . over."

When an answer came, the Russian's voice had taken on a threatening, chilling edge. "American pilot . . . we know what you are doing. Turn back now, or we will shoot you down. I repeat, you will be shot down if you do not change course immediately."

Meakin flipped off the intercom. So that was it, the Russians were on to him and the little game. There seemed little point in keeping up the pretense. However, he had been ordered to stall for as long as possible. Somehow, he couldn't believe that the Soviets would be willing to shoot him down without a lot more warning. It would be tantamount to an act of aggression. That being so, he probably still had a good few minutes to play with. He switched on his intercom again. "Hey, you guys—give a man a break, huh? Geneva convention and all that stuff."

The reply was terse. "You have been warned. Under international law you are now guilty of an act of espionage. We have every right to bring your aircraft down."

Meakin shrugged, replacing the intercom. He looked ahead

through the canopy of the Skyhawk. The Russian coastline was looming up, no more than two minutes flying time away. More than enough time to prepare himself for ejection, and set the self-destruct devices which would blow the Skyhawk into small pieces. After that, it was all up to the diplomats. Forcing himself to look at the bright side, Meakin figured that the Russians would have a pretty hard time trying to make a charge of espionage stick. He was in full flight uniform, his aircraft had been identified as a standard American Air Force machine in some sort of trouble. With the aircraft destroyed, the benefit of the doubt would be on his side, if it had to come before an international court. It was unlikely that the Russians could hold him indefinitely.

He uncoupled his safety straps, checked the aircraft controls one last time and tightened his parachute harness. Then, with a quick, decisive gesture, he stabbed the self-destruct button with his forefinger. He had thirty seconds to eject before the Skyhawk became a ball of flame.

Taking a deep breath, Meakin punched the ejector mechanism button.

For a couple of seconds, nothing registered. Meakin was dumb, uncomprehending. Then it hit him. He knew, then, with a sickening realization, the ultimate coarseness of a corrupt system, a nation which had come to rely on its machines, its material wealth.

People didn't matter anymore. Only the hardware, the technology, the expertise. Not people. Pilots were nothing, the machines they flew, everything.

There was one little modification to the Skyhawk which Commander Brant had failed to mention. The explosive charges which detonated the ejection mechanism had been removed.

Seconds before the Skyhawk blew itself apart, Hank Meakin indicted his country and everything it had come to stand for with one short, explosive curse.

On the bridge of the *Retribution*, Brant watched a small bright blip disappear from his radar screen and turned away, staring out over the sea. He wished that he could throw up, right there and then . . . His first officer was looking at him questioningly.

"Everything all right, sir?"

Brant looked at him dully for a few seconds. "Oh, yes, everything is just as it should be," he murmured in answer. The First Officer failed to sense the bitter irony concealed beneath the flat tone of the words.

"Any orders, sir?"

Wearily, Brant nodded. "Set a course for Tokyo," he snapped. "I'm expecting further orders. If the radio room comes through, I'll be in my quarters."

Brant walked off the bridge without acknowledging the officer's salute.

CHAPTER FORTY-ONE

The dark blue of the sea slipping away beneath the belly of the Foxbat gave way to the aquamarine of the coastal shallows, then to the pale gold of the beaches.

Passing over land, an alien land, brought a host of mixed feelings to Vologsky. There was a sense of achievement, certainly. He had undertaken to flee nearly half-way around the world, and he had made it. There was relief, in knowing that he had faced all the dangers which had been set up against him, and survived. Yet, for all that, there was a strange feeling of doubt which clouded everything, making all his achievements seem belittled, even pointless. The emptiness of space itself would be a positive, solid environment against the limbo which he was flying toward. Mikhail Vologsky had left reality behind him on the runway of the base at Kharkov. When the wheels of the Foxbat had left that runway, he had abandoned all contact with his past life, his nationality, his very identity. Now he was facing the prospect of putting those wheels down again in somewhere new, unkown. When he jumped from the cockpit of the Foxbat, Vologsky knew he would be stepping on to a new world about which he knew virtually nothing. Life would continue, of course, but in a manner which he could only guess at. Vologsky anticipated that moment as a kind of death.

Below him, the scattered huts of the coastal fishing communities had begun to give way to the more complex structures of urban fringe developments. Vologsky glanced at his altimeter, and realized that he was flying at less than 700 feet. He eased back on the control yoke, gaining a little height. At just over 1600 feet, he banked the Foxbat gently so that he could take a wider look over the terrain beneath him. It was time to start thinking of a place to set the aircraft down.

Vologsky knew absolutely nothing about the geography of Hokkaido. His original intention had been to fly to the main island of Honshu, and he had carefully checked out the major military airfields there. On Hokkaido, he knew of no suitable landing place. It would have to be found by trial and error, from the air.

But it had to be a fairly quick decision. Moments before crossing over the land, he had noticed that his expected safety margins of reserve fuel had failed to materialize. He was already running on dregs, with perhaps no more than fifteen minutes of flying time remaining to him. Vologsky could only conclude that his evasive maneuvers, the running dog-fight with his pursuit aircraft and the sustained high-speed flight across the Sea of Japan at low altitude had burned up fuel at a phenomenal rate. Vologsky had no way of knowing that he had started out from Blagoveshchensk with less than full tanks. The ground staff there, used to the smaller and less powerful Sukhois, had no idea of the unfamiliar Foxbat's thirst. They had pumped in the normal fuel complement for one of their own aircraft to fly to Irkutsk . . .

The immediate prospects did not look good. Straight ahead of him, Vologsky could see the mountain range which ran from the north to the south of the small island like a spine, rising to the highest peaks in the Hidaka Sammyaku mountains. Beyond them, even Vologsky's limited knowledge of this part of the world told him that there was only the Pacific Ocean.

He swung the Foxbat round to starboard, following a course due south. Logic dictated that any major airfields would be situated near the coast, probably facing toward the main island of Honshu or out over the Sea of Japan toward the USSR and Korea.

Flying south had one other advantage. If Hokkaido offered no safe landing places, Vologsky's dwindling fuel reserves should still take him at least as far as the northern tip of Honshu island. At worst, he could make a crash landing on the beaches there, or even ditch the Foxbat in shallow coastal waters.

His present course was taking him out over water again. Vologsky glanced out of the starboard side of the cockpit, noting that the land curved away in a massive bay, over fifty miles across. He altered his course slightly, following the curvature of the landmass. Three minutes later, Vologsky saw the southernmost tip of Hokkaido, the Tsugaru Kaikyo straits which separated it from Honshu, and the main island beyond it. He began to lose height again, dropping down to under 500 feet.

He almost missed the airstrip. It was minute, right on the coast, about ten miles to starboard. Vologsky took one quick glance at his fuel gauge, registering nearly empty, and made up his mind. Small though it was, the airstrip would have to do. He set course toward it, planning to make a single overpass then go straight in for a landing. Its airspeed trimmed below 300 knots, the Foxbat began to drop toward the civilian airport of Hakodate.

A sudden jolt shook the fuselage of the aircraft, as the port engine misfired, coughing briefly before re-igniting. Vologsky knew that his fuel was now critically low. His remaining flying time could be counted in seconds rather than minutes now. There was no time for a preliminary fly-over. He had to take the Foxbat straight in for a landing if he was to get it, and himself, down in one piece. Hurriedly, Vologsky adjusted his flight-path, trimmed the flaps and engines and set the Foxbat's nose toward the ground. He lost height rapidly, knowing that there was no way he could get the Foxbat down to landing height before the beginning of the main strip. He was going to have to land on less than three-quarters of a runway designed only to cope with civil aircraft, a good fifty meters shorter than the Foxbat needed.

Vologsky put down the undercarriage and set as much drag on the flaps as he dared. It showed the aircraft only marginally, but greatly increased the angle of descent. As the beginning of the runway flashed under the Foxbat's nose, the aircraft was less than fifty feet above it.

At fifteen feet, Vologsky knew that there was no way he could make a clean landing on the amount of runway left to him, and cut both engines savagely. The Foxbat dropped like a stone, bounced three times and made solid contact, the rear tires squealing against the tarmac. Setting both engines on full reverse thrust, Vologsky tensed himself in the flightcouch, mesmerized by the sight of the runway's end now flashing toward him. He was not going to make it; he knew that with absolute certainty now.

The rolling Foxbat left the end of the tarmac and bounced over rough grassland. There was a savage jolt, the sound of rending metal which ceased abruptly as the nosewheel assembly was torn away from the fuselage. The proud Foxbat bowed her head as if in defeat, and the drooping nose-cone ploughed into soft earth.

The weather had saved her. For three days running, the coastal regions of Hokkaido had been plagued with torrential rain. The surface of the grassland was like a gigantic mudslick. It clung to the Foxbat's rear wheels and lubricated the forward motion of its dropped nose. Miraculously, the aircraft slowed and finally slid smoothly to a halt, with a shattered nosewheel assembly, but no other damage.

Hardly able to believe his luck, Vologsky stared blankly out through the perspex canopy toward the main terminal building, as the shocked civilian personnel began to react to their unexpected visitor.

CHAPTER FORTY-TWO

THE FINANCIAL TIMES.
Tuesday September 7 1976

DEFECTOR FLIES TOP-SECRET
SOVIET FIGHTER TO JAPAN

(Hakodate. Sept 6.) A Soviet pilot landed his top-secret MiG 25 combat aircraft at this Northern Japanese town today and told police he wanted asylum in the U.S.

Western military experts said the defection would give their nations an unprecedented chance to assess at first hand the capabilities of the aircraft, codenamed the "Foxbat" and ranked as the world's fastest combat aircraft.

Police at the civilian Hakodate airport say, however, they will not allow Japanese or American military authorities to approach the fighter.

SOPHISTICATED

The Soviet Union quickly demanded the immediate return of both the MiG and its pilot, informed sources said tonight. The Soviet Embassy told Japanese authorities it could not tolerate approval of the pilot's asylum plan by Japan.

In Washington, the State Department confirmed that the pilot, described by the Japanese as a First Lieutenant, had asked for political asylum in the U.S. The matter was now under consideration.

Washingon officials said the future disposition of the plane was up to the Japanese but it was thought little time would be wasted by either Japanese or U.S. military personnel in photographing the jet and its sophisticated electronic and aerodynamic equipment.

The fighter is now surrounded by 30 riot police in front of the airport's terminal building.

Police said that the Soviet pilot was being interrogated by them for possible violation of Japan's immigration control law. Japan has no law covering defection to this country.

Meanwhile in Brussels, there was no official comment at NATO headquarters but the experts said privately it was believed to be the first time a MiG 25 had come intact into the hands of a friendly power.

Reuter.

DAILY TELEGRAPH
September 9 1976.

DEFECTING MIG PILOT
SET FOR US

By A. E. Cullison in Tokyo.

The Soviet pilot who landed his top-secret MiG 25 Foxbat fighter in Japan is expected to leave for America today. The United States has granted him political asylum. The pilot, who landed the jet in Hakodate on Monday, has been questioned by American Embassy officials in Tokyo.

After establishing that he wanted to seek asylum of his own free will, the Americans told the Japanese authorities they would accept him.

SUNDAY TIMES
September 12 1976

FOXBAT: Why Japan
was terrified

By Robert Whymant, Tokyo.

For several hours after the Soviet defecting pilot landed in north Japan last week, Japanese defense officials feared Russia would send bombers to destroy the Foxbat MiG 25 with all its secrets. Military bases were put on alert and pilots stood by to scramble perhaps hoping to regain some of the face lost when the country's defenses were caught napping by the plane's arrival in the island of Hokkaido.

It has been a sobering lesson for the front line of Japan's air defense in Hokkaido, which at its closest point is clearly visible from the Russian Habomai islands. The whole of Japan is within the cruising range of the Foxbat, whose appearance last week was the first indication that squadrons of this advanced plane are stationed in the Far East.

Five a half hours after the Foxbat landed, Japanese defense chiefs were alarmed when two aircraft appeared on radar screens on Monday evening. Four Phantoms at Chitose airbase scrambled, then the unidentified planes veered off toward Siberia. Two hours later two other groups of three planes appeared and again flew off after about an hour.

It was during this tense period that the possibility of a Russian strike was considered strongest, the most likely agent being the SU-19 tactical fighter-bomber, for precision bombing of the Foxbat parked at Hakodate airport. Japan's radar defenses, without an airborne early-warning system, would have been unable to cope with the SU-19, which can fly at supersonic speed only a few hundred feet above the ground.

DAILY TELEGRAPH
September 13 1976

JAPAN TO SHARE FOXBAT SECRETS WTH US

By A. E. Cullison in Tokyo.

Japan said yesterday that American technical intelligence experts would be invited to take part in a piece-by-piece examination of the Soviet super secret MiG 25 "Foxbat" jet fighter flown to Japan last week.

Gen. Michita Sakata, of the Japanese Self-Defense Agency, denied reports that American Air Force experts had already examined the MiG 25.

But they would certainly be invited to join the Japanese in a full-scale examination.

Gen. Sakata said the MiG 25 is to be dismantled because the nosewheel, damaged when the pilot overshot the short runway at Hakodate Airport, in Hokkaido, prevents the jet from being flown to a local military air base.

CHAPTER FORTY-THREE

On Dwight Ennis' desk, the intercom buzzed softly. "Comrade Zhagov is here to see you, sir," purred a soft female voice.

Ennis groaned. "Again?" Visits from the Soviet diplomatic staff had been running at the rate of five a day for the past two weeks. It was only to be expected, of course. Formal complaints and diplomatic discussions would continue until the Foxbat was returned to its home soil.

"Alright, show him in." Settling back in his chair, Ennis adopted a relaxed, almost casual attitude. He considered it a perfect foil to the stiff, formal stance which the Russian always adopted on such occasions.

He smiled easily as Zhagov was escorted into his office. "Well, Comrade Zhagov, what can I do for you today?"

Zhagov responded to the smile with a frosty stare. "I am instructed to demand, once more, that your Government take immediate steps to bring about the return of exclusive property of the peoples of the Union of Soviet Socialist Republics. I am also instructed to request that you hand over the living person of Soviet citizen Mikhail Vologsky, in order that he may be repatriated to face the courts of justice, under the laws of his native land, on a charge of treason."

Ennis nodded vaguely. It was the standard speech all over

again. He had heard it perhaps a couple of dozen times now. He could only make the equally standard response.

"The United States Government regrets that it cannot interfere with the internal politics of a neutral sovereign state, namely Japan. With regard to the person of Soviet citizen Vologsky, he has applied for asylum of his own free will, and is currently being considered for that privilege on the basis of international human rights."

Zhagov's formal stiffness disappeared suddenly. He had said and done what was expected of him, and Ennis had responded. Protocol had been observed, and could now be dispensed with. He extracted a packet of American cigarettes from his pocket, casually lighting one with a gold lighter. He blew a long, thin plume of smoke into the air before speaking again.

"The cuckoo always was a most unsociable bird," he observed. "It brings nothing but misery and disaster to its unfortunate hosts. You realize, of course, that this business has set back diplomatic relationships between Japan and the USSR by several years?"

Ennis smiled. "Oh, I think that's rather an exaggeration, Comrade Zhagov," he muttered. "I think everything has been handled rather well, under the circumstances. The Japanese have played their hand admirably, and I must say that your own control of the military has shown commendable restraint. It would not have been wise to attempt a bombing operation on Hakodate airport."

Zhagov raised one bushy eyebrow in a mock gesture of reproval. "Such a thing was never considered, Mister Ennis."

Ennis smiled knowingly. "No, of course not. I take it that violations of Japanese air-space have ceased now?"

Zhagov skirted round giving a direct answer. "Everything has been reduced to a nice cool level. The sooner the Foxbat is returned, the sooner we can bury this thing completely. How soon *can* we expect the return of the aircraft, Mr. Ennis?"

There was no real point in continuing to fence, Ennis decided. They were both concerned with working to a common end, if not exactly on the same side. International diplomacy demanded that all the dust was swept under the carpet as soon as possible. "I understand that the Japanese Self-Defense Agency will be making arrangements to return the aircraft

274

within the month," Ennis answered candidly. "An interesting little toy, from all accounts."

"So I understand," Zhagov murmured. He smiled openly. "No more than that now, I suppose. A toy . . . a piece of advanced technology which has suddenly become obsolete. A prized plaything loses so much value when you realize that every child in the street has one just like it."

"Quite," Ennis said, appreciating the Russian's dry sense of humor. "Still, back to the drawing board, eh? It will give your aerospace scientists something to keep them occupied for the next two or three years."

"Perhaps." Zhagov grinned slyly. "Perhaps not. For all we know, the Foxbat may already have been outmoded."

Ennis chose not to pursue the matter. "That's hardly our problem, is it?"

Zhagov's smile faded. He looked at Ennis with a new seriousness in his eyes. "That brings me, rather neatly, to the crux of the matter," he said softly. "As you say, a piece of machinery is not really our problem. It has given up all its secrets by now. By its mute, mechanical nature, it can not say anything more, cause either of us any future embarrassment. Not so the pilot, of course."

"Yes," Ennis said with a heavy sigh. He knew exactly where the conversation was heading. He had been expecting it. "Our mutual friend Vologsky does present potential problems, I must admit."

"I assume that you have learned all you wanted to learn from your interrogations?" Zhagov said.

"Interviews. We prefer to use the word interviews," Ennis rebuked gently. "It has a softer, more suitably decadent ring to it, for Western ears." He smiled, briefly. "Yes, you are quite right, of course. The pilot Vologsky has been quite cooperative. He is of little further use to us now."

"He could, however, be of considerable use to troublemakers," Zhagov suggested. "Dissident elements might well persuade him to talk, gaining information which could be used to play this thing up for years to come. Such an event would not suit either of us, Mr. Ennis, I feel sure you will agree."

Ennis considered deeply for several seconds. "We cannot hand him over to you, of course. You realize that? There would be a public outcry."

Zhagov nodded. "I realize that. You must also realize that we would not really want to take him, for similar reasons.

The Soviet people are not deaf to world opinion, Mr. Ennis. We realize that it is not only the Americans and the British who feel sympathy for the little man, the underdog. No, making a public example of him would serve no useful purpose at all, in diplomatic terms. It would please the military, of course, suit the more hard-line elements."

"Your alternative, then?"

Zhagov smiled, knowing that Ennis knew exactly what he had in mind. It was just that the American was a little more squeamish than he in voicing it. "An accident, of course. Some obscure group of political fanatics could be blamed. It would be done with all discretion, of course. I assume that, for the present, Lieutenant Vologsky is still under close guard?"

Ennis nodded. "For the present."

"Then it will have to wait for a while. A month or two, when he has a little more freedom—when he could, most unfortunately, be in a position to fall victim to those . . . fanatics . . ."

Ennis thought deeply for several minutes. Zhagov had a point, of course. Vologsky was a great potential embarrassment to both countries. Japan had handled the whole Foxbat business admirably. There had been no hint of United States involvement with the defection of the Russian pilot. The story released to the world was simply that Vologsky had acted on his own initiative, for purely selfish reasons. Whether or not the lie was really believed hardly mattered. It had been accepted, that was the important thing. Only Ennis, a handful of top Government officials and Zhagov knew the truth, and they all had a vested interest in suppressing it. Vologsky did not have any such interest. Once he was given complete freedom, the press of the whole world would hound him for his story. He would be offered huge sums of money to throw out as much dirt as he could. It was not a pleasant prospect at all—but then neither was the alternative which Zhagov seemed to be offering. Ennis looked troubled as he turned his attention back to the Russian.

"You cannot seriously expect me to sanction cold-blooded murder?"

Zhagov shrugged. "You would leave the mechanics of the operation to us, of course. You would be free to take as much, or as little, internal political advantage as you saw fit.

I'm sure that you have some radical elements which could do with a public slap-down."

"Quite a few." Ennis allowed himself a slightly bitter smile. "But we cherish our democracy to the point of masochism, Comrade Zhagov."

"Ah." Zhagov smiled. "That is your affair, of course. However, you probably need time to consider my suggestions."

Ennis shook his head vehemently. "Your suggestion is utterly unthinkable."

Nevertheless, for several minutes after Zhagov had left, Ennis did think about it.

CHAPTER FORTY-FOUR

THE GUARDIAN
November 9 1976

DATE SET FOR RETURN
OF MIG 25 BY JAPAN

(Tokyo; November 8) The top secret Soviet MiG 25 jet fighter flown here by a defecting Soviet pilot on September 6 will probably be returned to Moscow on Friday, Foreign Ministry sources reported today.

The sources said broad agreement on terms of the return of the sophisticated warplane to the Soviet Union has been reached in talks between the two countries. They said the finishing touches will be given to details in a meeting between Foreign Ministry and Soviet embassy officials tomorrow.

Under the agreement reached the supersonic fighter will be transported to the Soviet Union by a Soviet freighter from Hitachi port, near Tokyo.

The Foreign Ministry sources said the Soviet Union has refused to accept Japan's demand for compensation for damage caused to Hakodate airport when the fighter made a forced landing. They said Moscow demanded that Soviet technicians be allowed to inspect the aircraft before the plane's shipment from the base to the port.

The Soviets agreed to a compromise plan that the Soviet technicians would be allowed to inspect the aircraft at the port with detailed examinations to be made aboard the Soviet freighter.

CHAPTER FORTY-FIVE

Vologsky wondered what had happened to the Foxbat. Was it still in Japan, or had they brought it to the United States? How had the Kremlin reacted to the news of his defection, and the loss of their prized warplane?

Not knowing the answers was the only real irritant. Yet, Vologsky reasoned, in that much alone there was a small degree of comfort to be taken. In terms of specific information, his new homeland was not so different to his old one. They brought him newspapers, of course. Every morning, he was free to read quite candid, even dangerously speculative world news and internal American politics. They even allowed him to watch the television without any apparent censorship. Vologsky had no way of knowing that what he saw was a carefully edited videotape. Yet in almost every newspaper or magazine, he would eventually come to a gap, a missing piece which had carefully been removed and destroyed.

His interrogation had been much less harsh than he had expected. In Japan, the authorities had been noticeably edgy and nervous. They had treated him with an embarrassed concern, just short of actual hostility. The Americans were different. They were solicitous, almost friendly. They seemed far more relaxed than the Japanese. They asked him questions and invited, rather than demanded, answers from him.

They seemed to go out of their way to impress upon him the benefits of their country, their system and their way of life, without any obvious attempt at indoctrination.

Yet the people, and their culture, were a strange mixture, heady and confusing. On the one hand, Vologsky had seen the gigantic edifice to childish fantasy which they called Disneyland. A whole city of fairy castles, gigantic animated figures and pleasure rides. They had devoted an entire day to dragging him around the unbelievable complex, of which they seemed inordinately proud. The exact nature and purpose of the place had not been made quite clear. Vologsky had failed to appreciate it, finding the whole thing infantile.

On the other hand, he had seen the heights of their scientific technology, and marvelled at the hardware, the expertise, and the naïve way in which they fell over themselves trying to show it off. At Cape Canavarel, Vologsky had wondered if such a thing as National Security existed in his new refuge. He had been shown around the command center, introduced to top officials, taken especially to watch the launching of a massive Titan IIIB rocket taking an observation satellite into space. That had been a special thrill; an omen of great hope for the future. Despite Georgi Kirov's final betrayal, Vologsky still dared, sometimes, to retain part of the dream.

Space . . . the ultimate freedom. If America would only give him that, the country would be vindicated, everything he had been through proved worthwhile.

There was hope. Already, Vologsky had been granted a great deal more freedom than he had expected. The CIA men surrounding him had been reduced in number, their close attention to his movements subtly relaxed. He was allowed outside his apartment more or less alone, for short periods of time. Perhaps other security men picked him up outside, but they were discreet about it. Vologsky had failed to positively identify any escorts on his last two sorties outside the block.

As now. Vologsky walked down the concrete steps and paused, staring down both sides of the crowded Washington street. He saw no one vaguely resembling a security guard in the immediate vicinity. He stepped to the curb, waiting for the green light before he crossed the street. Over the other side, a green, spacious park; an oasis of grass and trees in the automobile-infested jungle which was America.

Vologsky strolled toward it, sucking in the fresh air, feeling the faint warmth of the pale winter sun on his face.

Perhaps it was a morning for dreaming, for seeking a new life in which the old nightmares had no part. He seated himself on a wooden bench, tilting his head back to let the sun play on his forehead. He closed his eyes, letting his mind drift, recapturing the harsh memories.

There was no place for the tight-gutted tension here, the overpowering sense of loss, of life and freedom being torn away from him. The flight out of Russia was over now, the death-dealing chatter of the wing-cannon from the attacking Chinese F-9s just an illusion.

The staccato gunfire which he seemed to hear was in the past, part of another world he had left behind. Even the pain which burned, suddenly, in his stomach was not real. The screaming which he heard could not be human, just the noise of the F-9's engines as the aircraft dived upon him for another attack.

Only the feel of warm, sticky blood oozing from his body, and the sight which greeted his suddenly open eyes, told Vologsky that the nightmare was a final, horrible reality.

CHAPTER FORTY-SIX

WORLD NEWS AGENCY
November 14 1976
Dateline Washington 14/11/76
Immediate release to all Media.

SOVIET DEFECTOR SHOT
Washington Sources Finger Student Group

Mikhail Vologsky, the Soviet Air Force pilot who defected to
Japan with a top-secret MiG 25 fighter plane two months ago
has been killed here in Washington, it was revealed today.

Vologsky, who had applied for and been granted political
asylum in this country, was apparently shot four times at
close range shortly after 10 am this morning by a lone gun-
man, said by an eye-witness to be a young male Caucasian in
his early twenties, in a Washington park.

The FBI are saying little at this stage, although informed
sources here suggest that they are working on the theory that
the assassination was politically motivated, and could possibly
be the work of an extreme radical Marxist student organization which calls itself the Red Youth Organization for Terror
(R.Y.O.T.).

It is understood that Soviet Embassy officials have already made a request for the body of Lieutenant Vologsky to be handed over to them, so that he can be buried in his native land. According to Vologsky's own statements, he left no living relatives.